ON THE MEND

Carolina Waves Series Book One

TINA GALLAGHER

Galsalla Press

On the Mend: Carolina Waves Series Book One

Published by Galsalla Press

Cover Design: Qamber Designs

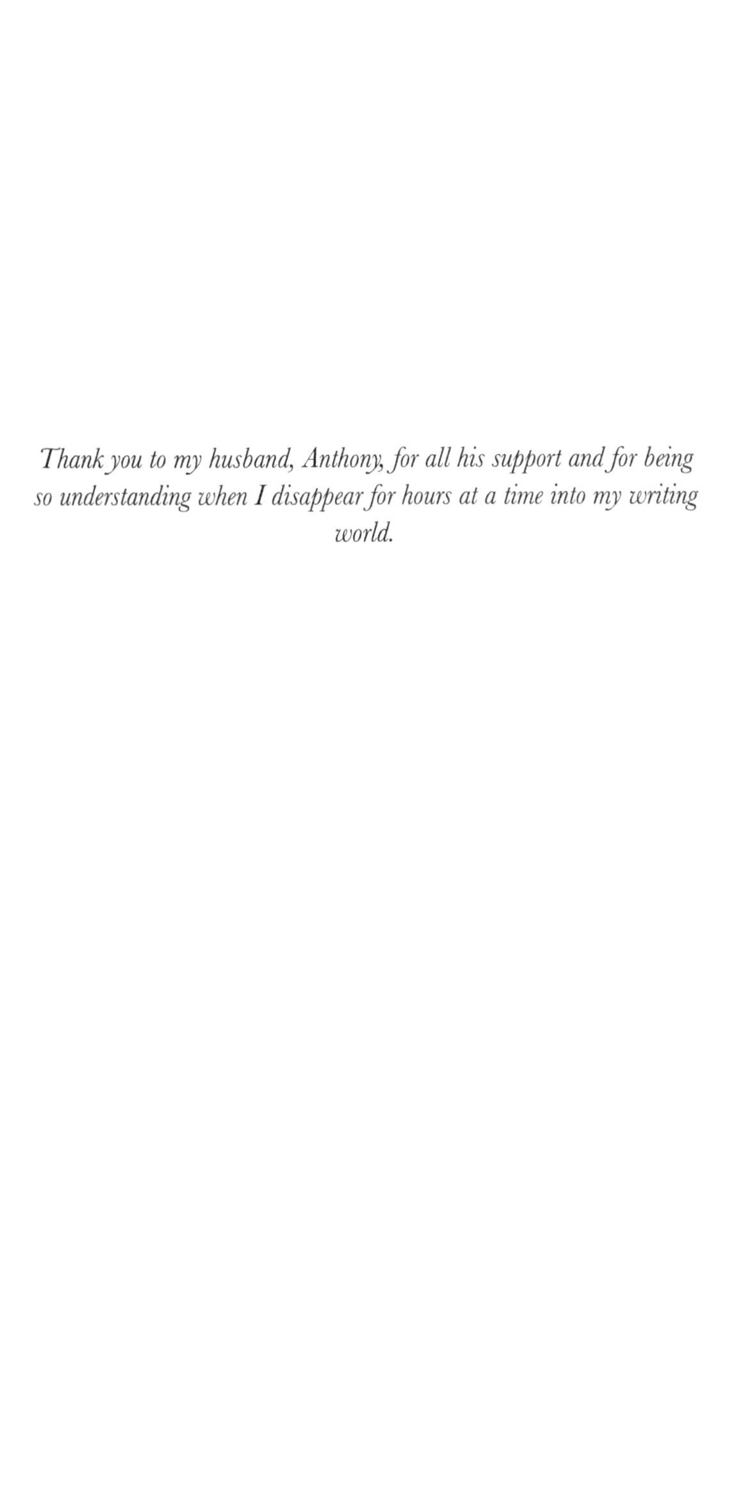

Thank you to my husband, Anthony, for all his support and for being so understanding when I disappear for hours at a time into my writing world.

Prologue

A GENTLE SMILE played on his lips as he stroked my cheek. "It's like my father always said, there are girls you fuck, and girls you marry. You are definitely a girl you marry."

I blinked. Had he meant that to be flattering? Was that crap supposed to be a compliment? Because he looked quite pleased with himself.

I'd found out Dan was screwing half of the females on campus, and that's all he had to say for himself? After two years together? What happened to the guy I'd loved? The one I thought I knew so well?

Until he'd shared his pathetic philosophy of women with me, I'd been hurt, near tears. Now he just pissed me off.

"Honey." Dan flashed his most charming smile and reached to take my hands in his. The smile disappeared when I jerked out of his grasp. "Don't be like this. I love *you*. I want to marry *you*. That's all that matters."

"You really believe that?" I asked.

"Bri, I don't know what to say." Dan dragged his fingers through his hair. "Tell me what you want me to say."

"Say goodbye, Dan. I don't ever want to see you again."

Chapter One

SABRINA

I SHUDDERED AT THE MEMORY. Even though ten years have passed since Dan uttered those words, just thinking about the conversation raises my blood pressure.

My supervisor must have been saying something while I was lost in the past, but I'll be damned if I know what it was. Only her silence alerted me to the fact she was waiting for me to say something.

"Could you repeat the question?"

Jodi rolled her eyes. "You know the question."

"I don't think I'm the right person for this job. Dan and I, we have a history." I added the last bit of information reluctantly. Don't get me wrong, I like Jodi, but she has a tendency to gossip.

"Dan mentioned that. It's one of the reasons he requested you."

"It is?" I couldn't hide my surprise. Dan and I hadn't parted on the best of terms. I can't imagine our past relationship would give me any extra points in the *Who gets to rehabilitate Dan McMullen?* contest.

"He's seen you work." Jodi sat forward and leaned her arms on her desk. "Granted, that was years ago, but it only stands to reason you'd get better with time." I smiled in acceptance of her subtle compliment.

"Isn't there someone else available?"

"Of course there is, but he asked for you. Personally, I might add." The last few words were finished off with a saucy smirk that turned into a full-blown smile. "I've never spoken to a professional baseball player before, never mind a hot one like Dan." She wriggled in her chair. "I get wet just thinking about it."

I'm not surprised by Jodi's reaction to Dan. His good looks and charm have captivated the sternest of females… myself included.

"What happened to his last therapist?" I asked.

"They didn't get along." Jodi shrugged. "Personality conflict, I guess."

"Who was it?"

"Tim Rawlins."

"He's very good."

"Yes he is," Jodi agreed. "But you and I both know that if a patient isn't happy with his therapist, the whole thing is a waste of time. Dan wasn't willing to work with, or for, Tim, but he sounds more than eager to cooperate with you." Jodi leaned back in her chair and crossed her legs. "So what do you say?"

"I say no."

She looked shocked by my blunt refusal, but quickly composed herself.

"I haven't told you the best part of this whole thing."

Both the look in her eyes and her cocky tone put me on full alert.

"What's that?"

"If you do this, you'll be made partner immediately following the assignment."

I don't believe it. I've been working at the Meyers Rehabilitation Clinic since graduating from college, and my ultimate goal has been to someday become a partner. Now it seems that goal depends on this one assignment.

"Why?"

"You know why, Sabrina."

I did. In all the years I've been working at the clinic, this is the first time we've been approached by a big name athlete. While the patient load has nearly tripled in the past decade, said patients consist mostly of local high school and college athletes, and post-operative patients. A good word from Dan McMullen, All-Star center fielder for the Carolina Waves, would really put us on the map.

"Just think. A few weeks out of your life for a partnership you've been working toward for nine years."

While I heard her words, my mind had already wandered back ten years. Back to one of the most humiliating nights of my life.

I rubbed my temples and groaned. "No one else can do this?"

"He wants you."

I thought of the partnership and groaned again. Why does my future depend upon Dan, of all people?

"Do we have a file on him?"

I didn't have to ask how Dan had injured himself. The video of him crashing into the centerfield wall of First Allegiant Bank Stadium as he chased a home run ball had aired on all major sports channels as well as the local news. The fact that he'd at least made the catch must be somewhat soothing to his ego.

Jodi waved a folder that had magically appeared in her right hand dramatically before handing it over.

"Do they have X-rays?" I asked as I scanned through various doctors' reports.

"They have some, but I haven't gotten them yet."

"Good. I'll want to see them before we start. When's he coming in?" I was still studying the pages in front of me, but Jodi's silence made the hair on the back of my neck stand on end. As I lifted my gaze to meet hers, she turned to face the window and mumbled a reply.

"What was that?"

Jodi cleared her throat. "We decided it'd be best if you went to Dan's house for therapy instead of him coming here."

"We? Who we? Not me we."

"Think about it." Jodi's business mask was fully in place once again. "Most of our clients will know who Dan is and once word gets out that he's here, people will be milling around like crazy. Not to mention the reporters. It would be a disaster to have him come here, and you know it."

"You have it all figured out, don't you?"

A smug smile crossed her lips. "It's my job to take care of the little details." She pointed to the items in my hand. "The directions to his house are on the back of the folder."

I flipped the folder over and had to agree with her statement. Jodi certainly knows how to dot all the I's and cross all the T's. The directions included mile markers, with street names and landmarks along the way. The precise description of the location of Dan's house could have been used for a real estate listing.

"Pack enough for a month or so."

"Pack?" I jerked my head up so fast, I nearly gave myself whiplash.

Jodi held her ground. "You didn't think we'd expect you to commute every day, did you?" She leaned forward, resting her elbows on the desk. "That's a good two hours each way, and God knows how long it would take you with all the construction going on now."

Jodi's patronizing tone nearly snapped my self-control.

"There's no reason for you to commute," Jodi continued. "Dan has enough room and all the equipment you'll need. And since you'll be in residence, theoretically you can work on his therapy twenty-four-seven. Which is a good thing, because he's really eager to get better."

"Twenty-four-seven?" I screeched. "Jodi, I have a life. I don't want to be cooped up in a house with Dan McMullen."

"I said theoretically." Jodi sighed. "It's not like you're going to be held prisoner." She chuckled. "Hell, if I was thirty, blond, and had a body like yours, I'd volunteer for the assignment myself." She sat back in her chair. "Think of it as a vacation. He has a pool, a hot tub, and acres of land. It'll be like being at your own private spa." Jodi paused for, what I'm sure was, dramatic effect. "By the time you come back, we'll have the partnership papers drawn up and ready to sign."

"You expect me to agree to this?"

"I believe you already have." Her tone was more confident than the look in her eyes.

"What about my other clients?"

"All taken care of." My angst must have been apparent because Jodi's look softened. "Sabrina, you have nothing to worry about. It'll be fine. You'll see." She flashed a brilliant smile. "As you said yourself, I have everything figured out. Right?"

I smiled sickly. "You seem to."

It was on the tip of my tongue to ask the answer lady

how I was going to survive living under the same roof with Dan McMullen. But of course, I didn't.

DAN

I CHECKED the clock for the fifth time in as many minutes. When Jodi told me Sabrina would be arriving today, I'd assumed she meant sometime in the morning. That just proves the old saying about what happens when you assume.

I still can't believe that at some point today Sabrina Kelly and I will be in the same room together for the first time in ten years. My thoughts are scattered in so many directions, I'm not sure which one to focus on first. Not a day has gone by in the last decade that I haven't thought about her, wanted to reach out to her. But it was never the right time. Or maybe I was just a coward.

Busting my knee may keep me off the field this season, but it's also given me the chance I need to get Sabrina into my life again. After my team-assigned therapist and I had a difference of opinion on my rehab, I grabbed the opportunity to contact the rehabilitation center Sabrina works for and set things in motion. Her manager, Jodi, was more than willing to do anything necessary to make me a client. Without getting into detail, I told her that Sabrina probably wouldn't be happy with the assignment, but Jodi assured me she'd take care of everything.

Maybe the fact that Sabrina agreed to do this means that she's forgiven me. Or maybe it just means Jodi made her an offer she couldn't refuse. Either way, I'm going to do everything I can to make her mine again.

Chapter Two

SABRINA

AT EVERY EXIT I APPROACHED, it took all my willpower not to veer off, turn around, and head back home. But I've never backed down from a challenge in my life, and am not about to start now.

I was repeating that last sentence in my head for at least the hundredth time as I turned my red CRV into the long driveway leading to Dan's house.

The driveway itself is impressive, with perfectly manicured lawns bordering either side. Massive trees scattered the acreage, and I looked around, digesting the beauty. I was doing just that when I spotted the immense stone and wood structure at the end of the driveway. My eyes lit on the old-fashioned front porch and traveled slowly across the entire house, taking in the two wings jutting out from the center building on either side. Two massive chimneys on each end of the structure told their own tale. Just the thought of curling up in front of a roaring fire with a good book eased some tension from my neck.

Apparently someone had approached my car while I was admiring the house, because when I looked away from it, I was startled to find a person—a child no less—staring at me.

"Hi."

"You're finally here," the little girl, who I figured to be eight or so, said.

"Oh, sorry. I didn't realize Jodi gave you an exact time. I stopped for a burger on the way."

Truth be told, I stopped more out of a desire to delay my arrival than an absolute need for nourishment.

"I'm sorry. Daddy always says I'm too impatient."

"No problem." Realizing how ridiculous it was to be carrying on a conversation through my open window, I waved her back and stepped out of the car. Extending my hand, I said, "I'm Sabrina."

She pumped my hand enthusiastically. "I know. Sabrina Kelly. I'm Lexi."

"It's nice to meet you, Lexi."

I opened the back driver's side door, reached in, and grabbed my backpack and oversized duffel bag in one swipe. Jodi assured me that Dan possessed all the equipment necessary for his therapy, so my personal belongings are all I have to contend with.

"That all your stuff?" Lexi's heart-shaped face tilted up, her light brown ringlets falling over her shoulders. It was then I noticed her amazing eyes. The unusual shade of green reminded me of the color of fresh sage.

"This is it."

"How long you gonna be here?" Her nose scrunched up as she asked the question.

I laughed. "Does that mean you think I have too much or not enough?"

"I take that much for a one-night sleepover party." She looked thoughtful. "But Daddy says I always pack way too much."

I'd almost done the same thing, but at the last minute I whittled it down to the bare necessities. I didn't even allow myself to pack make-up. I usually only wear it on special occasions and this doesn't qualify as one. I'm here to do a job, not to impress anyone. I made a point to remind myself to say that over and over in my head several times a day.

I was doing just that when Lexi opened the large front door and led me into the house.

"Hey munchkin." A tall, brown-haired, athletically thin man leaned down and gave Lexi a quick peck on the cheek.

I decided he must be the famous "Daddy."

"Sabrina's here, so I brought her in," Lexi said proudly.

"Good job." He stood to full height and extended his hand to me. "I'm Jeff Nealon."

Unnecessarily, I introduced myself. Lexi danced a jig next to me, looking like she was about to pee her pants.

"Why don't you go tell him Sabrina's here?" Jeff suggested to Lexi.

Apparently that's what she'd been waiting for, because she took off full speed down the hallway, throwing an "okay" over her shoulder.

"If I could bottle that energy and sell it, I'd make a fortune," Jeff said, as he lovingly stared down the hallway Lexi had just vacated.

"She's a beautiful little girl, and so polite."

"Thank you for saying so." Jeff faced me once again

and reached his hands out for my bags. "Why don't I show you to your room? Then I'll give you the grand tour."

"Sounds good."

It wasn't until I ascended the curved oak staircase that I noticed my surroundings. The golden walls looked cheerful, but not overpowering and perfectly complemented the dark wood of the foyer floor and stairs that were varnished to a high gloss. As we reached the second floor, a thick, beige carpet muffled our footsteps. Before I knew it, Jeff had opened a door and stood aside gesturing for me to enter. "This is it."

I stepped inside and took in my surroundings. The burgundy carpet and taupe walls created the framework for a room that was neither masculine nor feminine, but would most likely appeal to anyone who occupied it. Paisley throw pillows offset the bold stripes of the comforter in the same dark tones.

A large bay window offered a marvelous view of the front yard and myriad of trees surrounding the property. I imagine the view would be spectacular in the fall after the leaves have turned. Or even in spring, as the trees wake up after a long winter's nap. Thoughts of winter make me wonder how they'd look bare-branched against a grey, cloudy sky.

Not that the view right now isn't spectacular. The trees are full and lush, just waiting for someone to curl underneath with a picnic lunch or a good book and laze the day away.

I was so lost in my musings I forgot Jeff was in the room. I jumped when he spoke.

"The bathroom is through here, and this is the closet." He opened each door in turn. "The drawers and closet are empty, so feel free to make yourself at home." I nodded my response. Jeff led me back into the hallway and pointed at the door across the hall and down a few feet. "That's Lexi's room. She insisted you stay in here." He smiled. "If she gets in your way, just let me know."

"I'm sure we'll be fine."

Jeff pointed out the linen closet, instructing me to help myself to anything I might need. There was a small office next to that, which I was again told to make use of if necessary.

"And that's Dan's room." He gestured toward the door at the end of the hallway.

While Jeff was the picture of innocence, I could tell he expected a reaction. Apparently, he's aware that Dan and I have a history. I have to admit I'm surprised. In fact, I'm surprised that *the* Dan McMullen would take the time to mention my name.

Yes, we dated for two years in college and were nearly engaged, but I can't begin to imagine how many women there were before and after that. Hell, even during. Which had been the root of our problems.

Jeff resumed his tour when I neglected to react to the fact that Dan's room is practically next to mine.

While the house is large, it's also comfortable and has a homey feel. In fact, if Dan didn't live here, I might even relax and pretend I'm on vacation, like Jodi suggested. But he is, so I definitely won't.

"The gym is in the basement, which is where I'm assuming Dan and Lexi are. Any questions before we head down there?"

How did I get myself into this?

"Um, no. I don't think so." I smiled, attempting to hide the tension pulsing through my body. "But if you find me wandering around looking confused, please offer a helping hand. This place is huge."

"You'll have it down in no time. It's not that big."

My silly thoughts must have shown on my face, because Jeff asked, "What's so funny?"

I shook my head and chuckled. "The last time I saw Dan, he was living in an attic apartment with three other guys." I smiled at the memory. "They didn't even have beds. They slept on mattresses on the floor."

"Dan's come a long way since then," he said. "Remember that."

I chose to ignore the message I assume he was trying to send me.

"How about showing me that gym?"

DAN

I EASED my braced leg onto the couch, leaned back, and closed my eyes. This throbbing ache in my leg is starting to piss me off. I know my injury could have been a lot worse, but I'm just not used to sitting around. Not to mention having to rely on other people to do things for me.

Besides getting Sabrina back into my life, the only other bright side to this whole shit show is that I get to spend time with Lexi. I'm normally coming and going from February to September—October if the team is lucky —and I feel like I'm missing a good chunk of her child-hood. I spend as much time as possible with her when I'm home, but I still feel guilty. I guess that's the way all working parents feel, but that fact doesn't make it any less upsetting. I can't really complain though because I hit the jackpot with my career. I make a good living for playing a game I love.

Before I could delve deeper into my sorrows, I heard Lexi yell, "Daddy! Sabrina's here!"

I opened my eyes and watched my daughter run through the door and to my side. Pain radiated down my leg as I struggled to sit.

"Do you need help?"

"No baby, I'm good. Thanks though." I rubbed my thigh above the brace and tried to breathe normally.

"She's going to make your leg better, right?" Her nose scrunched in that adorable way, making me smile.

"She sure is."

"Good, because you seem sad since you got hurt."

"How can I be sad when I get to spend time with my favorite girl?"

She shrugged. "You just do."

I grabbed the crutches I'd placed on the floor and shifted my butt to the edge of the couch, mentally bracing for the pain that will envelop my left leg once I stand.

"I'm not sad. Just a little sore." Talk about an understatement. I stood with a grunt and tucked the crutches into my armpits. "Come on, let's go find Jeff and Sabrina."

"Can I stay here and play Xbox?"

"Are you sure?"

Lexi loves playing Xbox, but she's been semi-obnoxious with her enthusiasm about Sabrina coming to stay so I'm surprised.

"I'm sure."

"Ok, I'll come back when I'm done with Sabrina."

She jumped onto the couch I just vacated, grabbed the remote, and switched on the TV. I crutched my way out of the room as she grabbed the game controller and brought the console to life.

Chapter Three

WHAT A COMPLETE LETDOWN. My heart had pounded triple-time all the way from the kitchen, through the family room, across the hallway, down the stairs, and finally into the gym.

I'd expected Dan to be there, but he was nowhere to be found, and neither was Lexi. Aside from the tens of thousands of dollars' worth of equipment, the large room was empty. Jodi hadn't been misinformed. To say Dan's gym is well stocked is a gross understatement. He possesses everything I'd want, plus a few things I'd love to have.

"I talked to Jodi, and I think everything you'll need is here. But if there's something missing, just let me know," Jeff said.

"No, it looks great. This place is a physical therapist's dream."

"I'm glad you think so."

The voice came from behind me. Slightly deeper than I

remembered, it was unmistakable just the same. My traitorous body broke out in goosebumps at the mere sound of his husky timbre. I slowly turned to face him, hoping my erect nipples weren't obvious through my T-shirt.

"Hello Bri." His warm smile exposed twin dimples on either side of his face.

My heart beat so loudly, I was sure he could hear it all the way across the room. Between that and my unruly nipples, I'm giving the wrong impression here. To look at my flustered appearance, you'd think I'm still attracted to this man, which of course is ridiculous. Not that he isn't attractive, because he is. No one could deny that. Dan is blessed with the kind of All-American good looks that make women fall for him left and right.

Except for me, of course. All my feelings for him died when I found out exactly the kind of man he is, which is definitely not the kind for me.

My thoughts finally slowed, making me aware of the fact that both Dan and Jeff were staring at me.

Jeff turned on his heel and headed for the door. He slapped Dan's shoulder as he passed. "You have your work cut out for you, buddy."

His deep chuckle echoed behind him as he left the room.

Dan turned to face me once again with faint amusement lurking in his remarkable eyes. A deep sea green fringed with lashes so long they could get tangled, his eyes had haunted my dreams for years. And here they are now watching me, reading my every expression. For some reason, my poker face has never worked around Dan. Unfortunately, he can read my every thought and feeling just by looking at me.

Needing to take control of the situation, I mustered up all the hostility I could. "What did he mean by that?"

His amusement was replaced by a look I could only describe as earnest. He glanced down at his leg, which is encased in a brace from just above the ankle to mid-thigh, then met my eyes again.

"Are you saying this is going to be easy?"

I thought I detected a double entendre, but let it slide.

"From what I read in your file, you're in for the ordeal of your life if you want to be one hundred percent for spring training next year."

"But you think it's doable?"

I let myself relax and shift into professional mode. "With a lot of time and effort, yes, I think it's doable. But I'm warning you right now, it isn't going to be easy. You're gonna have to work your butt off."

"I'm willing to do anything."

He looked sincere enough, but his expression hinted that he was speaking about more than therapy. Then again, maybe I'm just being overly sensitive. Dan and I happened a long time ago. He could have any woman he wants, why would he bother with me?

"Good. Then we shouldn't have any problems." I moved to get a chair from the edge of the room. Placing it next to Dan, I gestured for him to sit. Once he was situated, I took his crutches and leaned them against a weight bench, then knelt down beside him. "I want to examine it before we start anything." I removed the brace and set it on the floor.

Why the condition of Dan's leg surprised me is beyond my comprehension. I've read his file, so I should have been prepared. Even if I hadn't been, I shouldn't feel nauseated just looking at it. After all, I am a professional. I've seen worse.

Even though three weeks have passed since the accident and corresponding surgery, the entire outside of his leg is still tinged a sickly greenish-yellow color. My eyes trailed the kaleidoscope from his anklebone up to his knee, where I studied the fresh pink scar surrounding the kneecap, to his thigh where the color disappeared into gray gym shorts. I quickly averted my gaze, but not before registering the fact that he's dressing to the left today.

"The scar looks good," I said, attempting to distract myself from the impressive package in front of me.

"I guess."

"What didn't you like about Rawlins?" I asked.

When he didn't answer, I looked up then wished I hadn't. His green gaze was devouring me. It's the same look that had melted the heart of a too-trusting college sophomore. At the time, it made me feel desirable and special and loved. Now it just annoyed me because I know it's fake.

He must have read my every thought, because his gaze turned serious, and a little sad. "Do you still hate me?"

That wasn't what I'd been expecting to come out of his mouth. I stood, eager to put some distance between us. "Why would I hate you?" I tried to sound carefree and airy, but even to my own ears, my voice sounded shrill.

"That's what I thought," he said around a sad chuckle.

Wanting to end this conversation…*needing to end it*…I repeated my question. "Why didn't you like Tim Rawlins?"

"The man is a control freak."

"Control freak?"

"He and I didn't see eye to eye on a lot of things." My arched brow asked its own question. "Like if I told him I couldn't do something, he'd insist I could."

"It's a therapist's job to push his patient."

"I realize that, but I know my limits, he doesn't." He ran a hand through his thick blond hair, which I couldn't help but notice had darkened a couple shades since college.

"Look, I'm not a wimp. I have a relatively high tolerance for pain. Hell, I can't count the number of times I played with a sprain or strain, or even a break, but some of the things the guy wanted me to do, I just couldn't." Gesturing toward his leg, he said, "And my leg hurt worse after each session. I'm not a doctor or a therapist, but that doesn't seem right."

"Did you tell him that?"

Dan nodded and flashed a crooked grin. "In no uncertain terms."

I couldn't hide my smirk. "I can only imagine."

"We also had scheduling problems."

"Scheduling problems? Didn't he stay here?"

"Yeah, and he wanted to work all throughout the day."

"And you had a problem with that?"

"Not all the time, no. If I didn't have other commitments, I had no problem working whenever he wanted. But if I had something more important scheduled, I wanted time to do it."

I had to bite back my sharp retort. I could just imagine what would be more important. I should've known I'd have to work around his sex life. "I thought you wanted to be ready for spring training."

"I do." His gaze was unwavering.

"Then you're going to have to decide whether or not you can fit therapy into your social calendar. If you can't, let me know right now. I'm here to work. If you're not willing to give me your all, we'll both be wasting our time."

"Why are you getting so pissed?"

"I'm not pissed. I just want to set some ground rules. I'm willing to do whatever I have to in order to get you back on your feet, but I can't do the work for you. And, in order to do the work, you have to be here, not running around with your little groupies." Even as the last sentence was spilling out, I wanted to suck it back in. But I couldn't, and I imagined it floating over my head like a comic strip balloon.

The look on his face was a cross between amusement and aggravation. He opened his mouth to speak, but before any words emerged, another voice interrupted.

"Can I go shopping with Mrs. Evans?" Lexi asked.

Dan turned to face her. "Did she invite you?"

Lexi's head bobbed up and down. "She said we could stop for ice cream on the way home."

"Well, don't let me to stand in the way of ice cream."

Lexi's smile encompassed her entire face. She wrapped her skinny arms around Dan's neck and squeezed, then pulled back, kissed him on the cheek, and said, "Love you, Daddy. See you later, Sabrina."

I couldn't hide my reaction to that if I tried. My mouth was still dragging on the floor after Lexi bounded out of the room. I remember her speaking to me before she left, and I'm sure I replied, but I have no idea what the exchange was about. The word "Daddy" kept ringing through my head.

"You okay?" Dan's deep voice brought me back to the here-and-now.

"I didn't know she was yours."

"I was about to explain that she was the reason for any scheduling problems." I nodded in acknowledgement of his words, not knowing what else to do. "I help coach her softball team and the games are every Tuesday and Thursday at 5:30, so I can't workout then. I help her with her homework when she needs it, which isn't too often." He smiled proudly, "She's pretty smart. And with summer vacation starting soon, that won't be an issue."

"She seems like a wonderful little girl." I laughed,

starting to relax. "In fact, I complimented Jeff on that fact when I arrived. I thought she was his."

"I'm sure he took full credit for her." He smiled wryly. "Actually, he deserves at least partial credit." My confusion must have shown, because he explained, "Jeff is Lexi's nanny, for lack of a better term."

"Jeff's the nanny?"

"Not your typical nanny, but that's what it comes down to. He does other things for me, but keeping an eye on Lexi when I can't is his main responsibility."

"Oh."

"You seem surprised."

"Yes. I mean no. I mean, nannies are usually…" I searched my brain for a tactful way to vocalize my thoughts.

"Women?" Dan finished for me. I nodded. He clucked his tongue comically, shaking his head from side to side. "I'm surprised at you, Sabrina. I really am. I thought you were a modern woman. I didn't expect you to be so chauvinistic." His eyes crinkled in amusement.

"I am not chauvinistic."

"Stereotyping a profession like that. I won't tell Jeff about this 'cause he's bound to get his feelings hurt."

"Oh please." I finally gave into the laughter that had been threatening to surface since the exchange began.

Dan laughed with me for a few seconds, before our eyes clashed, stopping us both. Our sober gazes held for the space of several heartbeats until Dan drew a great breath, breaking the moment.

"Well, at any rate, I tried going the so-called traditional route, but it didn't quite work out."

It took me a minute to decode what he was saying. My hot flesh instantly cooled. Of course he couldn't have a female nanny. He wouldn't be able to keep his hands off her so she could actually watch his daughter. Typical Dan.

"It's not what you're thinking," he said, through clenched teeth.

"I'm sure it's not," was my flippant reply.

"The first woman I hired seemed perfect, but I found out she was leaving Lexi in her playpen all afternoon so she could binge watch whatever on *Netflix*. The next one appeared in my bed one night, so I fired her." He read the question lurking behind my eyes. *"Before* anything happened," he answered in a low growl.

"The next woman was too busy trying to get me to notice her daughter to pay attention to mine. And last, but not least, was Gracie. I thought she was the answer to my every prayer. A real Mary Poppins, you know? Her sons were grown and living out of the area, and she said she missed being needed. She was wonderful with Lexi…took her for walks, to the park, fixed her hair nice." He shook his head and laughed, as though he still couldn't comprehend what had happened.

"Don't tell me she ended up in your bed."

"Please don't put that picture in my mind." He shuddered and looked pained. "Too late." He shook his head as if trying to erase the picture, like you'd do to an etch-a-sketch. "No, nothing like that. But," he held up his index finger to emphasize his point, "shortly after she arrived, personal little tidbits about me started appearing on the internet."

"Oh no." I groaned.

"Oh yes. It seems Gracie had a sideline going with a handful of sites."

"How'd you find out it was her?"

"My agent has quite a few contacts in the media. He

couldn't get a name out of anyone, but he did find out their contact was a member of my household staff. That narrowed it down to Mrs. Evans and Gracie. When I confronted her, Gracie broke down and confessed. Needless to say, I fired her."

"So where did you find Jeff?"

"He was living in Manhattan, working on Wall Street, one step away from having a nervous breakdown. I saw him at my mom's one Thanksgiving and told him I needed someone to watch Lexi and the job was his if he wanted it, even if it was only temporary. He showed up before spring training started. He's been here ever since. He also handles my investments."

"So he's a friend of the family?"

"He is family. Jeff's my cousin."

"Oh, I thought I…never mind."

"Jeff was in the Navy when we were together. That's why you never met him."

Wanting to stop this line of conversation before it really got started, I changed the subject. "Do you have any ice down here?"

"Ice cups are in the freezer over there."

I made my way across the large room and extracted a Styrofoam cup filled with ice. I took longer than usual peeling the excess off the sides before heading back to Dan's side.

Kneeling down beside him, I carefully rubbed the ice over his injured knee. "We won't do much today. I want to assess your range of motion at this point so I can fine tune a routine. Can you work in the morning for a few hours straight?"

When he didn't answer, I lifted my head. His green eyes were boring into me. My hand stilled.

"Aren't you going to ask?" His voice was a mere whisper.

"Ask what?"

"About Lexi's mom?"

Chapter Four

SABRINA

HE DID IT AGAIN…SHOCKED me into silence. I knelt there with my mouth hanging open, not knowing what to say.

"Weren't you going to ask?" He sounded incredulous and his eyes shadowed with an emotion I couldn't quite place, and certainly didn't want to name, since it looked suspiciously like hurt. His voice was quiet, almost hoarse, when he spoke again. "Or don't you care?"

For some reason, my eyes filled with tears. Maybe it's because I did care, and didn't want to. Maybe it's because he sounded so concerned about whether I cared or not. But I'll tell you one thing…it is *not* because I have any real feelings for this man.

On that thought, I spoke, and perhaps a bit too harshly. "Why would I be surprised that you have a child?" I placed the ice cup on the table next to Dan then stood and turned away from him, wiping my suddenly sweaty palms on a towel. "If anything, I'm surprised Lexi is the only one." I faced him once again, my brow raised. "Or is she?"

"Yes, she's the only one." His words were carefully spaced, squeezed out through clenched teeth.

"Hmmm." I shrugged. "Well, that's something," I said as I moved across the room toward the hamper to discard the used towel, more for something to do than out of necessity. "Then I suppose I should be commending you on your outstanding behavior."

The moment that comment slipped, I wished I could just take it back.

Why am I being such a bitch?

In order to avoid the piercing gaze I felt at the back of my head, I straightened a stack of towels. That took a total of ten seconds, in which time the room was so filled with tension, I was finding it hard to breathe. With nothing left to do, I turned around and faced Dan.

The look on his face was far worse than I had imagined it would be after my snide comments. His green eyes were bright with anger, but cloudy with so many other emotions I got lost trying to put a name to each and every one.

The anger I understood. My comments on the subject had been juvenile and totally uncalled for. But I had trouble explaining the other emotions I saw lurking in his gaze. The hurt, regret, and disappointment were easy to define, but I still hadn't put a name to several others when he finally spoke, putting an end to the almost deafening silence.

"Will you ever forgive me?"

I was suddenly thrust back in time staring not into the face of the man in front of me, but that of the twenty-one-year-old I had loved back in college. He'd asked me that same question once upon a time. The answer I gave him back then was fueled by anger, a broken heart, and the shattered dreams and illusions of a naïve twenty-year-old girl.

I closed my eyes and mentally counted to ten in an attempt to clear my head. When I opened them again, I saw Dan waiting expectantly for my answer. And the Dan I saw was the Dan of today, and not the one of the past, so I felt some sense of accomplishment.

"Dan, I want to apologize for my comments. They were totally uncalled for. Lexi is a wonderful little girl, and I'm sure you're the one responsible for that." The tension slowly drained from his body, and his blazing eyes darkened. I took those as good signs and continued, "I promise to behave from now on." I smiled and held my right hand up as though taking an oath.

Good. This is good. I'm going to make it through this.

Since he seemed to be relatively calm, I moved next to him, picked up the ice cup, and ran it over his knee again. That done, I manipulated his leg in a series of movements to judge his range of motion.

"Scale of one to ten," I said in my most professional voice, "how bad is the pain when you unbend it this far?" I moved his leg so it was a forty-five degree angle to the floor.

"Ten," he gritted out through clenched teeth.

"How about this?" I held his leg out straight and rotated it slightly.

He thought for a moment. "Seven or eight."

He was a good sport while I finished my evaluation, but his pale complexion and sweaty brow told me he was in pain.

I picked up the brace and put it back on his leg. "I

think that's enough for today. I'll work on a routine tonight, and we can get started tomorrow."

I took his silence for consent and started to gather my things. "Do you need help going upstairs?" When he didn't answer, I turned to face him.

"You never answered my question."

"Your question?" I knew damn well what question he was talking about, and could tell he knew that I knew, but I decided to play dumb anyway.

He spoke with exaggerated patience. "Do you think you'll ever be able to forgive me?"

Oh hell.

How am I supposed to answer that? My feelings on the subject are so jumbled I'm not even sure what the answer is. We were practically kids when the actual events took place, but I'd be lying if I said his actions haven't affected every relationship I've had since then.

In the two years we were together, I never once suspected he'd cheated on me. It just didn't seem like something he would do. He was so loving and attentive and we spent practically every waking moment together. I still can't imagine how he had time to cheat. But he did, multiple times, with multiple women. Once I confronted him, the ball started rolling and before I knew it, I had more information than I cared to.

The thing that pissed me off then, and still does now, is that he was totally unrepentant. He just chalked it up to the whole "boys will be boys" thing. I quickly stopped my train of thought so I didn't lose my temper again and start making snotty comments.

"Bri?" He sounded unsure as he said my name, snapping me out of my wayward thoughts.

I cleared my throat to speak, although I had no clue as

to what I was going to say. "Dan, all that happened so long ago. I'd be a real bitch if I was still hanging on to it."

He searched my eyes for a moment before nodding. I thought that was the end of the subject, but he apparently wasn't ready to let it go. "But you still hate me for it." It wasn't a question, but a bold statement and before I could comment, he continued. "I can't even begin to imagine how the whole thing affected you. I was so stupid back then. We had a great thing and I…" He shook his head as if trying to get the idea of exactly what he'd done out of his mind. "I'm so sorry about everything."

"Dan, like I said, that was a long time ago."

"I just don't want you to hate me anymore."

Trying to lighten the mood, I said, "Afraid I'll make you work your butt off tomorrow?"

"I can handle it."

"Think so?"

He nodded. "The only thing I can't handle is that wary look in your eyes."

"I—"

"Don't even try to deny it, because I see it every time you look at me."

How can I deny it? I *feel* it every time I look at him.

"Okay. While you work on your leg, I'll work on my look. Deal?"

"Deal."

He held out his hand to shake, and I had no choice but to do so. His hand felt warm, his grasp firm, and I couldn't ignore the fact that my entire body broke out in goose-bumps when it made contact with mine.

DAN

· · ·

WHAT A MESS. I don't know what I expected to happen when we came face to face again after ten years, but it wasn't that. Even though she tried to keep things professional, her body language screamed hate and anger. And the hurt and caution in her eyes tore me apart.

I slowly made my way to Lexi's playroom, where I'd left her playing Xbox. Hopefully she'd still be there because I don't know if I could make it any farther. Sabrina didn't do much to my leg and it's screaming in pain. What's it going to be like when we really get started with therapy?

I found my daughter zoned out, playing Xbox. I said her name three times before she looked in my direction.

"Hi Daddy."

I leaned down and kissed her forehead before settling on the couch next to her.

"What do you want to do tonight?"

My limitations have been as tough on Lexi as they have been on me. We're usually pretty active and there are only so many movies to watch and videogames to play before we turn into zombies. Board games and puzzles keep us more engaged, but they're definitely not a substitute for a long hike or game of catch. Thankfully Jeff and Mrs. Evans have kept Lexi occupied outside the house so she doesn't totally bounce off the walls.

"Can we watch a movie and make popcorn?"

"Sure. You pick the movie and I'll go make the popcorn."

"Don't forget, a little butter and extra love."

"Always extra love." I chuckled and kissed her forehead. "I'll be right back."

Mrs. Evans would be happy to make the popcorn so I

can rest my leg, but Lexi says mine is better, and I live to make her happy.

I may have fucked up many times in my life, but that little girl is one thing I did very right. She's amazing and I can't imagine my life without her. Now if I can get the rest of my life straightened out, things will be perfect.

LEXI CONKED out way before the credits rolled and I called Jeff to carry her to her room for me. Instead of picking her up and heading out, he sat in the chair across from me and smiled.

"So how'd it go with Sabrina after I left?" The look I gave him turned his smile into a full-blown laugh. "That well, huh?"

I dragged a hand down my face, then rubbed the back of my neck. "She still hates me. I guess I deserve it, but I thought—I'd hoped—she would have gotten over what happened back then."

"Have you ever met a woman before? In my experience, they don't get over anything."

"I guess."

"Well, I don't know Sabrina, so take this for what it's worth." He stood and walked toward Lexi. "I don't think she hates you as much as you think."

"What makes you say that?"

"Just a feeling." He reached down, picked Lexi up, and settled her against his chest. "Remember, the opposite of love isn't hate, it's indifference…and Sabrina *definitely* isn't indifferent to you. So all you need is a little time to bring her back to Team Dan."

"Hopefully you're right."

"I'm always right, remember?"

That said, he went to tuck Lexi into bed, leaving me to my own thoughts.

Jeff is pretty good at reading people…hopefully he's right about Sabrina. Thankfully she's staying here during my rehab. I'll have a lot of time to convince her I'm not the same jerk I was back in college.

Chapter Five

SABRINA

"SO THIS IS where you hide out."

His voice came from directly in front of me and I opened my eyes to look up at him. I'd been so focused on my stomach crunches I didn't hear him approach.

"I'm not hiding," I panted out not stopping the exercise. "I'm exercising."

"Hmmm. I can see that."

His voice held a hint of a smile, but I refused to take the bait and ask him what he found so amusing. I also refused to think about the fact that I am only wearing gym shorts and a sports bra, my usual workout attire. I forced myself to do one last crunch and sat up on the bench.

Grabbing my towel off the floor next to me, I wiped my face and looked at Dan. "Did you need something?"

He seemed distracted as his eyes toured my body. Hell, I'd be distracted too if I had to look at me. My haphazard ponytail, sweat-slicked skin, not to mention seen-better-days workout gear can't be pretty to look at.

"I'm taking Lexi to practice then we're going out for ice cream. We thought you might like to come along."

"Oh, I don't…"

"Look Bri, it's Lexi's request. I know you'd rather avoid me as much as possible, but she wanted me to ask you."

"I'm not avoiding you." His eyebrow arched. "Dan, I see you every day, multiple times a day. How do you figure I'm avoiding you?"

"You only see me when you have to. It's been nearly two weeks and, other than our workouts, I haven't seen you at all. That's a pretty mean feat considering we live under the same roof."

"It is a big house," I said, attempting to use humor to diffuse the situation. When he didn't smile, I said, "I'm just busy."

"Uh huh."

I nearly lost it right then and there. Why does this man have the ability to get me so riled up?

Fine, let him think I'm avoiding him. What do I care? I was about to tell him as much when Lexi came bounding into the gym, her green eyes shining.

"Can she come?" She directed the question to Dan.

He pulled her close for a quick hug then left his arm draped across her shoulders instead of letting her go. "I don't know, honey. She didn't answer me yet."

Lexi shifted her gaze to me. How could I say no to that face?

"I'd love to." I looked down at myself and winced. "Do I have time to take a quick shower? I'm pretty rank."

Dan looked at his watch. "Can you be ready in twenty minutes?" He looked skeptical.

"No problem."

I called myself every kind of fool as I showered, brushed my teeth, got dressed, and pulled my hair into a French braid. I do not want to socialize with Dan. He's too good-looking, too charming. Like a moth to a flame, I feel myself being pulled toward him even though I know I'll inevitably get burned. It's best if I just steer clear of him whenever possible.

I slipped on my sneakers, grabbed a jacket, and set out to find Dan and Lexi. This outing is about Lexi, not Dan. I'll just have to focus all my attention on her.

Dan stepped into the foyer as I reached the bottom landing. His eyes lit on mine for a second before slowly making their way down, then back up my body. By the time they met mine again, my body was covered with goosebumps, and the room is not the least bit chilly. If anything, the temperature has risen significantly in the past minute or so.

Dan looked at his watch, then back at me. I couldn't help notice the hint of appreciation in his eyes. "You did that in twenty minutes."

It was more a question than a statement, and obviously a compliment. I felt myself blush.

"Do you want me to drive?" I asked, hoping to distract myself from his perusal.

"No, I can manage." He yelled for Lexi as we walked toward the front door. She ran past us and out the door seconds later. "Do you have your glove?" Dan yelled.

I watched Lexi skid to a halt, turn around, and trace her steps back into the house. She ran in the door, past Dan and me, and up the stairs.

"Does she ever slow down?" I asked as we walked to the car.

"No." Dan chuckled. "She even tosses and turns in her sleep." He chuckled again. The loving look in his eyes nearly melted my heart. "She sneaks into bed with me every once in a while and beats me to a pulp."

I was running his last sentence through my brain when Lexi burst out of the house, glove in hand, and jumped into the back seat of the Land Rover. Dan refused my help and struggled into his seat. He adjusted his leg and settled in before putting the key in the ignition and turning it. He shifted the car into gear and looked back at Lexi. "All buckled up?"

"Yep."

He lifted his foot off the brake and steered us down the driveway. "I'm just thankful that, if this had to happen at all, it happened to my left leg and not the right. I'd go crazy if I had to depend on other people to chauffer me around."

"How does it feel?"

"Sore, but not unbearable."

"Good. That's how it's supposed to feel."

I have to admit that I've been pretty impressed with Dan's sessions this past week. He's dedicated and hard-working, and I haven't heard him complain once. In fact, I usually have to stop him from pushing too hard.

"I can't wait 'til I don't have to wear this damn brace anymore."

"Daddy!" Lexi admonished from the back seat.

"Sorry honey." Dan's eyes crinkled in amusement. "I meant to say 'this darn brace.'"

"I'm sure you did," Lexi answered, sounding like a little old lady.

I couldn't help but laugh. Dan McMullen apologizing for saying *damn*.

"Lexi's my language patrol," he explained.

I looked back at her and smiled. "You must have your work cut out for you."

"It's not so bad anymore."

"I try to behave," Dan said.

"Sometimes he forgets after a long road trip if I'm not with him, but he's usually pretty good."

I had to remind myself that these words of wisdom are coming from an eight-year-old.

Dan glanced over at me. "I don't say anything really bad anymore."

"Lexi is obviously doing a fine job."

I SHOULDN'T HAVE COME. This outing was a big mistake. Instead of focusing my attention on Lexi like I'm supposed to be doing, more often than not, I find myself watching Dan. His patience with the girls is amazing, and they obviously adore him. Then again, they *are* female.

"Hey Bri."

Dan's booming voice broke into my thoughts. I looked up and he waved his arm in a "come here" gesture. How can he look so sexy and virile with a brace on his leg, a crutch supporting his weight, and twelve eight-year-old girls surrounding him?

The short walk from my place on the bleachers to the field seemed to take forever. The women on the other set of bleachers whispered as I walked away. I wondered how many of them Dan has been with.

"You beckoned?"

He looked at me for a moment before answering. "Would you be willing to pitch some batting practice for the girls here?"

"Batting practice?"

He nodded and scratched his jaw with his thumb. "Our usual practice pitcher is out of town and George here isn't so good at it." Dan gestured toward the man in question then took the opportunity to introduce us. "I obviously can't do it," he added, his eyes gazing at me with an exaggerated plea. "So whaddya say? Think you can still do it?"

"Got an extra glove?"

Dan handed me his and smiled. "Okay girls, take your positions. Megan," he pointed at an adorable red-head, "you're up." He leaned toward me and whispered, "Go easy on them, Bri, they're just kids."

His warm breath caressed my cheek. My knees went weak and for a minute I thought about leaning into him for support. Before I could do anything so crazy, the buzzing started up in the bleachers once again, restoring my sanity.

I took a step back and looked him in the eye. "Don't worry. I'll be gentle." Dan looked confused, then angry. I walked away before he could comment. Sometimes my poker face is better at relaying my feelings than any words could be.

DAN

THIS WOMAN IS TESTING my sanity. I love her more than life, but it pushes all my buttons when she gives me that look.

When Lexi asked if Sabrina could come to get ice cream with us, I thought it would be a great way to spend more time with her. And the fact that she could pitch batting practice beforehand is just icing on the cake. Unfortunately, I forgot about the moms. I'm sure Sabrina thinks I've slept with them all. I mentally snorted. Not a chance.

Since starting my career, the women I've met who want me for *me* have been few and far between. Back then, I didn't care so much. I was trying to get over Sabrina and fucking her out of my system with as many random women as possible seemed to be the best way to do that. Eventually I figured out that wasn't working and slowed down. Then I met Marie and my life changed forever.

I watched Sabrina and swallowed. The woman literally takes my breath away. It's not just her physical beauty, it's *her*. And watching her pitch batting practice to Lexi's team is making my heart ache. She's glowing. I forgot how much she loved playing softball and how good she was. I wonder if she still plays.

She jogged from the pitcher's mound to home plate to adjust Gianna DelVecchio's stance.

"Now as my arm goes back," I heard her say, "you get ready to swing. Okay?"

The little girl nodded.

Sabrina ran back to the mound, giving me a very nice view of her backside.

"Okay, here we go," Sabrina said just before she went into her windup.

Gianna swung and made contact…a rare occurrence. The ball sailed over second base and into center field. Sabrina and the girls cheered as Gianna's smile engulfed her face.

Gianna managed to make contact with a few more pitches, seeming to gain confidence with each hit.

"Last pitch," Sabrina said. "When you hit it this time, run the bases."

Gianna hit it over third base and it rolled into left field. She took off toward first base and Sabrina followed behind her. The little girl giggled as she rounded the bag and spotted Sabrina. The other players ran from their positions and fell in line behind and they all crossed second base, rounded third, and jumped on home plate in quick succession.

The team circled Sabrina and she gave them all high fives and said what a great job they did. I watched as Lexi threw her arms around Sabrina's waist and squeezed tight. She looked up and said something I couldn't hear. Sabrina leaned down and whispered into Lexi's ear. Whatever she said had my daughter grinning from ear to ear. Watching the two of them together made it difficult to swallow. I didn't think it was possible to love Sabrina more than I had when she arrived, but she just proved me wrong.

Chapter Six

SABRINA

"YOU ATE THE WHOLE THING?" Lexi asked, her eyes wide.

"Yep," I answered then spooned the last bit of hot fudge into my mouth.

"Wow."

"You ate your whole sundae, too."

"Yeah, but yours was huge." She held her arms out to demonstrate her last word. "Plus it had brownies in it." She looked at me as though seeing me for the first time. "How do you stay so skinny?"

I almost snorted the word back at her. Skinny? Me? I don't think so. The best compliment I can hope for is that I'm athletically fit. But skinny? Not in this lifetime.

As a child, I was what my mother referred to as "pleasantly plump." Thankfully, my "baby fat" melted away by my junior year in high school. However, getting rid of all my fat wouldn't do anything to shrink my frame.

"Big boned" is another term my mom used to describe my physique. So while muscle may have replaced fat, my large frame still makes me look more like a linebacker than a ballerina.

"I exercise," I said when I realized Lexi was actually waiting for an answer.

"Oh." She pondered that for a second before shifting her attention to Dan. "Daddy, can I have some money to play video games?" She smiled sweetly and held out her hand. "Please?"

Dan reached into his pocket and pulled out a five-dollar bill. He started to hand it to her, but pulled it back at the last second. "Okay, but stay where I can see you."

"I will," she said as she grabbed the money.

With my buffer gone, my nerves returned. Dan and I have had a lot of sparks flying between us all day—some good, some bad, but sparks just the same—and I don't want to face them, or God forbid talk about them.

"Thanks for practice today."

"No problem."

"Do you still play?"

I shrugged. "Once in a while, but nothing organized."

"Why don't you join one of those bar leagues?"

"I joined one once and everyone got so drunk before the games, it's a wonder they didn't kill themselves on the field. Besides, most of those leagues are slow pitch, and I don't enjoy that as much." I paused then added, "I joined a fast pitch, co-ed league once, but surprise, surprise, I sat on the bench with all the other women. I don't know what the purpose of a co-ed team is if only the men play."

"That's too bad. You should be playing. You're very good and I know how much you enjoy it."

"I had a good time today. Maybe I'll think about

coaching." I took a drink of water. "How do you manage to coach with your schedule?"

"Normally I'm just an assistant and I make games and practices whenever I can. But when this happened, I knew I'd have some time on my hands so I gave Mark—he's the guy who usually pitches—a break."

"You seem to enjoy it."

"I really do." His face showed the surprise he'd felt about that fact. "The kids are great. They're so honest and trusting, not to mention eager to learn." He scanned the ice cream shop until his gaze fell on Lexi amusing herself with a video game. Dan smiled as he watched her skinny arms shift and steer. A lump formed in my throat at his expression.

"So, where *is* Lexi's mom?"

He looked as shocked as I felt by the question. I will admit it's been at the back of my brain, dying to be asked, but never in a million years did I think I would blurt it out like that. I suppose subconsciously I want to hear so I can harden my heart a little. Tales of Dan's conquests should do a good job of that.

"I'm not sure where she is right now," he answered so quietly, I had to strain to hear him over the background noise. His eyes met mine and I definitely regretted asking the question. While the subject obviously troubled him, he looked happy that I'd asked.

His words came back to me. *Or don't you care?*

"Does Lexi know her?"

He shook his head and leaned back in his seat, looking weary. "If she had her way, Lexi wouldn't exist," he said as he pinched the bridge of his nose between his thumb and forefinger.

What the hell is that supposed to mean?

A crooked smile flashed on his face. "I love the way your every thought shows on your face."

I stiffened. "Yeah, well I don't."

The last thing I want is Dan McMullen being able to read my mind. Unfortunately, he's one of the few people who can look at me and know exactly what I'm thinking. My mother can do the same thing, along with a few friends. Why Dan is still included in that handful of people, I'll never know.

He chuckled and looked around the shop again in order to locate the topic of our conversation. Once he found her, he looked at me once again. "When Marie found out she was pregnant, she planned on having an abortion."

I shifted my eyes from Dan to Lexi and felt like someone had punched me in the stomach. She's such a beautiful, wonderful little girl, the thought of her never having a chance at life definitely struck a chord.

"Yeah," Dan snorted. "That's pretty much the way I feel every time I look at her." He looked me straight in the eye. "I'll admit I didn't jump for joy when Marie told me she was pregnant, but when she asked me for money for an abortion, I nearly went through the roof."

"Were you married?"

"No."

I opened my mouth to ask if he'd ever heard of birth control, but stopped myself. It seems cruel to tell the man he should have used something to prevent his beautiful daughter from being born. He wasn't looking as those thoughts were running through my head, so imagine my shock when he responded to them anyway.

"I've always been careful, Bri. *Always.*" His eyes bore into mine driving his point home.

"So what happened?" I tried to keep the sarcasm out of my tone, but don't think I was very successful.

"No birth control is one hundred percent effective." I arched my brow. "Dammit Bri, the condom broke. Okay?" he growled. He sighed and rubbed the back of his neck. "Regardless of how or why Marie got pregnant, the fact is, she did. I've always believed in a woman's right to choose, but I don't know, when it was *my* baby she was choosing to get rid of…" He shook his head and glanced over at Lexi. "I just couldn't let her do it."

"How did you stop her? I mean, it's not like she would have needed your permission."

"No she didn't, and she reminded me of it every time I failed to march to the beat of her drum."

"I can't imagine you marching to anyone's drum but your own," I said, more with admiration than sarcasm.

He chuckled. "You'd be surprised." He took a long drink of his sweet tea and looked serious once again. "I wanted to get married and try to raise the baby with some sense of tradition, but she didn't want any part of that." He shrugged and took a deep breath, letting it out slowly. "When I look back, I realize how dumb that idea was. We would've killed each other." He shrugged again. "But at the time, it seemed like the thing to do."

He paused again and ran his index finger up and down the condensation on his glass. I sensed his reluctance to speak as sharply as I felt his need to open up to me. What I couldn't understand is why. Why is he telling me all this? Why does he seem to care what I think? And why the hell do *I* care at all?

"If you don't want to tell me—"

He cut me off before I could finish my sentence. "No, I want you to know the whole story."

Why? The question rang through my head again, but I didn't ask for fear of what his answer might be.

Dan took a deep breath and started to speak, but smiled at a point behind my shoulder instead. "Hey munchkin, all out of money?"

Lexi sat down next to me and nodded, grabbing her soda and taking a long draw on the straw at the same time.

"Did you kick some alien butt?" Dan asked.

Lexi laughed and rolled her eyes. "You are so old, Dad."

"Hey." He pretended to look offended, but his eyes crinkled in amusement.

Lexi looked at me wide-eyed and nodded. "He is, you know."

"Sorry Dan, I'll have to go with Lexi on this one."

Even though Dan and I were the same year in school, I'm a year younger. We were both born in September just before the cutoff for Kindergarten, and while my mother decided to send me as soon as I was eligible, Dan's held him back a year.

"You're insulting yourself then, because we're the same age."

"You must have me confused with someone else. You're more than a year older than me."

Dan rolled his eyes. "A whole year. Big deal."

"A year and a few days," I explained. "And a year is a year, Dan." Lexi and I shared a conspiratorial smile.

Dan laughed and shook his head. "Let's get going before you two really decide to gang up on me."

DAN

. . .

"SO HOW'D IT GO TODAY?" Jeff asked.

"Good," I answered. "Great actually."

Jeff chuckled. "You are really gone over this girl. It's fun to watch. I've never seen you like this, even with Marie."

"She's the only one I've ever been like this over. Everyone after her was just to distract me from how miserable I was without her."

"How's it going? Does she know you want to get back together?"

I shook my head. "She finally doesn't look like she wants to run from the room when I enter. I need to be patient so I don't scare her away."

"That's not really your strong suit."

"I'll be anything for her." Jeff's look made me chuckle. "I know, it's bad."

"I hope it works out for you," he said. "You deserve to be happy."

"I just don't know if I deserve her."

"So you fucked up when you were in college. We're all young and dumb at some point."

"It was different with her. I asked her to marry me. We looked at rings."

"You never told me that."

I shrugged. "What difference did it make once she was gone?"

Before things got too heavy, we turned our attention to the Waves game I'd put on before Jeff joined me. My teammate, and one of my best friends, Jack Reagan hit a line drive into the gap between left and center fields, scoring Cal Chase from second base, giving the Waves a 1-0 lead over the Rays. Jack ended up with a double.

Jack is the person who convinced me to hire Sabrina as my physical therapist. He'd listened to me whine about her more than once over the years, usually when I had too much to drink. When things went south with Tim Rawlins, the trainer the Waves set me up with, he told me I should contact Sabrina.

I'll admit that I'm guilty of stalking her online and I know she's well respected in her field. Heck, she was amazing back in college. So I know if anyone can get me back into shape, it's her.

The inning ended with a pop fly to first base, but the Waves had managed to score two more runs, bringing their lead to 3-0.

"They're looking good this year," Jeff said.

I nodded, not wanting to talk about the team. It really sucks that I'm not out there playing.

"She asked about Lexi's mom."

For a second, Jeff looked confused by my abrupt change of subject, but he quickly caught up.

"What did you tell her?"

"The basics."

"What did she say?"

"Not a whole lot, but the look on her face said it all." I rubbed the back of my neck. "I was gonna tell her everything, but Lexi came back to the table."

"Everything?" He raised his brows. "The whole story?"

I nodded. "The whole story."

"Not many people know that."

"No, but I want her to."

"Well, if nothing else, it should make her realize you're not a total asshole."

"Gee thanks."

"You know what I mean."

"I do," I said. "And I hope you're right. Because if this doesn't work out with her…" I shook my head, "…I don't know what I'll do."

Chapter Seven

I HAD JUST CURLED up in the window seat, book in hand, when I heard a knock on my door. I set my bookmark as I walked across the room and opened the door. I'm not sure who I was expecting, but when Lexi stared back at me over the threshold, I was somewhat shocked. She looked adorable in a pair of purple Tinkerbell pajamas, her hair curling around her heart-shaped face.

"Can I ask you something?" She looked so serious, I was almost afraid to hear the question.

"Sure." I stepped back and gestured for her to come into the room. "What's up?"

Lexi walked over to the bed and climbed up, setting herself at the corner of the mattress with her legs dangling over the edge. She looked at me warily for a second before speaking. "How did you do that to your hair?"

My hair? That's it?

Oh, thank God.

I ran my fingers down my braid. "Well, it's kind of like a regular braid, but you start with a little bit of hair and keep adding more as you go." It was a pathetic description of how to do a French braid, but the best I could offer.

"Do you think you could do it to mine?"

"I don't see why not." I walked over to my dresser to get a brush.

"You don't have to do it now," she said, though I could tell she wanted me to do just that. "I'm going out with my friend Cindy tomorrow, and I thought that maybe you could do it for then."

I tucked one leg beneath my rear end as I sat behind Lexi on the bed. "How about if I practice now and then I'll be really good at it for tomorrow?"

"Okay." I heard the smile in her voice. She scooted further back onto the bed, her legs straight out in front of her.

I pulled the brush through her hair a few times to remove any knots then went to work on the braid.

"Daddy and Jeff can do a regular braid, but not this kind."

"Well, as long as they know how to do a regular braid, I can teach them how to do this for you."

"Do you really think so?" She attempted to turn her head around to look at me, but I held her steady.

"If I can do this, anyone can."

"Did your mom teach you?" Her wistful tone made my heart ache.

"No, a friend taught me when I was in high school. The whole basketball team wore our hair like this for games. I practiced on anyone who would sit still for me, but it took me a long time to be able to do my own hair."

We chatted about hair and other girly things while I

finished the braid. "All done." I wrapped an elastic at the end. "Why don't you check it out?"

She jumped off the bed and ran to the dresser in order to peer into the mirror above it.

"Here." I stood and went to my purse to retrieve a compact. "Turn around." Lexi turned, and I held the hand-sized mirror up in front of her and explained how to look into it so she could see the back of her head. She struggled at first, but her beaming smile told me when her eyes finally made contact with what she wanted to see. Before I knew what was happening, she thrust herself at me and wrapped her arms around my waist.

"Thank you so much." She looked up, her green eyes shining. "I love it. You can do it again tomorrow, right?"

"Definitely."

"Thanks so much, Sabrina," she repeated, and squeezed me tight once again.

"Hey, what's going on in here?" Dan's voice bellowed from the doorway.

"Sabrina did my hair for me, Daddy. See?" She turned around so the back of her head faced him. "Don't ya just love it?"

"It's gorgeous," Dan said, dragging out the last word, which caused Lexi to break out laughing. "But aren't you supposed to be in bed? I distinctly remember tucking you in a while ago."

Her laughing stopped abruptly. "But Daddy, it's not like I have school tomorrow."

"No, but you're going out with Cindy tomorrow morning and I don't want you to be a grumpy pants."

Grumpy pants? Did I just hear Dan McMullen, athlete extraordinaire, master seducer, say grumpy pants?

Lexi's bottom lip stuck out in a pout. "Can Sabrina tuck me in?"

Dan looked surprised by the question, then his eyes met mine and he said, "That's up to Sabrina."

Lexi turned to face me, her eyes hopeful. "Will you?"

"Sure honey, come on."

We walked across the hall to her room and she climbed into bed. Once she settled in, I pulled the covers up and tucked them under her chin.

"Thanks Sabrina. Good night." She rolled onto her side and snuggled up.

"Good night Lexi. Sleep tight."

She closed her eyes and I backed out of the room, turning the light off as I passed through the doorway. I suppressed a scream as I backed into the solid wall of Dan's chest. His arm grabbed at my waist to steady me, but if anything, his touch made me feel more off-kilter. I sucked in a deep breath before turning around to face him.

"Sorry." I took a step back, putting some much needed space between us. I looked down to his leg. "Did I hurt you?"

"No, not at all." He took a deep breath. "I was hoping we could finish our conversation."

I didn't have to ask what conversation he was talking about. "Okay."

"Downstairs?" His eyes glanced towards Lexi's door. Without another word, Dan started toward the stairs and I followed.

Flopping onto the couch, Dan laid his crutch on the floor next to him. He stretched his injured leg onto the couch, his back resting on the arm, his other foot on the floor. I settled into the oversized chair across from him and watched as he rubbed his thigh directly above the brace.

I stood again and walked over to him. "Let's take this off for a while." My fingers went to work on the Velcro closures. I removed the brace and tucked a pillow beneath his knee. "Better?"

"I thought I had to keep it on at all times."

I shrugged as I settled into the chair once again. "Yes, to keep your leg immobile, you should, but I'm here to make sure you don't make any sudden moves." I said the last sentence in a cheeky tone.

"I'm sure you will," he said around a smile. Suddenly my words took on an entirely different meaning. I felt myself blush, but kept quiet. "Well, in any case, I thank you for giving me a reprieve from that thing."

"You're welcome."

Dan's gaze met mine again and the light-hearted tone disintegrated. He looked so serious I almost didn't want to hear what he had to say.

"Also, thank you for taking care of Lexi. I really appreciate it."

"You don't have to thank me for that. It was nothing."

He shook his head. "It wasn't nothing. I mean, it might have been nothing to you, but it was definitely something to her." He ran his fingers through his hair, then clasped his hands behind his neck and stared at the ceiling. When his eyes met mine again, they were so filled with sorrow, my throat tightened.

"I try my best, so does Jeff, but we're just not…" he gestured, then shrugged, "…women." I would have laughed at that statement if the subject matter weren't so serious. "Anyway, that braid thing you did…her friend Cindy wears her hair like that a lot and Lexi loves it. I bought a book on how to do it, but couldn't make heads or tails of the directions."

My heart softened with every word he uttered. "I can teach you how to do a French braid," I offered, before he spoke again.

"Really?" He looked nervous about the fact.

"It's easy. As long as Lexi is willing to sit still and you're willing to practice, you'll have it down in no time."

"I'd appreciate that."

Dan's gaze shifted to his toes and he pinched his bottom lip between his thumb and forefinger. He seemed to be pondering something and I settled myself further into the chair, tucking my legs beneath me, while he did.

"It just kills me that the two things she wants most, I can't give her." I arched my brow. "A mother and siblings."

I was shocked by his admission and had to fight my first instinct to utter some awful sarcastic reply. The fact that I didn't say the first thing that came to mind scared me more than the fact that I find him more attractive by the minute. When it comes to his relationship with his daughter, Dan is so sweet it's hard not to respond.

Time to move onto a topic of conversation that makes him sound more like the scoundrel I know him to be.

"You never finished telling me about Lexi's mother."

He took a deep breath and let it out slowly, dragging his fingers through his hair at the same time. "When Marie found out she was pregnant, she wasn't happy." He looked straight at me and explained. "She's a model and was afraid the pregnancy would ruin her figure." He rubbed his brow. "I don't know how much of this you want to know."

"Whatever you feel comfortable telling me."

He seemed to think about that for a minute before he spoke again. "When she told me she was pregnant, I was shocked, as I think I mentioned before." I nodded and kept silent, encouraging him to continue. "She was furious and actually searched me out in the locker room before a game."

"She just barged into the locker room?"

He chuckled. "Not exactly. She knocked on the door

and had someone get me. She told me about Lexi in the tunnel. Needless to say, my mind was not on the game that day. I kept thinking about the baby. By game's end, I had decided that the best thing would be for Marie and me to get married and raise her. She had other ideas," he added dryly. "She didn't want me or my baby." He chuckled, but there wasn't a trace of humor in it. "And she told me so in no uncertain terms."

"So what did you do? I mean, obviously you convinced her to have Lexi."

"I bribed her," he blurted out, then stared at me as if waiting for me to lash out at him. When I didn't, he relaxed a little and continued. "I offered her a half million dollars plus training expenses afterward so she could get her figure back." He rolled his eyes.

"And she agreed?"

"Not at first, but eventually yeah, she did. A half million dollars is a lot of money."

"But you said she was a model." I hear model, I automatically assume big bucks.

"She was, but she wasn't a supermodel or anything. Besides that, like athletes, modeling careers are generally short." He shrugged. "So she took the money and ran."

"Literally?"

"Practically. She took off two weeks after she gave birth to Lexi."

"And you haven't seen her since?"

"She came back when Lexi was one. It was in the legal agreement my lawyer drew up that she had to sign off rights after giving birth, but she had a year to reconsider. He had to contact her to come in and sign again. Lexi and I were there too. She barely looked at her."

"What a bitch." When I realized I said that out loud, I cringed. "Oh God. I didn't mean to say that."

Dan laughed. Not a small chuckle, but a full-blown belly laugh. "I always could count on you to tell it like it is." He wiped at his eyes and sobered. "Whatever she is or isn't, she's gone and I'm left to explain things to Lexi." He shifted his weight and the therapist in me went on instant alert.

"Are you okay?" I jumped out of my seat, but he stilled me with a raised arm.

"I'm fine. I mean, my leg is fine, but my butt went numb."

I settled back into the chair. "Sorry, there's no therapy to fix that."

He snapped his fingers. "Shucks." Our eyes met and held and my entire body broke out in goosebumps. I quickly averted my gaze.

Why does he affect me like this?

Dan must have sensed my unease and he continued his story. "Up until recently, it wasn't an issue. Lexi had me and Jeff and Mrs. Evans, not to mention my entire family. I don't think she realized anything was missing. A lot of her friends' parents are divorced, so I guess that's why she never questioned it. But somewhere along the way, she realized that her friends have both a mother and a father somewhere. So we were eating one night and she just blurts out, 'where's my mommy' and I nearly choked on my burger."

"What did you tell her?"

"I thought about telling her she died, but I've seen enough movies to know the lie would come back and bite me in the ass one day. So I just told her Marie left. I think 'went away' was the exact phrase I used.

"I'm just not sure how much more to tell her at this point. She's only eight. I don't want to lie to her, but I think she's too young to know the truth." He pinched the bridge of his nose as he continued. "I don't want to weave some fairy tale for her to believe in, but I also don't want her to know the ugly truth. I'm sure there's a middle ground somewhere in there, but I'll be damned if I know what it is." He dropped his hand to his lap and his eyes met mine once more. "The problem is that once she gets a question in her head, Lexi doesn't quit until she gets an answer."

DAN

I STARED at the ceiling and replayed my night with Sabrina over and over in my head. When I saw that braid thing she did to Lexi's hair, it felt like someone punched me in the gut. And then when she tucked her into bed, it was almost too much.

I thought I got it together during our walk downstairs, but then I ended up spilling my guts to her. I still can't believe it. Only my family knows the whole ugly truth about what happened with Marie. And I didn't do it to convince her that I'm some kind of saint…sharing it with her just seemed right. Her reaction made me love her even more.

It's obvious she cares about Lexi, but part of me is worried about what will happen if I can't make this work. It's obvious that Lexi has gotten pretty attached to Sabrina. What happens if once she's done here, she just goes away and we never see her again? I'll have to talk to her about that.

This is a complication I hadn't thought through when Jack helped me concoct the plan to get Sabrina into my life again. Besides Mrs. Evans, there hasn't been a woman around my house on a regular basis. I haven't had a real girlfriend since Marie and I didn't think it would be right to get Lexi attached to someone I'm not serious about. So I guess it's inevitable Lexi would gravitate toward any female, especially since she's asked about her mother.

I shook my head. That's not totally true. I don't think Lexi would give her affection to just anyone. She's a pretty smart kid, and seems to know when someone is being nice to her to get to me and when they genuinely like her. I think she's spent enough time around the ballpark to tell the difference. My chuckle echoed in the quiet room. Lord knows Sabrina falls into the latter category. If she had her way, she'd spend more time with my daughter than she does with me.

Although things have been better lately. That wary look isn't in her eyes anymore and her words have lost their sarcastic bite. I think it's safe to say we're friends now. Now I just need to convince her to take that friendship to the next level.

Chapter Eight

I COULDN'T FALL asleep for thinking about all the things Dan had told me. I've always considered myself a modern, free thinking woman, but I can't understand how a woman could nourish a child inside her body for nine months, give birth to her, and then walk away like she doesn't exist. It's bad enough when a man walks away from his flesh and blood, but to me, it seems so much worse when a woman does it.

I really admire Dan for all he's done for Lexi. The mere fact she was ever born speaks volumes about his stubbornness and determination. He was only twenty-three when Lexi was conceived. I assume most men would have simply let Marie get the abortion she craved instead of shackling himself with a baby while he was in his prime… especially when he was just starting his career.

His little settlement with Marie must have taken a large chunk out of his earnings back then. Maybe I'm not giving the males of our species enough credit, but I think what Dan did was extraordinary.

My problem now is that I have to remember to keep these soft feelings for Dan the father out of my dealings with Dan the sexually active, couldn't-be-faithful-to-save-his-life man.

The sun was not welcome through my window the following morning, nor was the knock on my door that had actually stirred me from a restless slumber in the first place. I nearly shouted "come in" in order to avoid actually getting out of bed, but remembering where I was, I quickly decided against it.

"Just a minute," I yelled as I reluctantly flipped back the covers and dragged myself out of bed. I cringed when got a glimpse of myself in the mirror. My hair looked like a rat's nest and it's a wonder I can focus through my red, puffy eyes. My shorts and tank top aren't something I usually greet people in, but right now, I'm too damn tired to care.

I opened the door and found Lexi on the other side. "Good morning, Sabrina."

I didn't want to contradict the child, so I simply said, "Hi, Lexi. How's it going?"

"Great." Her eyes glanced first up then down the hallway before she whispered, "Daddy told me not to wake you, but you said you'd do my hair today and Cindy'll be here to pick me up soon."

"What time is it?" I asked around a yawn.

"Nine o'clock." As if on cue, the grandfather clock at the top of the stairs started ringing its hourly tune.

"Oh man, I'm supposed to have a session with your dad now. I can't believe I overslept."

Lexi shrugged. "No big deal. He's downstairs eating breakfast. So, can you do it?"

She jumbled the last two sentences together and it took my sleep-riddled brain a second to figure out what she was talking about.

"Your hair?" She nodded enthusiastically. "Sure. Come on in."

Lexi hopped onto the bed while I retrieved my brush and an elastic from my dresser. I climbed on the bed behind her and brushed the knots out of her hair.

"You look tired," she said.

I nodded and started braiding. "I had trouble falling asleep last night." As if to punctuate my words, I yawned again.

"Are you married?"

Whoa! Where did that question come from?

"No."

"Neither is my dad. Do you have a boyfriend?"

"Not right now."

"Neither does my dad." She chuckled. "Have a girl-friend, I mean."

I think I know where this is going and I'm going to do my best to change course. "So what are you and Cindy going to do today?"

"Her mom is taking us to Magic Land. I'm gonna go on the rollercoaster. Do you like rollercoasters?"

"I love them," I answered truthfully, securing her braid with a purple holder.

"So does Daddy." Lexi turned around to face me, her green eyes dancing. "Maybe we can all go to Thunder Mountain together. They have the best rollercoasters."

"It's gonna be a while before your dad can go on a rollercoaster."

"Oh yeah. I forgot." Some of her enthusiasm faded for a second before she thought up another uncomfortable topic of conversation and it rekindled. "You used to be Daddy's girlfriend."

Although she said it more as a statement than a question, I answered her anyway, hoping that would end the conversation. "Yes."

"How long were you his girlfriend for?"

I nearly groaned in frustration. "About two years."

"Two years!" she shouted and hopped on her knees. "That's an awful long time."

I shrugged. "I guess so."

"Why aren't you his girlfriend anymore?"

Because your father was a lying, cheating scumbag.

"Well, that's a tough one," I said instead. "We just kind of broke up. He was graduating and going off to play ball and since I was a physical therapy major, I had another year of school." I trailed off there, hoping she'd let it go.

"You coulda gone with him. Uncle Jack's girlfriends go with him all the time."

No such luck.

I didn't want to get into a discussion about Uncle Jack…whoever he may be…and his girlfriends, so I simply said, "Things were different then. Besides, I was still in school. I couldn't go anywhere."

"Don't you think my dad is cute?" Before I could answer, she added, "All my friends do."

"Yes, he's cute," I answered, hoping once again, to put an end to the conversation.

Lexi opened her mouth to speak but three sharp knocks on the doorframe stopped her. She leapt off the bed and opened the door wide. "Daddy, how do you like my hair?"

"It's great. Are you all ready to go?" Lexi bobbed her head up and down. "Good, 'cause I saw Cindy and her mom pulling into the driveway." As if he had it timed, the doorbell rang signaling Cindy's arrival. "There they are. Grab your gear and I'll meet you downstairs."

"I'm sorry I overslept, Dan. I'll meet you downstairs in a half hour."

"No problem." His eyes made a lazy tour down then back up my body. "Nice jammies."

His intimate tone, not to mention the appreciative look in his eyes made my heart beat double time.

"I'll meet you downstairs," I said sternly and backed him out the door. Lexi came bounding out of her room. I wished her a good time before stepping into my room and closing the door.

ONE NICE THING about working with a single patient is that getting a late start doesn't disrupt an entire day's worth of appointments. Essentially, I'm at Dan's disposal twenty-four-seven and since Lexi's gone, Dan is free all day.

Our first workout of the day is going remarkably well despite its late start. Dan really is giving it his all and I have no doubt in my mind he'll be one hundred percent for spring training next year. His pain level is still relatively high, but I've seen a big improvement in his range of motion in the month we've been working together. I was telling him that very thing while I iced his knee.

"When can I stop wearing this thing?" he asked, pointing to his brace.

"I'd say not for a while, but you'll have to ask your doctor."

He grunted in response, but otherwise remained silent. I felt his hot gaze on the back of my head, but chose to ignore it…well, ignore it as much as I could.

"There you go," I said when the ice melted down to the end of the Styrofoam cup it was encased in. "All done."

I made the mistake of looking at him. His eyes glowed with a hint of amusement, and something more.

My face grew hot and the hair on the back of my neck stood on end. He took my hand in his and rubbed his thumb slowly across my knuckles. His eyes dropped to our co-joined hands and for a moment I thought he was going to raise my hand to his lips, but he didn't. His gaze met mine again and he smiled.

"I just wanted to let you know that I think you're cute too."

I felt all the blood drain from my face in a rush and my over-heated skin froze like the ice I still held in my hand. My mortification was obvious and Dan spoke again in what I'm sure was an attempt to make me feel better. But the fact of the matter is, no matter what he says, I'll still feel like an idiot.

"I'm sorry. I wasn't eavesdropping, but I overheard part of your conversation with Lexi." He looked at me for the space of several heartbeats before he continued. In that short span of time, I couldn't help but wonder just how much of the conversation he'd heard.

"I want to apologize for Lexi and I promise I'll talk to her. She shouldn't be asking you things like that and backing you into a corner like she did."

"Did you hear the entire conversation?"

He shook his head. "I'm not sure how much I missed. The first thing I heard was why we're not together anymore."

"That was about midpoint." I walked around picking up towels, putting things away. Even from halfway across the room, I felt his gaze pull at me. How can I be so attracted to a man whose core values are the exact opposite of mine? Somewhere deep inside I must be warped.

"Did I miss anything important?" he asked.

"No, I don't think so. She just kind of verified that we, uh, dated in college."

I walked back over to him to place his brace back on his leg. I know he's quite capable of doing it himself, but I'm more accomplished at the task and always do it for my patients. That way, I'm assured it's on properly.

"We did more than date, Bri. We were practically engaged."

I held back the snort of laughter that was just dying to be released along with at least a dozen seething replies. Dan and I have been getting along well and I don't want to upset the peace. I didn't want to continue this line of conversation and told him so. He looked like he was going to argue, but then relaxed his posture.

"Just one more question," he said.

I ran my fingers through my hair and looked at the ceiling. "What?"

"How did she know about us?"

"I don't have a clue, but she did know. When she said 'you used to be Daddy's girlfriend' it was a statement, not a question." I shrugged. "I figured you told her."

He shook his head and pinched his bottom lip between his thumb and forefinger. "No, I never told her."

"Then, I don't know." That said, I felt the subject was closed. "Okay, I'll see you around three?"

He nodded but continued to look confused. I took the opportunity to make my way out of the room.

"Bri." His voice stopped me in my tracks, but I didn't turn around. "Thanks for not making me sound like a jerk."

I didn't know what he was talking about and turned around and told him so.

"When Lexi asked you why we broke up." He shrugged. "Instead of telling her what an idiot I was, you just told her we were going in different directions. I appreciate that. I really don't want her to know how I used to be."

I tuned out that last part. I don't want to hear all about how he's changed. "You're welcome."

I turned on my heel and left the room.

DAN

I HOBBLED out to the pool, cursing the entire way. This damn brace is driving me crazy. If my career didn't depend on my leg making a full recovery, I would have taken it off weeks ago.

Dropping into a lounge chair, I grabbed the pillow from the chair next to me and propped it under my knee. Settling back, I took in a deep breath and slowly let it out. These sessions are getting a little easier, but still hurt like hell. But at least the pain makes me feel like I'm making some kind of progress. It also helps distract me from my attraction to Sabrina. Otherwise, I'd be sporting wood every minute we're together.

Before I could think about that too much, my phone rang.

"Hey Dan, it's Chris."

"Everything okay?"

She chuckled. "Lexi is fine. But I ran into some friends who are camping nearby. They invited us to their site for dinner and to roast marshmallows later. I was wondering if Lexi could sleep over tonight since we'll be getting back pretty late."

"Oh, sure," I said. "As long as she's up for it."

"They're both really excited."

"Do you need me to drop anything off for her?"

"No, she has a toothbrush at the house and she can borrow something of Cindy's to wear."

"Sounds like she's all set."

"Yep, we're good. I'll have her give you a call later."

"Thanks Chris."

I disconnected and dragged my fingers through my hair and closed my eyes.

"Hey, you busy?"

Jeff blocked the sun from my face as I heard his voice.

"Yeah, can't you tell?"

"I have some papers for you to sign. Do you want to do it here or inside?"

"Are there a lot?"

"About ten."

I sighed. "Inside, I guess. It's easier."

We made our way to Jeff's office and he gestured for me to sit in the chair behind the desk. Jeff produced a folder and set two papers in front of me before starting to explain what I was signing.

I held my hand up to stop him.

"Just tell me where to sign. I don't need to know the details."

"Seriously?"

"Seriously. You're moving money around, right?"

"Yes."

"That's all I need to know. The rest is Greek to me."

I spent the next few minutes signing and initialing where Jeff pointed. When I was done, he put the papers back in the folder and placed it on the desk.

"You know, you should pay more attention to these things."

"I used to and it hurt my head," I said. "Thankfully, I

have you for that now and based on the bottom line, I'd say you're doing a good job."

"I could break things down for you."

"Nope, I'm good."

"I just don't want you to think—"

"Jeff, you're the expert at this. I wouldn't ask you to understand how to do what I do."

He snorted. "Yeah, like that's so difficult."

"You know, I can kick your ass, even with this brace on."

"No need for that." He held his hands up in mock surrender.

"Thank God." I chuckled. "Are we done here?"

"Yep."

I grabbed my crutch and stood.

"I have to find Mrs. Evans and let her know it's just Sabrina and me for dinner tonight."

"How come?"

"Lexi is sleeping at Cindy's and you're out."

"Why don't you give Mrs. Evans the night off and take Sabrina out?"

"Huh?" I caught the edge of the chair with my crutch and stumbled. I righted myself and said, "Seriously?"

"Why not? You both have to eat and she has been friendlier toward you lately."

"I don't know." I rubbed my forehead.

"What's *your* plan?"

"For what?"

Jeff rolled his eyes. "For getting Sabrina back."

"I don't really have one."

"You got her here. Now you gotta take your shot and your time's running out. She'll be gone before you know it and then what will you do?"

"I've been trying not to think about that," I mumbled.

"Ask her out to dinner and take it from there." He chuckled. "And I can't believe I have to coach you through this. You're the ladies' man, not me."

"That's not really going to help me here."

"Tell Mrs. Evans you won't need dinner, then go work your magic."

"I guess I could." I shrugged the crutch back into place under my arm.

"Try to sound a little more enthusiastic when you ask her," Jeff said. "Good luck."

"Thanks man, I'm probably gonna need it."

Chapter Nine

SABRINA

I CLOSED the book I was supposed to be reading and rested it on my knees. For nearly two hours I sat perched on the window seat, book in hand, staring at the words on the page, but not reading any of them. The only words filling my head were Dan's.

No matter how hard I tried, I couldn't put them out of my mind. Not only the words, but the manner in which he said them. He actually looked sorry and slightly embarrassed. That's more than I got when I confronted him ten years ago. Back then he'd been a bit cocky and not the least bit apologetic.

Is he really sorry, or is it just an act?

Should I even care?

No, I shouldn't.

Do I care?

Unfortunately, and totally against my will, I do.

But why? Why after all these years do I care whether or not Dan is sorry?

If I'm being totally honest with myself, the answer to that last question is because he's the first boy I ever loved… truly loved, not just had some schoolgirl crush on. There wasn't anyone before him and there sure as hell hasn't been anyone since. No one who matters anyway.

Let's face it. Dan has left some sort of indelible mark on me that I can't erase. Subconsciously, I've compared every man I've dated since college to him. And sad to say, not one has measured up.

I flopped down on my bed and stared at the ceiling. As depressing as my thoughts are, they're one hundred percent true. Instead of blocking all these facts out, I've decided that I better face them if I'm going to be strong. Face things with my eyes open, as they say. Dan has been making subtle moves on me all week and I'm determined to not fall for his charming smiles and sweet words. I can't risk it.

My watch alarm chirped signaling that it was time for Dan's next therapy session. Time to face him again. I got off the bed and headed for the door. With every step I took toward the gym, I steeled myself against him.

I can do this.

I gave myself a pep talk all the way through the house, to the gym. Three more weeks, four at the most and I'll be gone…five on the outside. At any rate, this is only temporary. Soon I'll be able to leave and pick up my life right where I left off, a bit richer in the process.

The partnership I'll obtain upon my return to the clinic will definitely put me into a new tax bracket. But it's not just the money, it's the satisfaction of reaching my goal that's spurring me on. In the end, it will all be worth it.

Before long, this time with Dan will be a distant memory, but the partnership will last forever, or at least until I die. I just have to keep my focus.

When I stepped into the gym, my jaw nearly hit the floor. I kept my focus all right. I focused right onto Dan's bare chest and bulging biceps as he curled hand weights. I have to admit that, despite his various flaws, Dan is one fine specimen of manhood.

Being a physical therapist, I've seen all sizes and shapes of men in various states of undress and haven't batted an eye. And as I look at Dan, I still haven't batted an eye, because I haven't blinked once.

His back and shoulders are broad and I find myself fascinated as his muscles flex and relax with his movements. The angle he's sitting at also gives me a view of his magnificent chest and six-pack abs, which are covered with tawny hair that disappears in a straight line into his gym shorts. That line is like an arrow directing my eyes to his shorts and what lies within them.

I had just dragged my gaze from the area of his anatomy that I have no business staring at when Dan noticed my presence. He turned his head so quickly in my direction, I couldn't help but wonder if he felt my eyes on him the entire time. I covered my embarrassment with hostility.

"Don't you know that you should never lift weights without a spot?" I marched toward him.

He actually looked amused, which pissed me off even more.

"I think I've heard that somewhere before." He lifted the weights into my line of vision. "But as you can see, these are only twenty pounds each, so unless I accidentally bash myself in the head with them, I think I'm safe."

What he was saying was true, but I didn't want to admit it, so I ignored the statement entirely. I retrieved a Styrofoam ice cup from the freezer and prepared to get down to business.

Kneeling beside him, I removed his brace, and iced his knee. As I did so, I explained a few slight alterations I made to his routine. "If it's too much, let me know. I don't want you to push yourself too hard."

"Do you want to go out for dinner tonight?"

His abrupt change of subject, as well as his question, threw me off guard. "What?"

"Would you like to go out to dinner tonight?" he repeated in an overly patient tone.

"Oh." I stood and wiped my hands on a towel. "I don't think so."

Annoyance, then determination shone in his eyes. "Come on, Bri. Except for Lexi's practice, neither one of us has left this house. Jeff has a date and I told Mrs. Evans she could go home since Lexi isn't here." He flashed a smile that lit up his whole face. "So it's just you and me."

I thought about that for a minute. Since I can't boil water without scorching it and the last time I'd seen Dan cook, he burned the food way past the point of recognition, we'd probably have to order out anyway. And, given a choice, I'd rather eat somewhere in public with him than at home alone. It's definitely the lesser of two evils.

"Okay."

"Okay?"

I laughed out loud at his shocked expression. Apparently he thought he was really going to have to turn on the charm to persuade me.

"Great."

"But first we have to finish your workout."

"Right."

"That's why I'm here, you know. To get you all better," I reminded him, lifting his foot and moving his leg in a series of pre-workout warm-ups. He flinched as I held his heel and rotated it from side to side.

"Does it feel any better than it did earlier?"

He shook his head. "No."

"How about this?" I pulled on his heel in an attempt to straighten out his leg.

"Argh! It hurts like hell."

I sat back on my heels and looked at his leg then up to his face, covered with a fine sheen of sweat. I would have liked to try the new routine, but didn't think he was ready.

"Okay," I said as I stood. "Nix the new routine. Just run through the usual, and if at anytime it hurts above a five, stop immediately."

"Yes ma'am."

I ignored that and started him moving in an attempt to keep the tone professional. If we're going to be alone tonight, I want it to be on my terms, not his.

I SAT on my bed and called myself every kind of fool. Why did I agree to go out with him tonight? Even when we have Lexi as a barrier, the sparks fly between us. What will it be like when I don't have anything other than him to focus on?

I stood and walked to the closet. Now, what to wear? We'd decided to go to a little Italian restaurant in town that Dan said looks like a hole in the wall but serves the best food he's ever tasted. So I don't need anything fancy, but I don't want to look like a grub either. Then again, I don't want to look like I'm dressed for a *date* date.

I wish I could see what Dan is wearing. I've only seen him in sweat pants or shorts since I've arrived, but he assured me that he'd get into something decent for our night out.

Why do I care?

On that last thought, I yanked a pair of khaki capris, a white sleeveless shell, and black cardigan sweater off their hangers with more force than necessary. The hangers rattled against each other before settling into place.

After donning my clothes and slipping my feet into a pair of sandals, I studied the result in the mirror. I decided to let my hair hang loose, and brushed it until it framed my face. I know that by the end of the night it will be driving me crazy…which is why I usually pull it back…but for now I'm happy with it. I wish I had some make up to dress up my face a little, but lightly glossed lips will have to do. I picked up my purse and headed out the door.

There seemed to be an awful lot of noise coming from the family room, but I figured Dan was watching a game with the volume up too loud. How wrong I was. I recognized the men sitting in the room and hoped like hell none of them recognized me. No such luck.

"Sabrina, is that you?" Moose Johnson asked.

I nodded reluctantly as the once buff football player ambled over to hug me. His beer belly banged into my chest as his beefy arms circled around my back. Just when I thought I was going to pass out from lack of oxygen, he released his grip. "You didn't tell us Sabrina was here, Dan."

"Sabrina's here, Moose," Dan said, deadpan. Then he explained, "She's my physical therapist."

I heard a chorus of "holy hell," "no shit," and "get outta here" before Dan spoke again. "We're actually heading out to dinner so—" Their collective protests cut him off.

"Dan, come on," Moose said, looking like a pouting child.

Another of Dan's chums from college chimed in, "You gotta be kiddin'." John Levecchi was a mere inch taller than me and in college had been thin and wiry. The guys had nicknamed him "Chugger" because of his ability to drink more quantities of beer than any of them, despite his small stature. From the looks of John's distended abdomen, all that beer had finally caught up with him.

Moose—who if he has a real name, I don't know it—and John were starting to whine when what sounded like the voice of reason spoke up. "There's no need to go out. Murph is bringing pizza," Kent "the Kentster" Ainsworth said.

Kent had been Dan's roommate freshman year and that fact is his only claim to fame. I met Kent a few months before Dan and I started dating and even then I thought he was a snake, but for some reason, Dan took a liking to him.

He was the bane of my existence for the two years Dan and I dated and is the person who told me about Dan's philandering. Not out of the goodness of his heart, you understand. No, no, when he told me, Kent had me pinned against the wall, trying his best to get in my pants. He had been slightly drunk at the time, but not so far gone that he didn't know exactly what he was doing.

At first, I tried to treat the whole thing as a joke, which I had hoped it was. When that didn't work, I got down to some serious pushing and shoving.

"Kent, cut it out. You know I'm seeing Dan," I'd said. Although I wouldn't have touched him with a ten foot pole, regardless. But I didn't feel the need to be cruel. Unfortunately he did.

He'd snorted. "Yeah, I know, but it's not like he's not out enjoying a little variety."

"Get out, Kent," I'd said forcefully. I didn't believe him, but my stomach knotted at the thought.

His laugh had sounded evil and his sneer scared me. "You actually think Dan is being faithful?" He'd looked at me with mock pity. "Oh God, you do, don't you?" He laughed, but there was no humor in the sound. "Dan's been getting some of the best pussy on campus while he has plain little Sabrina to escort to Mom and help him with his homework. Did you actually think someone like you could keep Dan happy?"

That was about all I could take. I'd fled from my own room so Kent wouldn't see me break down. His words had cut clear to my core and released every doubt I had ever had about myself and my relationship with Dan.

I'd never understood why Dan was with me instead of the walking Barbie dolls who'd drooled over him as they followed him around campus. But, as Dan later confirmed, he was having the best of both worlds, just as Kent had said.

"Sabrina," Dan's voice broke into my sour thoughts. "Are you okay?" He used his crutch to push himself up from the couch and make his way toward me.

Kent slapped his hand against Dan's chest. "She's fine. Aren't you?"

I wanted to scream at him, I wanted to blame him for everything that went wrong between Dan and me, but in my heart I knew I couldn't. Kent is a weasel and I certainly don't trust him, but Dan is the one who cheated on me all those years ago. I just can't help but wonder how Dan would react if he knew how I found out. He had asked, but I never told. It didn't seem important at the time. I guess it still isn't.

"I'm okay, Dan."

"See, told ya. Why don't you sit back down, Dan the Man? Murph should be here any minute with the pizza and some girls to go with it." He glanced at me as he spoke the last few words, a smirk playing on his thin lips. "You've been cooped up way too long buddy." He bobbed his eyebrows. "You've got a reputation to keep up, don't forget."

"Sabrina?" Dan looked like a drowning man.

If he was looking to me to be the bitch and demand we go out to dinner, he was looking to the wrong person. I've been the party pooper more than once with these guys when Dan didn't have the guts to tell them he couldn't go out because he had to study or just didn't want to go out. I'm not doing it now.

"Actually, I'm not all that hungry."

Dan was about to say something when Murph barged through the front door, his arms laden with pizza and five of the most gorgeous women I've ever seen trailing in his wake. I didn't stick around to be introduced.

DAN

WHAT IN THE *ever-loving fuck just happened?*

After wrestling myself into khakis and shrugging into a button down shirt, I'd made my way downstairs to wait for Sabrina. When the doorbell rang and I found Kent, Moose, and Chugger on the other side of the door, I was anything but pleased. I let them in, hoping to convince them to leave before Sabrina made an appearance.

Besides the fact that I know Kent was never her

favorite person, I'd been looking forward to our night out. Apparently she hadn't been at all, because instead of backing me up when I told the guys we already had plans, she totally bailed on me.

After Sabrina went back upstairs, Murph showed up with an armload of pizza and a bunch of women. The way Kent took over as if he lived here kind of pissed me off, but I fought the urge to freak out. Even though they showed up unannounced and uninvited, they are old friends. I never want to be one of those pricks who forgets his old friends just because he finds more interesting people to play with.

A cute redhead settled on the couch next to me.

"How's the leg?" Her high-pitched voice nearly burst my eardrums.

"Coming along."

When she leaned closer, pushing her right tit into my left bicep, I shifted, putting space between us. She stuck out her bottom lip in what I assume is supposed to be an alluring pout, but it just pissed me off. I shifted further away from her and she got the hint. Face pinched, she walked across the room and sat next to Moose, who had a brunette on his other side.

Kent sank into the other side of the couch and handed me a beer.

"It's good to see you, man. How's it going?" He gestured toward my leg with his bottle.

"It's getting there."

"I'm sure Sabrina is whipping you into shape."

"Yeah. She said I should be good to go for next season."

"That's good. Really good," he said. "Hey, why didn't you tell me she was here?"

I wasn't sure how to answer that. How do I ask him

why the hell I would tell him anything about my daily life without sounding like a total dick? And the truth is, I don't talk to Kent all that often. Between Lexi, my family, and baseball, my plate is pretty full. A few phone calls a year is all I can handle. Plus, Kent and the guys still like to hang out in bars and chase women, and that's just not me.

He looked around the room.

"Where's everyone tonight?"

"Jeff is out, Lexi is spending the night at a friend's house, and I gave Mrs. Evans the night off."

"Then it's a good thing we stopped by, right?" He slapped my shoulder. "I'd hate to think of you here all alone."

I mentally snorted. If Lexi was home, this would never be happening. Not the women, anyway.

"I was taking Sabrina out to dinner."

Taking a long draw on my beer, I tried to tamp down the disappointment. Sure, I kind of coerced her into accepting my dinner offer, but if she really didn't want to go, she could have just said no.

"So you and Sabrina," Kent said. "You're a thing?"

I looked over at him.

"A thing?"

"Yeah, you know, like back in the day."

"Kent, she's my physical therapist." He's one of the last people I'd confide in.

"You guys just seem kinda cozy here all alone."

"What's your point, Kent?"

"Just curious…" he waggled his eyebrows and continued, "…you finally get to fuck her?"

I jumped up, grabbed Kent's arm, and pulled him off the couch. In the back of my mind, I registered the fact that conversation behind me stopped, but I didn't care.

"That is none of your fucking business." My low tone intensified the words.

Kent's Adam's apple bobbed up and down and he let out a nervous chuckle. I loosened my grip on his arm and stepped back, noting the twinge in my knee.

"Hey, Dan, I was just—"

I cut him off before he could finish and piss me off even more.

"I think you should leave now."

Chapter Ten

SABRINA

THE SUN HAD BARELY CLEARED the horizon when I made my way down to the kitchen. After leaving Dan to the mercy of his friends, I went for a long walk before retiring to my room to finish the novel I'd brought with me. It was a love story with a happy ending so, needless to say, it didn't lift my spirits much.

Empty beer bottles and pizza boxes trailed from the family room to the kitchen and dirty dishes and discarded napkins littered most every surface. I looked at it all with disgust and took pity on Mrs. Evans, who undoubtedly would be the one to clean up the mess.

I tried not to think of the events of the previous night as I scooped coffee into a filter. The smell of ground beans filled my senses and my mouth watered in anticipation of my first cup. Normally one cup would be my limit, but after my restless night, I figure I might need at least two or three to keep me going today.

The coffee had just started brewing when I heard the back door knob jiggle. Expecting Mrs. Evans, I was surprised when Jeff walked through the door.

"Hey Sabrina." He was obviously surprised and a little embarrassed to see me. "What are you doing up so early?"

I laughed and took in his slightly disheveled appearance. "I could ask you the same question." I watched in amusement as a blush crept up his neck, turning his entire face crimson. I can't believe he actually blushed.

"Would you like some coffee?"

"Sounds good." He settled onto a stool at the breakfast bar. "What the hell happened here?" he asked as he shifted a beer bottle aside.

"Dan had a party last night," I answered, retrieving two mugs from the cupboard.

"Dan had a what?" He looked around at the evidence. "I thought you two were going out to dinner."

"We were, but then some of his friends showed up." I attempted to sound nonchalant, but don't think I was very successful.

"And?" he asked pointedly as I set a steaming mug in front of him.

"And what?" I took a sip of the potent brew.

"Don't 'and what' me, Sabrina. I know how much Dan was looking forward to having dinner with you."

I did not want to process that last bit of information. "They brought pizza," I said as if that explained it all, but just in case it didn't, I added, "They brought girls, too."

Jeff cursed under his breath and took a long drink of coffee, then gritted his teeth as if he just downed a shot of whiskey.

"That Kent guy, right?"

"Moose, Murph, and Chugger, too."

"I never liked Kent," he said.

"Yeah," I snorted, "join the club."

"He's a wannabe. It's like he's riding Dan's coattails through life." He looked me in the eye. "Was it always like that?"

I nodded and swallowed a mouthful of coffee. "Pretty much. Kent used to leech onto Dan every weekend because he knew he couldn't get into any good parties without him. Once Dan and I got together, he'd arrange for Kent to get into places without him just so we could have an actual date." I shrugged. "And speaking of dates, I don't think Kent ever had one that Dan didn't either arrange or date first."

"What about you?"

My eyes widened at his question and I nearly choked on my coffee. "What about me?" I asked although I knew what he was asking.

"Did you date Kent after you broke up with Dan?"

I crinkled my nose in disgust. "Please Jeff, you're making me sick."

"I'll take that as a no." His blue eyes twinkled.

"That's an absolutely, positively, gag me, not in this life-time no." I shuddered at the thought. "Not that he didn't try." I have no idea why I added that, but once it was out, there was no taking it back.

Jeff stilled and placed his mug down with a dull thud. "Kent hit on you?" I nodded. "After you and Dan broke up?" I shrugged. "What does that mean?"

"Jeff, I don't want to talk about this. It's ancient history."

"Yeah right," he snorted. "Before or after Sabrina?"

I blew out an exasperated breath. If Jeff is anything like Dan—and I can see now that he is—he won't quit until he gets an answer. And I'd much rather answer him now than later, in Dan's presence.

"Before, during, and after." I crossed my arms over my chest and flashed him an are-you-satisfied-now look.

"Does Dan know?" He took a sip of coffee.

"No."

"You know the shit would hit the fan if he did, don't you?"

I had to resist the urge to snort and say, "Yeah right." Instead I carried my mug to the coffee maker and refilled it. As I added cream I said, "Like I said, that was a long time ago."

"Doesn't matter. You were important to Dan, still are. He cares about you more than he's ever cared about any other woman."

"And God knows he's had his pick," I muttered under my breath. Unfortunately, Jeff heard.

"Like you said, Sabrina, that stuff happened a long time ago. Dan's changed a lot since then. This…" He waved his arm around the room pointing out the mess from the impromptu party, "…isn't Dan anymore. I don't know if it ever really was."

I remembered many quiet evenings at either Dan's apartment or mine wrapped up in each other's arms. Sometimes we'd watch a movie, sometimes not, but regardless, the quiet times were always the best.

Sure, we'd go to parties and out to dinner, but Dan seemed more relaxed at home. However, that didn't stop him from going out with or without me, didn't stop him from…

"I don't want to talk about this anymore."

"You just don't want to face the truth."

"You want truth? Huh?" I felt my temper rise and couldn't control it. "The truth is that your sainted cousin and I dated for two years in college. He gave me a pre-engagement ring, talked incessantly about the future…*our* future…and all the while he was screwing every girl who came along."

"Every girl but you."

All the blood drained from my face. Those very words had been on the tip of my tongue. Can Jeff read my mind too?

"That. Is. Irrelevant."

"Regardless." He shrugged. "It obviously bothers you."

I wanted to deny it, but couldn't. "Hell yes, it bothers me," spilled out of my mouth before I could stop it.

He smiled. He actually had the gall to smirk at me while I stood in front of him, my chest heaving. The thing that bothers me most is that it's not just an ordinary smirk. Oh no, it's one of those I-know-something-you-don't-know smirks.

"Well," he started in a cheery tone, "it's a good thing you don't care about Dan anymore."

I was about to respond when I heard the topic of our conversation making his way down the hall. I shot Jeff a look that warned him not to say another word on the subject. Apparently he got my message loud and clear because he held his hands up as if in surrender, then grabbed his mug and leaned back in his chair.

Dan ambled into the kitchen wearing only a pair of loose gym shorts, looking better than a body had a right to this early in the morning. His eyes were bloodshot, but other than that, he looked sexy as hell with his slightly rumpled hair and shadowed jaw. I know from experience how that stubble would feel against my fingers and skin. My stomach flipped at the thought.

"Morning." His voice sounded raspy. "What are you guys doing up so early?"

"I just got in," Jeff said.

Dan gave him a "way to go" look before turning his

attention to me. "What about you?" Dan settled himself onto a stool. "Why are you up so early?"

The sight of his bare chest was very distracting, and I had to make a conscious effort not to stare. Only the rest of him was just as bad. His cheek still held the crease from his pillow and his hair looked adorably mussed, like someone ran their fingers through it. I froze. Maybe someone had. There were girls here last night after all. That thought cooled me off fast.

"I woke up and couldn't fall back to sleep." I dumped my now-cold coffee into the sink and rinsed out the mug, setting it on the drain board before turning around. "Come downstairs whenever you're ready. I wasn't expecting you up this early and planned on getting a workout in myself."

"Lexi usually bounces in on me at the crack of dawn." His eyes twinkled with amusement. "The one day I get to sleep in and I wake up early anyway." He pointed to the coffee maker and looked at Jeff. "Did you make that?"

"No. Sabrina did."

"Good, then it's safe to drink."

"Hey, mine's not so bad." Jeff sounded offended.

"Jeff, your coffee could double as paint stripper."

"Wimp."

Dan chuckled but didn't comment.

"Let me down a cup of coffee and change." Dan pushed up from his stool and made his way around the island to the coffee maker. I backed out of his way. "I didn't sleep too well last night myself. Hopefully some caffeine will give me a jump start."

I bet you didn't sleep well.

What I actually said was, "I'll see you downstairs."

DAN

"WHAT THE HELL happened here last night?"

"Damned if I know," I said, settling onto a stool. "One minute I was ready to go out with Sabrina, the next my old college crew showed up, and she flaked on me."

"Flaked?"

I took a sip of coffee and nodded. "Said she wasn't hungry and went upstairs."

Jeff looked at me like I was a few cards short of a deck.

"What?" I asked.

"I think your pretty face has made getting women too easy for you, because it doesn't seem like you have a clue." Before I could ask what the hell he was talking about, Jeff asked, "Why were they even here?"

"They just stopped by. Said they were in the neighborhood."

"With pizza and women?"

I shrugged. "It's been years since they stopped by like that. Not since Lexi was a baby." I chuckled at the memory. "They didn't stay as long that time. She was teething and screamed the entire time they were here."

"Too bad no one screamed this time. Maybe you would have made it to dinner."

He walked over to the sink, washed his mug, and set it in the draining rack. "I'm gonna take a nap. See you later."

After topping off my coffee and pouring a bowl of cereal, I surveyed the clutter around me. I'd never allow Lexi to leave a mess like this for Mrs. Evans, so I shouldn't either.

I settled into my Cheerios and thought about what Jeff said. Maybe he's right—maybe women have come so easy to me, I don't know how to deal with a challenge. And Sabrina's been challenging from the day I met her.

I swear I fell in love with her the minute I saw her in the trainer's room taping ankles. It took me weeks to convince her to go out with me. Even then, every subsequent time I asked her out, I was never confident she'd say yes. She just didn't seem to be that in to me. It was only after we were dating a few months that I felt secure.

Life would be so much easier if I could just forget her, but I can't. For whatever reason, she's it for me, always has been.

I finished my cereal and took a last gulp of coffee. After cleaning and setting my bowl and mug to dry, I grabbed two large garbage bags from the pantry.

Time to clean up my mess.

Chapter Eleven

I CONCENTRATED ON MY WORKOUT. Breathe in. Lift the weight. Breathe out. I repeated the mantra in my head through my thigh and bun reps, then altered it slightly for stomach crunches. My riotous thoughts distracted me from keeping a count, so I simply kept doing crunches until my muscles ached.

After stretching and mopping off my face and arms, I walked across the room and snagged two five-pound weights off the rack. Bracing my legs shoulder width apart, I started my routine, but no matter how hard I tried to concentrate, my mind wandered back to the things Jeff said.

Regardless what he thinks, or how smug he acts, I do not care about Dan anymore...not in that way anyway. Sure, as his therapist, I'm concerned about his wellbeing, and I have to admit we've had some pretty good conversations since I've been here. I suppose I'd consider him a friend more than an enemy at this point, but it's not like I want a relationship with him or anything.

Then why were you so upset at the thought of him with another woman?

I wasn't.

Yeah right.

Straddling the bench, I sat then rested back, my feet still on the floor. Stretching my arms out alongside me, I slowly raised them until the weights touched then lowered them to the side again. I've been doing these exercises for over a year now, and I haven't noticed any lift to my boobs, but I figure it must be doing some good somewhere. My mind wandered shortly after I finished my first set of ten.

I can't believe I was actually fooled into thinking Dan changed. Last night just proves he hasn't. Sure he spends most of his time with Lexi now, but as soon as she's not around, he reverts back to his old ways.

But he didn't invite them over. They showed up on their own. He made plans with you, not them.

Yeah, he made plans with me, but he didn't hesitate to cancel them.

He didn't cancel, you did. If you said you wanted to go out to dinner, he would have sent them packing.

I don't need any favors from him.

He wanted to go with you and you know it.

Then why didn't he say so instead of just sitting there like a moron?

Ask him.

I shook my head again and tried to concentrate on my weights, deciding that I must be schizophrenic because having arguments with yourself inside your head is just not normal.

"Don't you know that you shouldn't lift without a spot?" Dan shot my own words back at me.

I paused, my arms raised straight out over me and tilted my head back to look at him. Big mistake. He'd cleaned up all right. His clean-shaven face held a shiny softness and his hair still looked damp from a recent shower. Navy performance shorts replaced the old gray gym shorts he'd worn earlier and a white T-shirt boasting the blue and yellow Carolina Waves logo stretched across his magnificent chest.

Not wanting to be at a disadvantage, I stood and faced him. "It's okay. I'm a professional."

Instead of commenting, Dan let his gaze roam over my body. "You look cute."

In ratty shorts, a sweat-soaked tank top, my wet hair half-in and half-out of its ponytail, and my face as red as a beet? I don't think so.

I turned away from him and went to place the hand weights back on the rack. That done, I did a few cool-down stretches. Dan's eyes tracked my every move.

Removing my ponytail from its holder, I finger-combed my hair and once again pulled it off my face into some semblance of order. "Let me grab a drink and we can get started." I felt his eyes on me as I walked to the refrigerator and grabbed an orange juice for myself, and an ice cup from the freezer for Dan's leg.

When I turned around to make my way back across the room, I nearly fell down when I crashed right into the solid wall of Dan's chest. I didn't even hear him come up behind me. How can a man wearing a leg brace and using a crutch move so quietly? His right hand clamped around my elbow in order to steady me.

"Whoa," he said.

"God Dan, don't sneak up on me like that."

"Sneak?" he chuckled. "Bri, I couldn't sneak these days if my life depended on it."

"Well *I* didn't hear you." I took two quick gulps of juice and squared my shoulders. "And please don't call me Bri."

Dan is the only person who's ever called me that and I used to love it. I thought it was sweet. You know, like Ricky Riccardo calling Lucille Ball "Lucy." Then again, he was a cheating pig, too.

"You never minded before."

"Well, now I do." I had to resist the childish urge to cross my arms over my chest and stomp my foot to emphasize the point. At the thought of my arms, I realized that Dan's hand still had possession of mine. I pulled it out of his grasp.

"You're pissed," he sighed, rubbing his brow.

"I'm not pissed. I just don't want you to call me Bri. No one calls me Bri." I knew what he was talking about, but chose to play dumb, with the hope he'd drop the subject before it got started.

"I've always called you Bri," he pointed out. "And you know that's not why you're pissed. You're mad about last night."

I finished my orange juice in one long gulp and threw the empty bottle into the recycling bin, but didn't say a word.

"Why didn't you say you wanted to go out to dinner? Insist that we go out to dinner? The guys would have understood. After all, they dropped in uninvited and unannounced."

"Then why didn't you tell them to go?"

"Because you said you didn't want to go out. You said you weren't hungry."

He cannot be this dense.

"Did *you* want to go out to dinner?"

"I wouldn't have asked you if I didn't." He looked at me and sighed. "Yes, I wanted to go out with you."

"Then you should have said that instead of sitting there like a mute."

"But you said—"

"I know what I said, Dan. Why should I have said anything else? Huh? If you had really wanted to go out with me instead of having a party with your friends, you should have said so. I was the bad guy enough back in college, I refuse to play the role now."

The aggravation drained from his face and was replaced with something that looked suspiciously like understanding. Since he seemed to be a captive audience and I was on a roll, I continued. "You need to say what you mean and take responsibility for your actions." I could have gone on, but I figured I made my point and realized that I was starting to sound like a shrew.

I took a deep, cleansing breath, which was a big mistake because my lungs filled with the clean fresh-from-the-shower scent of Dan. At that moment I realized how close he was standing. My eyes widened and met his smoldering gaze.

The air between us crackled. I wanted to step back but couldn't. Tried to look away, but I couldn't seem to do that either.

Dan's eyes bore into me and of course he could read my every thought, anticipate my every move. I swallowed hard and attempted to put some space between us. He shook his head and took a step closer, fully invading my personal space. I was about to protest—at least I like to think I was—but he placed his index finger across my lips and shook his head again.

"I promise I'll take responsibility for my actions."

My befuddled brain didn't have a chance to process the

meaning of Dan's words before his mouth claimed mine with a kiss that started out frantic, but quickly turned into something softer, slower, more languorous, but no less potent. Somewhere in the back of my mind I realized that I'd dropped the ice cup I had been holding. It landed on the floor with a dull thud.

I knew I should step back and push Dan away, but all I could manage was to take my now-empty hand and wrap it around the back of his neck. I curled my cold fingers into his hair, threading them through the damp strands, seeking the warmth of his skull. Dan's moan echoed against my chest.

He took a step closer still, backing me up against the refrigerator. His fingers plowed through my hair and tilted my head back and to the side, opening my mouth further to his sensual exploration. I had expected a full-blown, tongue-tangling kiss, but instead, he nibbled at my bottom lip before fully placing his mouth over mine once again and applying a wonderful suction that nearly brought me to my knees.

My mind whirled and my resistance—yeah right, resistance—weakened as Dan's mouth opened and closed over mine in a steady rhythm. The taste of him filled my senses as his tongue swept into my mouth. It was both familiar and new, as were the sensations he stirred within me. Only Dan has ever made me feel this way, this out of control, this wonderful.

The kiss went on and on, long and hard, soft and gentle, our tongues tangling in a hot, sexual union. He was literally making love to my mouth and I loved every single minute of it. A groan erupted from Dan's chest and he pulled back slightly, looking down at me with heavy-lidded eyes.

"Oh God, Bri," he groaned before dipping his head and starting all over again.

I couldn't say how long the kiss lasted or how long it would have gone on—or God forbid, what else would have happened right there against the refrigerator—if the distinct sound of Lexi's feet pounding down the stairs didn't break through the sensual fog that surrounded us.

If I want to be totally honest—and I'm not sure I do—I didn't actually hear anything until Dan broke the kiss. His head had cocked to the side as he listened, but his burning green gaze never left my eyes. In their depths I saw his desire so clearly, I couldn't turn away.

Lexi's steps danced closer and Dan squeezed my waist gently before taking a step back. His eyes were still on mine, but when I licked my lips, they dropped to my mouth. He closed his eyes and took a deep breath in through his nose and let it slowly out his mouth.

Part of me was terrified of the desire I saw etched on his face, but another part felt thrilled. My own body hummed with a need I haven't felt for ten years. And if the bulge in Dan's shorts was any indication, he was pretty turned on himself.

"Daddy!" Lexi ran across the room and flung herself at Dan. How he caught her, I'll never know. My legs feel so weak a good breeze could blow me over.

"Hey munchkin. Did you have a good time?"

Lexi's head bobbed up and down. "Uh huh. Hi Sabrina."

"Hey Lexi. How were those rollercoasters?"

She looked me over before answering. "They were awesome." Her eyes left me and returned to Dan, giving him the same once-over. "Sabrina likes rollercoasters too, Daddy."

"I know."

Right then my stomach felt like it was on a roller-coaster. Why does Dan affect me like this? I've made love with guys before and haven't felt this flutter. I needed to gain control of myself. Letting Dan kiss me was a big mistake with a capital B.I.G. Kissing him back was even worse.

"Do you want to put this off until later?" Dan raised a questioning brow and I felt myself blush. "I thought you might want to postpone your workout so you could spend some time with Lexi."

His "yeah right" look made me feel like a coward, but I suppose that's exactly what I am where Dan is concerned.

"Did you eat breakfast, honey?" he asked Lexi.

"Mrs. Evans is making it now."

"Give me a half hour?" he said to me.

"Sounds good."

That should give me enough time to get my head together.

Dan's eyes narrowed and I knew that once again he'd managed to read my thoughts, and from the look in his eyes, he wasn't happy with them. In fact, he now looked determined to keep me from ever getting my head on straight again.

DAN

LEXI DUG into the plateful of perfect pancakes Mrs. Evans had set in front of her.

"So you had fun?" I asked.

She nodded and swallowed. "We got to go on all the rides, then we went to the campground." She shoveled another forkful of pancakes into her mouth and chewed.

In between bites, Lexi told me what happened during every minute we'd been apart. Or so it seemed. My daughter is nothing if not descriptive, not to mention enthusiastic. And I love that about her…normally I hang on her every word. But right now, I'm struggling to focus on what she's saying.

I hadn't planned on kissing Sabrina, but the pull between us was so strong, I couldn't resist. And it was so damn good. Better than I remembered, if that's possible. She's the perfect combination of sweetness and fire, even now. And she tastes amazing.

When she curled her fingers into my hair, I was half a heartbeat away from pinning her to the refrigerator and ripping her clothes off when I heard Lexi's feet on the stairs. It was either some kind of parent radar or divine intervention that made me hear her, because every cell in my body had been focused on Sabrina. Whatever it was, I'm thankful. It would be horrible for Lexi to walk in on Sabrina and me doing God knows what.

I caught the tail end of Lexi's last sentence and switched gears to finish our conversation.

"I'm glad you had a good time," I said.

"It was the best," she said. "Maybe you can come next time."

"We'll go once my leg is better."

"Maybe Sabrina can come, too."

I gave her the universal, non-committal parent answer, "We'll see."

After our kiss, things will either work out with Sabrina or she'll run as far and fast as she can. I'll hope for the former and figure out how to stop the latter from happening.

Chapter Twelve

"WE HAVE to talk about it, you know."

The milk I'd been pouring missed the glass and spilled all over the counter. "Jesus Dan, you scared me." I ripped a paper towel off the roll directly in front of me and blotted up the mess. I glanced over at him. "How do you move so quietly with a crutch and that brace on your leg?"

He shrugged and leaned against the counter. "Maybe I'm not quiet. Maybe you're just too wrapped up in your thoughts to hear me." He chuckled. "Besides, if I give you fair warning, you might run the other way."

I didn't dispute that claim because he just might be right. "Want some?" I gestured toward the milk container.

"If you're pouring."

I grabbed a glass from the cabinet above my head, filled it with milk, and handed it to Dan. His fingers brushed over mine and sparks radiated from my hand to every pleasure point in my body reminding me why I wanted to avoid him in the first place.

"You can't avoid me forever, you know."

"I've been with you all day."

"Not because you wanted to be." He looked and sounded like a pouting child, but his words rang true.

After our morning session, I'd wanted nothing more than to put some much-needed space between Dan and myself. Unfortunately, Lexi had other plans. First she asked me to play catch with her, which seemed harmless enough until she asked Dan to watch just to make sure she was doing everything right. After that, her sage green eyes turned pathetic and pleading as she begged Dan and me to play a game of Uno with her. When I attempted to say no, she really turned on the charm and added logic for good measure. After all, Uno really is quite boring with only two people playing.

Lunch followed what seemed like a hundred hands of the card game, followed by Dan's afternoon therapy session. Shortly after that, Lexi tracked me down and asked me to give Dan a French braiding lesson.

I managed to escape after dinner, sneaking out the back door to explore the grounds. Part of me felt guilty, but I know Lexi would have wanted to tag along if she knew my plans—most likely inviting "Daddy" along—and I really needed the time to clear my head.

The kiss Dan and I had shared still has my head spinning, and that combined with the whole Mr. Mom thing he has going on might skew my vision of him. Rose-colored glasses are lovely, until you're into someone heart and soul and are forced to take them off and see him in his true light. That happened to me once with Dan and I can't allow it to happen again.

The walk had helped clear my vision of him. Now if I

can only keep it that way for the next few weeks, I'll be okay.

"Did you hear what I said before?" Dan asked.

"What's that?"

"We have to talk about it."

"Talk about what?"

He blew out a frustrated breath and ran his fingers through his hair. "The kiss."

"There's nothing to talk about." I drained my glass in one gulp, rinsed it out, and placed it in the dish drainer. Just to keep myself occupied, I retrieved the sponge from the sink and wiped down the counter.

Dan grabbed my wrist, forcing me to stop. "Would you slow down and talk to me?" His green eyes bore into mine. "Please?"

I'm not sure if it was the "please" or the frustration in his tone that convinced me to put the sponge back into the sink and lean against the counter, waiting for him to speak.

"Thank you." He let go of my wrist and took a step back. "That kiss was pretty amazing." I gave him what I hoped was my best bland expression. He must have sensed that I wasn't going to comment, because he continued. "There's something between us, Bri. There always has been." His smile turned nostalgic. "I remember the first time I laid eyes on you. Do you remember that?"

I nodded and swallowed the lump that had formed in my throat. Apparently my remembering wasn't good enough, he wanted to reminisce.

"You were taping ankles in the training room. I couldn't keep my eyes off you. I knew then Sabrina, at that moment, we were meant for each other."

Tears stung my eyes, threatening to spill. I wanted to stop him, but the lump in my throat prohibited me from saying a word.

"I know you feel it too. You got just as caught up in that kiss as I did, and if Lexi didn't come home, who knows what would have happened?" His eyes seemed to glow in the dim light of the kitchen and I felt drawn to him. So drawn it terrified me.

"I've never forgotten you. Never forgotten what it was like between us. I nearly died when you left me. It was like losing half of my heart."

Thank the good Lord he said those last two sentences because I'd been starting to melt. His last words actually made me see red. *He* nearly died when *I* left him? Ha! What a laugh. I was such a mess, my mother nearly had to sedate me. Thank God it happened at the end of the school year, otherwise I probably would have taken the semester off…that, or flunk out.

Dan must have seen the storm in my eyes because he started speaking quickly, as if he was trying to get it all out before I exploded.

"I know I was a jerk back then. I know I hurt you as much as I hurt myself, but I'm not the same person." He rubbed the back of his neck and looked at the floor before his eyes met mine again. "What I'm trying to say is that I want you back. I mean, I'd like another chance if you're willing to give me one. I'll treat you right this time Bri, I swear I will."

I have to admit he was giving an award winning performance. He looked sincere enough, but then he always did. I wanted to rant and tell him about how devastated I was back then, how much he'd hurt me. But for some reason I couldn't. I felt numb inside. Numb and cold. I wanted nothing more than to go to bed.

"No," I said quietly.

He blinked comically. "Excuse me?" Apparently he's not used to having women say that word to him.

"No, I'm not willing to give you another chance." I waited a second for my words to sink in, then added, "Now if you'll excuse me, I'm going to bed."

I left him standing in the kitchen with his mouth hanging open.

DAN

WELL FUCK, that didn't go like I'd hoped.

What can I do? How can I make her understand?

Before I could delve too deeply into those questions, Jeff came through the door.

"Early night?"

"Tori didn't feel well so she came home tonight instead of tomorrow."

Jeff was currently dating the mom of one of Lexi's friends. They were keeping things under wraps until they figured out where things were going. Since Nancy is a single mother, their alone time is pretty limited. But he seems happy. At least someone's love life is looking bright.

"You look like somebody kicked you in the balls," he said. "What's up?"

I looked down at the glass of milk in my hand. Unfortunately, it didn't hold any of the answers I need. Turning to the sink, I poured it down the drain and rinsed my glass.

"I asked Sabrina to give me another chance and she said no."

"Okay, so you still have work to do."

"Yeah, I guess." I rubbed the back of my neck. "I don't know."

Jeff chuckled. "It really is interesting seeing you like this."

"I'm glad you're enjoying yourself." I scowled. "You know, it's not like my love life has been perfect. Did you forget about Marie? That turned to shit as soon as she got pregnant."

"True. But before Marie, you had the life. You were the first guy my age to get laid, and you continued getting it on the regular."

"Yeah, and that's what got me into this mess with Sabrina," I said. "God, I was such a dick."

"Don't beat yourself up too much. You know the old saying, 'A stiff prick doesn't have a conscience.'"

"But I do. And part of me knew it was wrong while I was doing it, no matter what my father said."

"Well, you can't change the past. Just keep proving yourself," he said. "Sabrina is pretty smart. She'll figure it out eventually."

I STARED AT THE CEILING, hoping a game plan would appear. The last time I felt this unhinged was when I was pleading with Marie not to have an abortion. I'm a take-action kind of guy and it drives me crazy when I don't have control over the outcome of a situation. With Marie, I had something she wanted…money. With Sabrina, I can only offer myself and she doesn't seem to want any part of me.

That's not exactly true. When she lets her guard down, I can see the attraction is still there, she just doesn't trust me. I can show her I'm worthy of her trust, but there's no way I can make her take a chance on me.

When it was obvious I wasn't going to fall asleep any time soon, I got out of bed and ventured downstairs to watch TV. After flipping through the channels a couple times, I settled on an old *Seinfeld* rerun I'd already seen a million times. Good. Something mindless to distract me from this whole situation.

Unfortunately, it didn't work. I just couldn't shut my mind off. If I wasn't trying to come

up with a plan of attack, I was beating myself up about the past and how badly I fucked up.

Then there's this damn leg. I know my injuries could have been much worse, but not being able to play ball leaves a lot of time for me to do nothing but think.

I pushed back on the recliner until I was lying down and settled my arm over my eyes, willing sleep to come. Hopefully Sabrina is getting a good night's sleep. One of us will need a clear head in my therapy sessions tomorrow.

Chapter Thirteen

SABRINA

SLEEP ELUDED me for most of the night. My mind was racing, filled with so many thoughts I couldn't keep up with all of them. Dan's words dredged up so many things I never wanted to think about again.

Things had been good between us—perfect in fact—if only he could have kept it in his pants. I laughed out loud at that last thought. The fact that he couldn't keep it in his pants didn't bother me as much as the fact that he had no problem keeping it there with me, yet whipped it out for every other female on campus.

I'd been more than willing to have sex with Dan. I'm not proud of it, but there were nights I practically begged him to make love to me, but he never would. His hands on my body, his soft lips on my mouth, my neck, my breasts nearly drove me crazy.

One night in particular comes to mind. Dan and I had attended his senior prom. *Prom night. Can I be more cliché?*

And instead of going to one of the many parties being thrown across campus, Dan and I went to my apartment. My roommate had gone home for the weekend, so we had the whole place to ourselves.

We didn't speak as we walked to my bedroom. Dan took my face in his hands and kissed me so sweetly, tears had welled in my eyes. By slow degrees, the kiss changed tone and turned hungry, almost demanding. Somehow we ended up on the bed with Dan on top of me. Our hands were all over each other and before I knew it, Dan had divested me of my dress. His shirt, tie, and vest had followed suit.

I'd always loved his chest and my hands roamed freely, relishing the feel of the crisp hair that dusted the soft skin and steel muscles beneath. I lifted my head off the pillow and nipped at his pec and sucked on his nipple. He groaned.

His hands gripped my waist and rolled over so he was lying flat on his back with me straddling his hips. I felt his hard length pressing into me through his pants and my panties and I actually shivered with excitement. Dan's limber fingers flicked open the front closure of my bra and my breasts spilled into his waiting hands. It was my turn to groan when he lightly brushed his thumbs over my aching nipples.

I bent my head and kissed him for all I was worth. My whole heart and soul was put into that kiss, into every stroke of my tongue, telling him without words how much I loved him.

Dan's hands continued caressing my breasts and the sensations he created were amazing. My hips bucked in rhythm over his and every nerve in my body was on full alert. I shifted, better aligning our bodies and continued to move over him.

Dan's hands left my breasts and grasped my hips, stilling my movements. It took some doing on his part, because my body seemed to be on autopilot and wouldn't relent. He shifted onto his side and I slid next to him. I looked into his glowing green eyes, slumberous with passion and my heart felt like it expanded in my chest. I was so filled with love. His love.

He kissed me lightly on the mouth and then pulled back. "You are so beautiful," he whispered, before placing a lingering kiss at the hollow of my throat. "Absolutely beautiful." His mouth traced a path to my ear. "And I love you very, very much." His warm breath whirled in my ear and I shivered.

The tone of our actions changed from hot and frenzied to loving and reverent. Dan's hand slid around my waist and moved down my rear end to the back of my thigh and ultimately landed behind my knee, which he grasped and lifted until my leg rested on his hip. His fingers traced their way back up my thigh, squeezed my bottom and stroked my stomach before tucking themselves into the waistband of my panties.

I trembled as his fingers grazed over me. He misunderstood my reaction. Kissing the tip of my nose, he said, "It's okay."

I was going to explain that I wasn't worried, but his hand slipped down further into my heat and I couldn't think. Dan growled deep in his chest as he slipped one finger inside me. In and out, in and out, in and out he pumped, and I arched my back, not sure of how to put out the fire he'd started within me.

I felt my panties being dragged down my legs, leaving me exposed to his eyes, to his touch. Dan moved me onto my back and rolled slightly, pinning my leg beneath his. His thick erection pressed against my thigh and I wanted to touch him, make him feel the sensations I was feeling, but his chest blocked my access.

Again, Dan moved his hand down between my thighs and slid not one, but two, fingers inside. Pumping into me, his hand settled into a rhythm that nearly drove me insane. My once languid body tensed, searching for release. When Dan moved his thumb over and stroked the tiny nub of nerves, I came unglued. All the tension within me seemed to concentrate and twist into a tight knot at my very center before unraveling and exploding into sparks of sensation throughout my body. When I came back to my senses, Dan was watching me, a sweet, gentle smile on his lips.

"You're amazing and so fucking beautiful." He leaned down and kissed me softly. "I love you," he whispered.

He ran his hand up my stomach to my breast. I was shocked when he ran his still slick fingers over my nipple, then proceeded to suck. I felt his groan as his tongue curled around the distended peak.

"So sweet," he muttered against my swollen flesh.

He seemed to be slowing down, which I couldn't understand. I wasn't half as naïve as all that. I *knew* what should happen next, even if I'd never actually done it before. And while what I had just experienced was amazing, I was sure it would be even more incredible experiencing it with Dan inside me.

I shifted so I could reach down and unbutton his pants. I needed to touch him, taste him. I couldn't believe my compulsion to do so, but it was there.

The button of his pants popped free and I slowly ran the zipper down its track. Dan held his breath as I reached inside and ran my hand up and down his length through his underwear. He felt so big, I wondered if he was going to fit inside me then laughed out loud at the thought. Of course he'd fit.

Feeling bold, I reached inside his waistband and touched him. Dan sucked in a breath and let it out in short choppy moans. I moved my hand up and down his hard length, fascinated by the various textures…the softness of the skin, the steel beneath. How something could be so hard, yet so soft was beyond me, but I was enthralled.

I grasped him in my fist and allowed my thumb to reach up and explore the plump head. Softer than the rest of his penis, I was amazed to find a warm bead of moisture at the tip. I slowly rubbed it into his skin and was surprised when it was quickly replaced by another.

I moved my hand in a rhythmic up and down motion, hoping he liked it, hoping I was doing it right. Dan's hand closed over mine and I waited for him to tutor me, to show me how to pleasure him. Imagine my surprise when he unlocked my fingers from around him and removed my hand completely. He placed my palm flat on his chest over his pounding heart. His eyes were unfocused as he pulled in a long breath through his nose and let it out slowly through his mouth. Eventually his breathing steadied and his eyes focused on mine once again.

"Why?" I croaked, not trying to hide my confusion. Tears burned at the back of my eyes.

Dan cupped my cheek with his large hand and brushed his lips over mine. "I love you honey, and I want you so much it literally hurts," he said around a wry smile.

A tear escaped and rolled down my face. "I don't understand. Why did you stop?"

He stroked the stray tear from my cheek. "Because when we make love for the first time, I want us to be married."

"Married?" It was both the sweetest and most ridiculous thing I had ever heard. This isn't 1950. "But why?" I felt like a broken record, but I truly didn't understand.

"I just think it would make it special."

"But," I felt my lips tremble, "don't you think it would be special anyway?"

He wrapped me in his embrace, tucking my head beneath his chin. "Oh God honey, I think it would be amazing."

I pulled back so I could look at his face. "Dan, I love you. I want to be with you. I want to make love with you."

He shook his head. "I…"

Before he could say another word, I ran my hand down his chest to his still erect penis. "Come on, Dan. We've been together for two years. I love you. Please make love to me."

When Dan and I started dating, I'd never questioned the fact that our relationship wasn't very physical. We kissed and touched, but he rarely went past second base. I assumed he was being respectful of my inexperience, but obviously there was more to it.

For a moment I thought he was going to crumble, but instead he said, "I can't, Bri. I just can't." He sprang from the bed and adjusted his pants. "I'm sorry. It'll be worth the wait. You'll see."

I felt like an idiot…a totally humiliated idiot. He should have been the one trying to get me to say yes, not the other way around.

"I better go," Dan said, his voice laced with regret.

"But…"

He gave me a quick peck on the cheek, careful not to touch me anywhere else, or allow me to touch him. "I'll see you tomorrow."

He left without looking back.

A week later, I learned about his various indiscretions. Ever since then, I've wondered who finished what I had started that night.

Chapter Fourteen

"WHERE ARE YOU GOING?" Lexi asked.

"Home." Before I could explain, my cell phone rang. "Just a minute," I told her as I answered it.

My mother was on the other end of the line wanting to know what time I planned to arrive. And, since it was my mother, the call lasted slightly longer than I'd intended. When I turned back to Lexi, I found her father standing where she had been, looking gorgeous, out of breath, and furious.

"You're leaving?" he accused more than asked.

"I…" I started to explain, but stopped. I don't have to explain anything. Instead of answering, I went back to packing.

"So that's it?" he said. I peered over to find him, as I knew he would be, hands on his hips, looking dangerous. Not that I would think for a minute he'd physically hurt me, but mentally, emotionally…that's another story. "You're just leaving? Quitting?"

I turned and fully faced him. The look on his face almost made me laugh. Disbelief, anger, and what I could only describe as panic molded his normally perfect features into a comical mask. As much as part of me wanted to keep him in the dark, I decided to confess my plans.

"I'm going to my mother's," I explained in a patient tone. "I'm off this weekend, remember?"

"But Lexi said you were going home."

"Don't you call your mother's house home?" My brow arched. He nodded and some of the tension drained from his body. "I didn't get a chance to explain it to her because my phone rang. I didn't mean to upset her."

Dan walked to the bed and sat on the edge, right next to my suitcase. "Well, she *was* upset." He rubbed his eyes. "Dammit, I didn't mean for this to happen."

"What?"

"I didn't think she'd get so attached to you." He pinched the bridge of his nose between his thumb and forefinger. "Obviously she has."

I didn't know what to say to that, so I returned my attention to packing.

"I'll have to talk with her while you're gone," Dan said, more to himself than to me.

"You know the routine well enough to attempt it on your own tomorrow." I looked at him to make sure he was listening. "But don't push yourself too hard. If it hurts above a five, don't do it." He looked distracted, but he nodded. I rethought my plan of action. "On second thought, give yourself a break tomorrow. I'll be back Sunday. We'll fit in a session then."

That seemed to catch his attention. "When are you coming back?"

"Sunday evening. I'm not exactly sure what time. If you have plans…"

"No. No plans."

"Okay, I'll see you then." I zipped my duffel bag.

"It's a date."

I know it's just an expression, but the words still bothered me. "No, it definitely is not a date."

Dan almost smiled, but must have thought twice when he saw the aggravated look on my face. "Okay then, it's an appointment."

I could live with that and told him so. Tossing my bag over my shoulder, I asked where Lexi was. "I want to say good-bye."

"She's in the kitchen with Mrs. Evans."

Dan followed on my heels as I started out of my room.

I found Lexi perched on a stool at the island, eating a bowl of cereal. "Hey, Lex." When she turned to face me, it was obvious she'd been crying. I felt awful, but quickly reasoned with myself that I have nothing to feel bad about. Not really. She simply misunderstood. And even if I was leaving for good, it boggles my mind that she'd be so upset. After all, I've only been here a few weeks. What's going to happen when I am leaving for good? It makes me wonder what Dan's women treat her like if she's gotten so attached to me in so short a time.

"You're really going?" she asked, her face sullen. Her big green eyes shifted to my duffel bag.

"I'm going to visit my parents, but I'll see you Sunday night."

Her eyes brightened. "You're coming back?"

I nodded then nearly fell as she launched off the stool and threw herself at me, wrapping her arms around my waist. "I'm so happy," she mumbled against my stomach.

I might normally have been annoyed, or at least slightly

embarrassed, but Lexi is so sweet, I can't help but find it endearing.

Somehow I managed to pry her arms from around my body and step back. "Take care of your dad, okay?" She nodded. "Make sure he doesn't do too much."

"I will."

"I'll see you Sunday."

"Okay."

"Have a safe trip," Dan added.

"I will," I said around the lump in my throat.

I took one last glance at Lexi my chest tightened. I closed the door behind me and headed to my car.

I wish I had a daughter like her.

Whoa! Where did that come from?

I slammed the car door with more force than was necessary. Don't get me wrong, I like kids. I love holding little babies and breathing in their sweet scent, enjoy talking with toddlers, and just hanging out with older kids, but what I love most is handing them back to their parents when I'm done. I don't consider myself very maternal. Sure I can take care of children for short periods of time, but that's vastly different from being responsible for their every need, their very lives for that matter. Never, in all the years of friends and relatives having children, have I wanted one of my own. So, why now?

That question occupied my mind all the way home.

DAN

AFTER SABRINA LEFT, I hung out with Lexi in the pool, which basically consisted of me sitting on a raft watching her swim around. I had to talk to her about her reaction to Sabrina going home, but needed her full attention first.

"Hey Lex, you about ready to get out?"

She picked her head up and looked at me through pink goggles.

"Five more minutes?"

"Sounds good," I said. "You coming to the game with me tonight?"

The Waves are at home for the next ten days and I figured I'd stop in and watch a game. I've put off visiting the stadium this long because I know it won't be as simple as stopping in and watching them play. I'll visit the guys in the locker room, talk to PR, and probably end up in the booth giving the journalists—and the fans— a rundown on my progress. I've also put it off because I didn't want to have to hobble around the stadium on crutches…or God forbid, have someone drive me around on one of those little golf carts.

"Yeah," she said.

"Do you want to stop for some fritters on the way?"

"Yes!" She jumped up and down and pulled her goggles off.

There's a little shack on a backroad near the stadium that make the best crab fritters I've ever tasted. True South Carolina native, Lexi loves them, too. We usually go every day before a home game, but for obvious reasons, haven't been there at all yet this season.

"Let's get out now and dry off. I want you to try to relax a little, maybe take a short nap, before we go. It might be a late night."

I know my chances of Lexi taking a nap are slim to none. That only happens when she's sick. But, if she at least rests for a while, so can I. Paddling my way to the edge, I slid off the raft, and carefully walked up the stairs. I had gotten permission to take my brace off while showering, and figured it would be okay to remove it so I could float in the pool for a bit. I don't want to make any sudden moves and totally fuck up my leg again.

I wrapped a towel around my waist and grabbed another one for Lexi. When she made her way to my side, I dried the excess water from her hair, then wrapped the towel around her shoulders. She hopped into a lounge chair and sat back. I sat on the edge of her chair, still trying to figure out what I was going to say about her reaction to Sabrina going home for the weekend.

"I want to talk to you about something," I said.

She rubbed the towel across her cheek. "About what?"

"How upset you were when Sabrina told you she was leaving."

"I thought she was going for good."

"I understand that, but you know that just because she wasn't leaving for good this time, eventually she will be, right? Sabrina is my physical therapist and she's here to get my leg fixed so I can play again. Once that's done, she'll go home." It killed me to say all that. Lord knows I don't want Sabrina to go, but I have to prepare Lexi in case it does happen.

Lexi looked down at her lap and twisted the towel in her fingers.

"But I don't want her to go." She looked up at me. "I like Sabrina. And…" Looking back down toward her lap, she pulled the towel tighter around her shoulders.

"And what?"

She shrugged. "I just like her and don't want her to go." She scrunched her nose. "When she does leave, do you think she'll call this time?"

I'm sure she was going to say something else, but didn't push it. This conversation is awful enough. Besides, whatever she's thinking will eventually come out. Lexi doesn't keep too much to herself.

"I know you like her, and I know she really likes you. I'm sure she'll keep in touch when she does leave for good."

"You think so?"

"Sure." I wasn't sure of anything where Sabrina was concerned, but Lexi seemed to believe me. "Come on, let's get changed and relax for a little bit. We'll put a movie in and snuggle on the couch."

LEXI ABANDONED me shortly after we entered the stadium. We ran into John Kasprzyk's wife Natalie and his daughter Ava, and the girls begged to hang out. Since they haven't seen each other since my injury, I let her go.

I made my way down to the locker room and was greeted with the ribbing I'd expected. When all the smack talk was done, I got the guys up to date on my progress. With all that out of the way, everyone settled back into their pre-game routine, and I joined two of my best friends, Jack Reagan and Cal Chase at the end of the room. My locker sat between theirs, so I settled into my chair to catch up.

"All that bullshit you said over there true?" Cal asked.

"Of course." I smiled. "Seriously, it's a lot better. Sabrina said I'll definitely be ready for spring training."

"And how are things going with Operation Sabrina?" Jack asked.

"I'm still working on that," I said.

Before Jack could ask a follow-up question, Eric Griffin, one of the team journalists, approached.

"Hey Dan," he said. "How's the leg?"

"Eric." I shook his hand. "It's good. Coming along."

"Would you have a few minutes to stop in the booth and let the fans know how you're doing?"

"Sure. I need to pick some things up at the office, but I can come up after that."

"See you then."

Once Eric left, I filled Jack and Cal in on my leg and they gave me the inside scoop on the season to date. I've been following the team, but watching the games doesn't give you the whole story. They seem optimistic about the Waves going to the Series this year. I'm happy for the team, but pissed off because I'm sitting on the sidelines.

"I'll let you guys finish getting ready. I have to stop and see Hannah before I hit the booth," I said, referring to the head of public relations for the Waves. "She emailed some potential appearances I want to find out more about. Since I'm here, I figured I'd talk to her in person."

"If you're up to it, a few of us are visiting the children's hospital next Tuesday," Cal said.

"Sounds good. Text me the details."

I'm glad to be mobile again so I can at least get back to some of the PR aspects of my job. And I know the children's hospital is near and dear to Cal's heart, so I'm happy to help him any way I can.

After saying my goodbyes, I left the locker room and made my way toward the PR office. It's an odd feeling, leaving the locker room before a game and heading away from the field. One I hope to not feel permanently for a long time.

Chapter Fifteen

SABRINA

I LOVE MY FAMILY, but right now they're driving me crazy. If anyone asks me another question about Dan, I think I'll scream.

Coming home seemed like a great alternative to staying cooped up with Dan, but now I'm not so sure. In honor of my homecoming—like I never travel the whopping sixty miles to visit—my mother invited some people over for a barbecue. Within half an hour, everyone knew about my working with Dan, and within an hour, they were aware of our past relationship.

Of course, my family and close friends had already known, but my mother's neighbors were awestruck by the fact. The funny thing is that some of them had met Dan back then, they just hadn't taken notice of him. I wasn't going to tell them that, though. My mother, however, had no qualms about doing just that.

"You remember John, he was here for Kevin's graduation party. You yelled at him for parking in front of your house."

John Roberts, my parent's neighbor of umpteen years, and possibly the most tactless and annoying man I've ever met, perked up at that piece of information. "Oh yeah," he said as he nodded slowly. "Now I remember. He was a great kid. Really down to earth." John turned his attention to me. "Don't take it personally that he didn't stick with ya, Sabrina. With so many babes throwing themselves at him, you can't expect a guy to stick with just one. Especially someone like you."

See what I mean? No tact.

I forced a smile, excused myself to freshen my drink, and took the opportunity to sneak into the house. I didn't realize I'd been followed until my brother, Kevin, put his two cents into the conversation I'd been having with myself.

"What the hell was I thinking?" I asked myself, out loud.

"You were probably thinking that you could run away from Dan again." Kevin's voice startled me so much I actually jumped. My heart threatened to pound out of my chest.

"Kevin!" I screeched. "You scared the crap out of me."

"Did I intrude on a private conversation?" His eyes twinkled.

"As a matter of fact, you did."

"Sorry," he said, looking anything but.

He sat at the kitchen table and pushed the chair across from him out with his foot, inviting me to sit. I looked at him for the space of several heartbeats before obliging.

"You okay?" he asked, his brow furrowed.

I attempted to swallow the lump that had formed in my

throat so I could give him a verbal answer. It wasn't working, so I simply nodded.

"Sure?"

My shrug said all that I couldn't. Kevin is the only person who knows the whole ugly story. Being two years older, he has always been my confidante and protector. He even offered to "pound the shit out of the bastard" ten years ago, which I found really touching, because they had become good friends while Dan and I were together. Although the offer was greatly appreciated, I declined.

"You know, my offer still stands," he said, only half-teasing.

"I don't know, Kevin, he's bigger than he used to be."

Dan tops off at six foot two and Kevin stands half an inch taller. Physically, their bodies are similar, broad shoulders, narrow hips, powerful arms and legs; if anyone could "pound the shit" out of Dan, it would be Kevin. But for some reason, I don't want Dan hurt. Sometimes it kills me to watch him work through the pain in therapy, a reality I don't want to explore.

"Yeah, but I have rage on my side."

"Rage?" I laughed. "I like that."

Kevin ran a hand through his blond hair and sighed. "Talk to me, Sabrina. You're obviously upset."

"It's just all the questions, the comments. I had to get away from them." I looked toward the door.

Kevin wasn't buying it. "What's going on with Dan?"

"Nothing," I answered, perhaps a bit too quickly.

"Are you two back together?"

"God no!"

"Then what's wrong?" His blue eyes, a shade lighter than my own, cast me a warning glare. "And don't tell me nothing, because I know it's something."

Sometimes it really stinks when people know you so well.

"He kissed me." I cast him an are-you-satisfied-now look, hoping he'd drop the whole subject.

"Anything else?" I shook my head. "Just a kiss?"

"Just a kiss." I didn't feel the need to tell him about the heavy petting that had been going on, nor the fact that I don't know how far things would have gone if Lexi didn't appear.

"So what's the problem?"

I wanted to tell him that there wasn't a problem, but (a) he wouldn't believe me and (b) I really need to talk to someone. I sucked in a deep breath and let it out slowly.

"I just don't want to go there." I averted my gaze from his. "I wouldn't be able to survive it again."

"You never got over him, did you?"

Tears burned at the back of my eyes. I didn't answer, couldn't answer, but Kevin knew. "Talk to me, Sabrina."

"Did you know he has a daughter?" Kevin shook his head, but remained silent. "She's adorable and Dan is absolutely wonderful with her. I've been watching them together and sometimes I'm almost convinced…" I couldn't continue.

"Convinced of what?"

"That he's changed," I confessed.

"Maybe he has."

"Do you really think that's possible?"

"I'm not the one who has to believe it. You are." He stared into my eyes, driving his point home. "Do you think he's capable of change?"

I thought about that for a minute. "We all change to some extent. We grow up, our thoughts and ideas change, but I think that fundamentally we remain the same." Kevin arched a brow, silently asking where I was going with my little speech. "Kevin, he screwed around on me during our entire relationship and thought nothing of it. I mean, that line he threw at me when I confronted him still pisses me off."

The last time Kevin and I had discussed this was ten years ago, just after the fact. I was too busy being consoled to ask Kevin's opinion. Better late than never. "Do you believe that?"

"Believe what?" Kevin asked, warily. I could tell he knew what I was talking about, he was just hoping he was wrong.

"That there are girls you fuck and girls you marry," I answered, matter-of-factly.

Kevin flinched, but I'm not sure if it was because I dropped the F-bomb or that he dreaded answering the question. He stared at the tablecloth, seemingly fascinated with its pattern. It was taking him forever to speak, and I started to wonder if he was going to answer at all. Finally, he lifted his head and looked me in the eye.

"To a point, yes, I believe that." I couldn't hide my shock at his words. He raised his hand in a "slow down" gesture. "Hold on, Sabrina. Hear me out before you freak out." I sat back in my chair and crossed my arms across my chest. My toe tapped a rapid tattoo against the tile floor as I awaited his explanation.

"Of course there are girls out there a guy would fool around with but not marry, but generally they're the girls who wouldn't want to get married anyway. I'm sure it's the same for women. Haven't you ever dated someone who you would never think of getting serious about?"

Since Dan, I haven't really thought of getting serious with anyone, but I chose not to mention that fact at this point in time. Plus I don't really want to discuss my sex life with my brother.

"Sure I have, and I understand that. But tell me, would you commit yourself to a 'girl you marry' and then fool around with 'a girl you fuck?' I mean, before you married Maggie, did you fool around behind her back?"

"No, I've never been unfaithful to Maggie, before or after our wedding. I haven't even looked at another woman since the day I met her. But that's just me. I could never look Maggie in the eye—or myself in the eye, for that matter—if I cheated on her." Kevin straightened and cleared his throat. "Some guys think it's okay to fool around, especially before marriage."

My heart felt like it was trapped in a vise and my stomach flip-flopped. I suppose part of me had wanted Kevin's reassurance that Dan could change, but the opposite had happened. His words only served to point out the fact that some men have scruples while others are morally bankrupt. Unfortunately for me, Dan falls into the latter category.

"Talk to him," Kevin said. "To give you closure, if nothing else. We both know you've never dealt with the whole mess. One minute you were comatose in your room and the next you were back to normal. It just doesn't happen that way." He reached across the table and took my hand in his. "Talk to him. Find out why he did it." Squeezing my hand to emphasize his point, he added, "I'm not sticking up for him here, but you never gave him a chance to explain."

"What is there to explain?"

He shrugged. "Maybe nothing. Maybe everything. I don't know and neither do you until you speak to him. I was here all those times he called and showed up begging to see you. Seems to me like he had something to say."

Footsteps sounded on the front porch, alerting us to

someone's imminent arrival. "That's my best advice, but you have to do what's right for you."

"Thanks, Kev," I said, just as the screen door screeched open and my mother entered the kitchen.

Kevin leaned forward and whispered, "Call if you need me."

Chapter Sixteen

SABRINA

AFTER ALL WAS SAID and done, the trip home hadn't been totally horrendous. I got to visit with my parents, saw some people I hadn't seen in a long time, and managed to get some good advice from Kevin. Whether I take said advice is a whole other story.

Just the thought of bringing up the subject with Dan makes me nauseated. Yet, I drove back to Dan's house confidently knowing the choice is mine. Unfortunately, my confidence only lasted until I turned into his driveway and made my way toward the house. The feeling of home-coming hit me like a Mack truck and scared me half to death.

"Sabrina, Sabrina, Sabrina!" Lexi ran out of the house to greet me. "You're back, you're back, you're back!" She threw herself at me and wrapped her arms around my waist.

"Hey Lex, how's it going?" I tried to sound casual, but

I really had missed her. How am I going to handle it when I leave for good?

"Did you have a good time at home?"

"Sure did," I said as I peeled her off me and retrieved my bag from the car. "What did you do this weekend?"

Lexi placed her hand in mine as we walked toward the house. "Daddy took me out to dinner last night."

"That sounds nice."

"It was. Then we went to the movies."

"Now I'm jealous," I replied as I opened the front door and stepped inside.

"Maybe we can all go out for ice cream tonight," she offered, eagerly.

"That sounds great, but I don't think so." I tucked her hair behind her ear then patted her shoulder. My mother used to do the same thing to me when I was a little girl. Recognizing the maternal gesture, I snapped my hand back.

"I want your dad to get in a therapy session so his leg doesn't freeze up."

"No rest for the wicked, I guess," Dan said, from the hallway.

I allowed my eyes to take a lazy tour of him. Damn he looks good.

"You said it, not me." I laughed. "Give me five to unpack and we can get started," I said. "That is, if you're not busy." My statement came out more like a question.

"I'm free, but don't you want to relax or eat or something?"

"I just came from my mother's house. I won't have to eat for a week."

Dan chuckled and leaned against the wall. "Does she still make enough to feed an army?"

I nodded. "She always says she'd rather have too much

than not enough." Dan's voice blended with mine on the last few words of my mother's favorite mantra.

I looked down at the floor and cleared my throat. What he had just done seemed somehow intimate and made me feel uncomfortable. "I'll meet you downstairs in five minutes."

Dan narrowed his gaze and stared at me for the space of several heartbeats before nodding. Wanting to escape the sudden tension between Dan and myself, I turned and ran up to my room. I threw both my bag and myself onto the bed and attempted to slow my racing heart.

Why does he affect me this way? Why is the air between us always so charged?

Whatever the reason, I have to steel myself against him and it. My conversation with Kevin convinced me of that more than anything. Dan's charm and sweetness can't make up for the fact that he just doesn't believe in the same things I do. Namely fidelity.

Feeling in control again, I changed into shorts and a t-shirt and made my way down to the gym.

Lexi's screeching laughter greeted me as I reached the bottom stair. I entered the gym to find her stretched out over Dan's head as he bench-pressed her. She giggled in delight as his arms thrust her up and down.

"Hey Sabrina," Lexi yelled before Dan pulled her back down to his chest.

He glanced at me before pushing her up once again. "One more and I'm through," he said, attempting to sound out of breath when it was obvious he was anything but. He pushed her up over his head. "Okay kiddo, we're done here."

"Daddy," Lexi chuckled. "You have to let me down."

"What?" He looked up at her, feigning innocence.

"Daaaaddddyyyy," Lexi said, through a laugh.

Dan lowered her to his face and kissed her forehead before arching his arms behind his head and setting her on the floor. "Why don't you go find Jeff?" he said. "I'll be up when I'm done here."

Lexi's eyes darted between Dan and me. She yawned and stretched her arms over her head. "I'm pretty tired. I might go to bed."

Dan's brow furrowed as Lexi kissed him on the cheek. "Are you feeling okay?" he asked.

I personally thought that was a silly question since she had just been laughing her head off. But then, I'm not a parent.

"I'm okay, just tired." She bounced over and kissed me on the cheek. "I'll see you tomorrow."

Dan watched her walk out of the room, his brow wrinkled. When he turned his gaze to me, the frown faded somewhat. "Did she look all right to you?"

"She looked fine," I said as I walked to the freezer and removed an ice cup. He still looked concerned when I returned to his side, so I added, "She's probably just tired."

"Not likely."

I'm not sure what he meant by that, and I didn't ask. I felt his eyes on me as I peeled the excess Styrofoam from the cup, then knelt and removed his knee brace.

"So how's everybody at home?" he asked, while I rubbed ice over his knee.

"Great." I focused on the task at hand instead of the man in front of me. "They all say hi."

"Really?" I nodded. "Huh."

After I finished icing his knee, I worked him through some range of motion exercises. "How does it feel?" I asked, wiping my hands on a crisp, white towel.

"Better every day." I arched my brow. "Seriously, I feel improvement all the time."

"How's the pain?"

He shrugged. "Depends on what I'm doing, but at least it doesn't throb all the time like it used to."

"How does it feel when you work out?"

"Sore, but not unbearable."

I questioned him some more as we worked through his routine. I watched as his range of motion decreased toward the end and stopped him. "That's enough for now," I said.

"I can do more." His boyish eagerness made me smile.

"Not tonight." He looked upset. "Dan, I don't want you to overdo it," I explained. "Slow and steady is the best way to build strength. You're doing great. We'll have you back on the field in no time."

"Promise?" I knew he was teasing, but answered anyway.

"Cross my heart." I made the symbol over my chest with my index finger. My cheeky reply seemed to please him. I iced his knee and replaced the brace. "All done."

"Did they really say hi?"

"Who?"

"Your family. Did they really say hi?"

"Would I have said that if they didn't?" I snapped.

"Don't freak on me," he said calmly. "I'm just surprised. I figured they'd all hate me."

I looked him straight in the eye, allowing him to see my anger.

"They don't know why we broke up, Dan. Well, Kevin does, but not Mom and Dad."

"Kevin knows?"

"Why do you keep questioning what I say?" I sighed and crossed my arms over my chest. "Yes, Kevin knows."

"I'm surprised he didn't beat me to a pulp."

"He did offer to pound the shit out of you." I felt tremendous satisfaction in sharing that information.

"So why didn't he?"

"I told him not to."

He cocked his head to the side. "Why?"

"Why, do you want him to do it? He told me the offer still stands."

Dan chuckled. He actually had the audacity to chuckle. "He could probably do it, too." His eyes twinkled. "I'm glad Kevin still looks out for you."

I wanted to yell at him, tell him his remark was chauvinistic and that I can take care of myself but, truth be told, I don't know what I'd do without Kevin. "Yeah, Kevin's the best," I said instead. "I guess I'll head up to my room. I'll see you tomorrow at nine o'clock sharp."

"Bri, we have to talk."

I tensed. "No, we don't."

"Yes, we do." I narrowed my eyes and Dan must have realized that I wouldn't budge on the point. He sighed and rubbed his eyes. "If not about us, then about Lexi."

"There is no us, and don't think you're going to use your daughter to get to me. It won't work."

At least I hope it won't work.

His expression hardened. "I would never use Lexi like that," he gritted out through clenched teeth.

"No, I don't suppose you would," I admitted, feeling small for making the accusation. "What did you want to tell me about Lexi?"

"She's gotten pretty attached to you." His expression sobered, his eyes reflecting the significance of the topic. I nodded, urging him to continue. "I talked with her this weekend, but I'm not sure I got through."

"What did you tell her?"

"That you're not staying. I told her you'd be leaving in

a few weeks." He flashed an adorable smile. "Unless you've changed your mind."

"I'll be leaving as soon as I think you're ready."

"I'll never be ready for you to leave," he said, deliberately misinterpreting my words.

"When I think you're healed enough, I'll leave," I clarified.

"At any rate, I tried to explain to her that you'll be leaving." He sighed and ran his fingers through his hair, causing it to stand up in a sexy, disheveled mess. "She asked if you'd call this time."

"This time?" Dan nodded.

"What does that mean?"

"I'm not sure, but those were her exact words."

"Do you think she's upset that I didn't call her while I was away?"

"I don't know." He shrugged. "Maybe." He opened his mouth to say something else but shut it, trapping the words inside.

"What?" His green eyes looked wary. "What were you going to say?" I asked.

"Just…" He took a deep breath and let it out slowly. "When you're leaving, when you do leave for good, could you please somehow soften the blow? As corny as it sounds, be gentle?"

"What do you want me to do?"

"Maybe text her, or at least let her email you. Call her a few times." He rubbed the back of his neck. "I know I'm not your favorite person in the world, and I can understand that, but I'd appreciate it if you wouldn't just vanish on her. She's way too attached to you at this point. I'm sure that as time goes by, you'll be able to fade out of the picture." He looked at me once again, obviously awaiting an answer.

My thoughts were so jumbled, I had to sort through them before I spewed everything out all at once. On one hand, his concern for Lexi is very endearing. I know how much pride Dan has and how difficult it must have been for him to ask what he just did. On the other hand, what kind of monster does he think I am? Does he think I'd just drop Lexi like a hot potato once this assignment is done? My anger won out over the softer emotions.

"Dan, my relationship with Lexi has nothing to do with you. My feelings for you, good or bad, have nothing to do with my feelings for her. If she wants me to text, I'll text. If she wants me to call, I'll call. If she wants me to visit, I'll even do that." Realizing who I was speaking to, I added, "If you don't have a problem with it, that is."

"No, I don't have a problem with it." He shook his head as he spoke. "Thank you. I just don't want her hurt."

"You don't have to thank me. Lexi is a sweet little girl and I've really come to care about her. You must really think I'm a bitch if you think I'd intentionally hurt her."

He rubbed the back of his neck again and groaned. "Are you deliberately misinterpreting everything I say?"

"What did I misinterpret?"

"Sabrina, I didn't mean to offend you. I'm just not sure how to handle this whole situation."

"Why is this different than any other time?"

He looked at me like I was insane. "There hasn't been another time."

"What about the women you date? Or hasn't she met any of them?" I wanted to bite my tongue for letting those questions slip out. I don't want to discuss his love life.

"There haven't been any women."

"Give me a break." I rolled my eyes and when they met his again, I was mortified to find that I'd actually spoken those words out loud. Judging by the look on his face, he was just as shocked, but slowly his eyes crinkled with amusement.

"I always could count on you to tell it like it is," he said, dryly.

"I didn't mean to say that." I felt my face flush.

"Why were you even thinking it?"

He cannot be this obtuse.

"Dan, I find it hard to believe that you've been celibate since Lexi's mother left."

"No, I haven't been," he admitted. "But I haven't really had a serious girlfriend since then. I mean, there have been women I've spent time with, but that's usually when I'm on the road." He paused and looked me in the eye, as if trying to decide if he should go on. Then he nodded and continued. "I don't think Lexi should be exposed to women I'm not serious about. And besides, whether you want to believe it or not, I've changed. I'm not the same indiscriminate jerk I used to be."

A thousand scathing replies popped into my head, but thankfully I didn't utter any of them out loud. Again, I don't want to hear about his love life.

"Good for you," I said, trying to sound sincere instead of sarcastic. Judging by the look on his face, I wasn't very successful. Needing the conversation to be over, I added, "At any rate, I'll do my best not to hurt Lexi when I leave. I'll see you tomorrow at nine."

Chapter Seventeen

I CAN'T BELIEVE the depths to which I've sunk. Pumping a small, defenseless child for information should be punishable by law. It really should.

Not that I set out to ask Lexi personal information about her father, it just sort of happened. At least I couldn't be charged with pre-meditated prying, just involuntary.

After Dan's workout, I found her eating cereal in the kitchen with Jeff.

"How's he doing?" Jeff asked. His eyes shifted to Lexi, then back to me warning me not to get into too much detail. As if I would.

"He's doing wonderful. I see improvement every day."

"Great." He topped off his coffee, and offered me a mug. I eagerly accepted.

"So how's it going, Lex?" I asked.

"Pretty good," she said around a mouthful of Cheerios.

"What are your plans for the day? Anything exciting?"

"Nope. Just hanging out. Daddy said he'd go swimming with me if you said it was okay."

"I don't see a problem with that. But no wild stuff," I added with a smirk.

"Do you wanna come too?"

"I didn't bring a suit with me."

"Couldn't you go in your workout clothes?"

"I suppose I could…" I was trying to think of an excuse when Jeff joined the conversation.

"You could buy a suit. The mall is only ten minutes from here."

"I could go with you and help you pick one out," Lexi offered in an excited tone. "I love going to the mall."

So that's how I ended up in my car with Lexi, asking her for information about Dan. In my defense, she brought up the subject, not me. After asking about his leg and his work-outs, she moved onto more personal topics.

"I think Daddy needs a girlfriend."

"Why do you say that?"

She shrugged. "He just does. I'm not the only one who thinks so, either."

"No?"

Out of the corner of my eye, I saw her shake her head, her curls bobbing. "My friends' moms think so too. They're always trying to introduce him to women, but he never goes out with any of them."

"Never?"

"Never," she added, her green eyes wide and solemn. "And some of them are real pretty, too."

"Did he ever have a girlfriend?"

She shook her head. "He says I'm his best girl and he doesn't need another one."

"And there haven't been any women just hanging around that he might have been dating?"

"No." She frowned. "And he never goes out, so I don't think he goes on dates." Her face brightened. "But I think he'd like you to be his girlfriend."

"Me? Why would you say that?"

"I don't know. I just think he would."

Thankfully, we arrived at the mall, distracting Lexi from the conversation.

LEXI PERFORMED A NOT-TOO-GRACEFUL dive into the pool.

"Getting better, honey," Dan yelled from his raft as her head popped to the surface of the water.

"Do you really think so?" she asked, swimming toward him, obviously not believing him.

"You're not doing belly flops anymore," he pointed out.

Lexi nodded, and was about to say something else when she spotted me standing at the side of the pool. "Sabrina," she yelled, directing Dan's attention my way. "How do you like Sabrina's suit, Daddy? I picked it out."

The royal blue two-piece Lexi had picked out was more sporty than skimpy, but I felt way too exposed as Dan's hot gaze roamed over every inch of my body.

"It looks great," was all he said to Lexi, though his eyes spoke volumes more to me.

"Can you dive, Sabrina?"

Dan answered for me, his eyes still glued to mine. "She can do better than dive, Lex, she can flip."

"You can?" Lexi bobbed up and down in the water, moving the raft Dan was floating on with her.

"I don't know. I haven't done that in a long time." Actually, it hasn't been that long, but just thinking about what I'd look like performing that particular maneuver in a two-piece suit made me cringe.

"I think she's chicken." Dan spoke to Lexi, though his gaze was still riveted on me.

I planted my hands on my hips and glared at him. "Don't think you can use that old trick on me Daniel, because it won't work."

"What?" He lifted his hand to his chest. His innocent "Who me?" gesture didn't fool me. "If you're afraid to do it, just say so. Lexi and I totally understand. Don't we?"

"Are you scared?" Lexi asked.

"I'm not scared."

Before I could add to that, she cut in. "So you're gonna do it? You do it and then I can try."

"Don't push her, honey," Dan said. "I don't think she wants to."

The man is infuriating. Sitting there on that raft, looking so sure of himself. Like he has any idea what I'm capable of. I'll wipe that smug smile off his face.

I stepped onto the diving board and bounced lightly to judge its spring. Feeling Dan's eyes on me the entire time, I stepped back, then quickly moved forward, jumped onto the very edge of the board and pushed off, propelling myself forward. I flipped once in the air, my body curled tight, before I straightened and plunged into the water. Allowing myself to sink all the way to the bottom of the pool, I checked that my bathing suit was in place before kicking off the floor and pushing myself to the surface of the water.

"How did you learn how to do that?" Lexi asked, her eyes wide.

"My brother taught me. But it takes lots and lots of practice," I emphasized. "And don't ever try doing it if you're alone."

"Can I try it now?"

"Why don't you practice doing somersaults under the water? That's the best way to get started." She clearly wasn't pleased with that, but didn't argue. Instead, she moved away from Dan and me and proceeded to practice her flips.

"So how was your trip to the mall?" His tone was casual, but the look on his face was anything but.

"Good. We had a great time. Lexi showed me all the hot spots." His eyes were devouring me and I dipped further into the water to shield myself from their heat. The smirk that spread across his face told me he knew exactly what I was doing.

"That's a nice suit you've got on."

"Thanks." I bent my knees until only my head was above the water. "Lexi picked it out. I don't normally wear a two-piece, but somehow I let her talk me into it." I'm not sure why I added that last part.

"You should always wear a bikini. You've definitely got the body for it." I couldn't hold back my snort of disbelief. "Honey, if you looked any better in that suit, I'd have to climb off this raft and hide in the water for fear of embarrassing myself."

I didn't have to ask what he was talking about. My eyes lowered to his crotch. Dan's low chuckle drew them back up to his eyes, which were filled with both amusement and hunger.

My body felt so overheated, I'm surprised I didn't set the pool water boiling. I stood with the intention of escaping, and the water level dipped to my waist. Dan's eyes lowered and he groaned then tipped himself off the raft.

"God, Bri." His voice sounded strangled.

My insides fluttered at his obvious attraction, as my brain fought for control. Of course, I feel flattered by

Dan's interest. Who wouldn't? I'm just surprised he's still so obvious about it after my blunt refusal. He asked me for a second chance. I said no. I thought he'd let it go at that.

Maybe by refusing, I've made myself a challenge. Dan has always been very competitive, and I'm pretty sure he doesn't have too many women refuse him. Maybe now it's a matter of pride.

"Sabrina, can we talk later?" His eyes looked soft and sexy, yet pleading.

Not a good idea.

"I don't think we have anything to talk about. That is, unless you want to discuss your therapy." I raised my voice an octave on the last word, turning the sentence into a question.

His eyes narrowed, but were full of determination. Just when he was going to answer, Lexi interrupted. "Can I try to flip off the diving board now?"

Anything to get away from Dan.

"Sure," I said. "Let's go."

For the rest of the afternoon, I stuck to Lexi, teaching her how to flip off the diving board. Dan climbed back on his raft and cheered her on. While he managed to look relaxed, I sensed his underlying tension, and the look in his eyes promised that our conversation was far from over.

DAN

I SLID off Lexi's bed, leaned over, and tucked her in. A full day in the pool had tired her out and she fell asleep before we finished reading her favorite book. I switched on her night light, stepped out of the room, and shut the door behind me.

Glancing at Sabrina's room, I noticed that her light was still on.

Should I knock on the door?

Deciding against it, I made my way down to the kitchen, grabbed a beer out of the refrigerator, and went outside to the patio. Settling into a lounge chair, I popped the top and took a long draw on my beer before setting it on the table next to me.

It had been a nearly perfect day. I was able to do more than float on a raft and it felt good to move around. Lexi had a lot of fun, especially learning how to flip off the diving board, thanks to Sabrina, who had actually relaxed and enjoyed herself. Not to mention how she looked in that two-piece.

Damn, when she came outside wearing that bathing suit, I'd almost embarrassed myself. Then later, when she stood up in the water and her hard nipples cleared the surface, there had definitely been movement down south. Thankfully I was able to jump off the raft and cool myself off.

I settled back in the lounge chair and closed my eyes, letting the memory form an image in my head. Even though she doesn't think so, Sabrina has an amazing body. Womanly with curves that had always fit so seamlessly against me. I know for a fact that her boobs are a perfect handful with the most sensitive nipples. The way they stood at attention against the thin material of her suit earlier had me fighting the urge to latch on and see if I could make her lose all control.

I sat forward, grabbed my beer off the table, and downed half the bottle in one gulp. That train of thought isn't going to get me anywhere. I think she wants me physically, mentally is another story. But there were times today when it had seemed like she forgot she hates me.

We'd spent the day in the pool, then went to the gym for a therapy session, and returned to the patio to cook steaks on the grill, followed by some more subdued antics in the pool.

It had been fun. Easy. And it gives me hope.

I finished my beer and went back into the house.

Time to find out.

Chapter Eighteen

SABRINA

I'D JUST PUT the last of my freshly-laundered clothes away when I heard an impatient knock on the door.

"It's open," I yelled, knowing without a doubt who would enter my room.

Dan crossed the threshold, closed the door behind him, and proceeded to stare at me. I felt uneasy with those amazing green eyes looking right through me, but I'll be damned if I'd show it.

"Did you need something?"

"I think I mentioned that I wanted to talk to you."

"And I think I told you we had nothing to talk about."

"Do you really believe that?"

"Yes, I do."

"Don't tell me you don't feel this thing between us, this thing that's always been between us." He moved toward me as he spoke. I forced myself to stand my ground, both literally and figuratively.

"Dan, if you want to discuss your therapy or your health, I'm all ears, but everything else is off limits."

"This *is* about my well-being."

My eyes shifted to his leg. "What's wrong?"

"My heart is broken."

"Oh please," I snorted. "Tell me another one."

"Bri, I want you back, *need* to have you back in my life."

"Why?"

He studied me for a moment. "Because I love you. I always have, and after ten years of trying not to, realize I always will."

Tears stung my eyes, but they were more from anger than anything else. "Why are you doing this?"

"I just told you—"

I couldn't bear to hear it again, so I interrupted him. "I know what you told me, but I've heard it all before." I spat. "The thing is, I'm not the same stupid, naïve girl I was ten years ago. I learned my lesson well and will never fall for sweet lines and charming smiles again. Not from you, not from anyone." I took a breath and glared at him. "The thing I don't understand is why you did it. I mean, if you wanted all those other girls, why bother with me at all? I couldn't hold a candle to any of them in the looks department and certainly not in the body department, so why did you have me around at all?"

"Because I loved you."

I was getting ready to lambaste him again, but he stopped me.

"And as far as those other girls, *they* couldn't hold a candle to *you*." He sighed and shook his head. "I told you before, I fell in love with you the minute I laid eyes on you." He flashed an adorable, crooked smile. "Then again, I suppose I only fell in lust with you when I first saw you. The love came shortly after we went out and I realized you were just as beautiful on the inside as you are on the outside."

My knees weakened, so I sat on the bed and hugged them to my chest. "Dan, please don't." My voice cracked.

"Bri." Dan sat down on the edge of the bed beside me. "I might've done some stupid things back then, but I never lied to you. Every word I ever said was true."

The look of sheer disbelief I threw at him said all I wanted to.

"Don't look at me like that. I didn't lie to you," he insisted. "Not even when I wanted to. Not even when you confronted me and I knew, just knew, I'd lose you if I told the truth."

I wanted to yell at him, wanted to tell him that it doesn't matter anymore…but I couldn't, because it does. A familiar ache settled in my chest and my eyes began to sting. One question kept ringing through my head…why? I didn't realize I'd spoken the word out loud until he answered.

"I was an ass. That's all there is to it."

A tear escaped, ran down my face, and plopped onto the back of my hand. I reached up and wiped away the trailing moisture, hoping he didn't notice. "It doesn't matter anymore, Dan," I said, softly.

"Is that why you're lying in the fetal position with tears rolling down your face?" I narrowed my eyes and gave him my best glare. His own expression softened. "Talk to me, Bri. I want to know what you're thinking and feeling. I want you to understand what happened back then."

I couldn't restrain myself any longer.

He's asking for it, so he's gonna get it.

"You want to know what I'm thinking?" I dropped my feet to the floor and straightened my spine. "I'm thinking that I'll never understand why you did the things you did. I mean, why would you screw half the campus and keep me as your girlfriend? I could see if you were screwing me too, but that wasn't the case." I laughed, but it held no humor, only disgust. Whether it was directed at myself or him, I couldn't say.

"When I think of all the time I wasted thinking you were a true gentleman, I feel sick. All the times you told me you loved me and wanted to wait until we were married to make love so it'd be special, I believed you."

Dan opened his mouth to speak, but I raised my hand halting his words. "Do you want to know what I'm thinking, or not?" He nodded. "I believed you. I believed every single word you told me." I wiped at the tears streaming down my face and glared at him, silently daring him to speak. He remained silent. "I should've trusted my instincts. I knew you were too good to be true. Guys like you don't date girls like me. I know that, yet somehow you made me feel like we belonged together, like we were made for each other."

Tears glistened in his eyes, but I forced myself to ignore them. "But what gets me the most is the way you just blew it off when I confronted you. Girls you fuck and girls you marry," I mocked, gaining a small amount of pleasure when he flinched at his own words. "Was that supposed to make it all right, Dan? Were those lovely words supposed to make me feel better about the fact that the man I loved with my whole heart and soul stuck it to every girl who crossed his path? Make me feel less embarrassed about begging you to make love to me?"

"Is that what this is about? You don't have anything to be embarrassed about, Bri."

"This is about your inability to keep it in your pants while we were together."

"Is it?" His brow cocked. "Or is it about the fact that I kept it in my pants with you?"

"Don't you dare try to turn this around. I may not be perfect, but I never once cheated on you, never even thought about it." I shook my head in disgust. "And the thing that really kills me is the fact that I fought you. Remember that? I didn't want to go out with you because I knew it wasn't natural. Ken dates Barbie, not the generic Dollar Store version. But you kept at me and convinced me to go out with you, made me fall in love with you."

"Are you finished?" he asked, nostrils flaring, his tone impatient. I nodded. "Good, now it's your turn to listen."

I wanted to remind him that he's the one who's supposed to be groveling, but his thunderous expression stopped me.

"First off, what is this Ken and Barbie shit you're talking about? You're a beautiful woman, Bri." His jaw tensed when I rolled my eyes. "Do *not* roll your eyes," he said through clenched teeth. "You're beautiful and smart and funny and I fell head over heels in love with you. The problem was…" He looked at me for the space of several heartbeats, lowered his head, and rubbed the back of his neck. "From the time I was twelve, my father drilled it into my head that there are girls you fuck and girls you marry, and that you don't fuck the girl you plan to marry until the wedding night." He ran his fingers through his hair. "Even once you married them, he said that you treated them with respect in and out of the bedroom. If you wanted raunchy sex, again you'd go find a girl you fuck."

I couldn't believe my ears. Does he actually believe this stuff? I asked him just that.

"My father raised me to believe it. In fact, when I was sixteen, he caught my girlfriend and me in the middle of some heavy petting on the couch. When she went home, he dragged me to my room, and lectured me for a half hour, then beat the crap out of me."

"He *what?*" I couldn't believe my ears.

"You heard me right. He was careful not to break anything or cause any real damage, but he certainly got his message across." He dragged in a deep breath and let it out slowly. "Until I met you, I never questioned his theory again."

"What's that supposed to mean?"

"It means I never thought twice about it until I fell in love with you. But once we were together, I felt guilty as hell cheating on you."

"So why did you?"

"I just told you."

"Let me get this straight. You couldn't fuck me because you wanted to marry me, so you went to other girls."

"Pretty much."

"Did it ever occur to you not to fuck anyone?" The look on his face answered the question. "*I* wasn't fucking anyone Dan, so why should you?"

I swear I haven't said the word fuck as much in my entire life as I have in this conversation.

"Would you please stop saying fuck?" he shouted, as if reading my mind.

"Why? You seem to like the action, why not the word?"

He sucked in what I could tell was a calming breath and let it slide out through his teeth. "I think we've gotten off track here. I just wanted you to understand what I was thinking back then."

"And it's different now?"

"Yes, it is." His eyes met mine and held, willing me to believe him. "When my parents split up, my mother broke down one night and told me why. For all the years my father was preaching his philosophy to me, it never occurred to me that he was also living it.

"I was shattered when you broke up with me, but I'll admit I didn't really see your side. I thought I'd give you time and you'd forgive and forget. Everything would be okay. After talking to my mother, I didn't believe that anymore.

"My mom told me how hurt and humiliated she was and how she couldn't understand why he'd done it. She also couldn't believe he had the nerve to ask her for a second chance." Dan sighed. "Right then I understood exactly how you must've felt."

"How's your mother doing now?"

He shrugged. "Okay, I guess."

"Good. I always liked her."

Dan's jaw dropped. "That's all you have to say?"

"What do you want me to say?"

"I want you to say that you understand what happened back then," he said. "I want you to say that you see me as the man I am today, not the stupid boy I was." He dragged his fingers through his hair. "But more than anything else, I want you to say that you'll give me another chance." His eyes glistened with tears and were so full of emotion I had to turn away before I got pulled into their green depths.

"Why?" I asked, my voice hoarse. "Why are you doing this to me? And why now, after ten years?" I knew I sounded like a broken record asking "why" but it was the one thing I needed to know.

"Because I love you," he answered, sounding like a broken record himself. He scooted closer and took my hand. His grasp was firm and I didn't have the strength to pull away.

"Look at me, Bri." Though his tone was soft, it was definitely a command. My gaze met his, hoping he couldn't see my weakness. Hoping he wouldn't know that I was barely holding on to my resolve.

"Why not you?" he asked. "You're everything I've ever wanted in a woman. As far as why now…" He shrugged. "I've wanted to contact you for the past ten years, but I went to see you a few times right after it happened and got the door slammed in my face. I decided to give you some time to cool off. With my crazy schedule, time just got away from me, and then Lexi was born. Next thing I know, it's ten years later." Dan looked down and clasped his hands together, staring at them as if they held the secrets of the universe. My stomach twisted when he met my gaze again with glistening green eyes.

"When I smacked into that wall and busted my leg, I knew it was fate. It was my one chance to get you into my life without coming on too strong. I've been dreaming about you for years, Sabrina, but those dreams held the girl I knew. I wanted to get to know the woman you've become." His eyes bore into mine. "And I find I love her more than that girl. You still have so many of the qualities I fell in love with back then, but now there's more. So much more." He reached over and squeezed my hand to punctuate his words. "I love talking with you. It doesn't matter what the topic is, I just like listening to your voice, hearing your opinions. I think I've already mentioned that I really like the way you look." His crooked smile set my heart racing. "And just watching you with Lexi brings tears to my eyes."

That last sentence broke the sensual spell. I felt as though a bright light was suddenly turned on. Of course he's interested in someone like me. He wouldn't want one of his little groupies raising his daughter. Safe little Sabrina would be perfect for the job.

"I warned you not to do that," I said in a venomous tone, jerking my hand away from his warm fingers.

"Do what?" He looked bewildered.

"Don't use Lexi to get to me."

"I'm not—"

"I know she wants a mother, but don't toy with my emotions just to give her that."

Dan looked furious. I was just about to scoot away when he jumped off the bed. He stood with his back to me for several seconds, combing his fingers through his hair, and taking deep breaths.

My own anger faded into a combination of weariness and regret. When Dan faced me again, his eyes still glowed with anger, though his face had softened.

"Obviously the damage I did back then can't be undone. You still think I'm an asshole and I guess I'll have to live with that." He sighed. "I won't bring this up again, I promise."

That said, he turned and left the room.

Chapter Nineteen

"I THINK THAT'S TEN," Dan said, halting his actions. "I can do more if you'd like," he offered.

I had expected him to be brooding and quiet at therapy this morning, but that wasn't the case. He's as affable as ever and I have to admit it's thrown me off, and as a result, I haven't been paying attention.

"No," I said. "No more."

Dan moved on to his next set of exercises and my mind wandered once again. Our conversation last night had been pretty intense. I can't believe he's acting so nonchalant, so…normal. I'd tossed and turned half the night thinking about it.

I admit that I'm afraid. If I let him in, I don't think I could survive it if he hurt me again. I worry that I'm a challenge, and Dan is nothing if not competitive. Have I made myself more attractive to him by turning him down?

I frowned. If that's the case, then what was our relationship in college all about? Sure, I gave him a hard time when he asked me out initially, but after that it was smooth sailing. If the thrill of the chase was the attraction, why did he stay with me for two years? And if he really was so in love with me, so attracted to me, why didn't he sleep with me?

The last question could be answered by what he told me last night. If his father had pounded those theories into his head—literally and figuratively—his actions are understandable. But, as I pointed out to him, he could have simply gone without. Is that concept so ridiculous?

If fidelity was so foreign to him then, why would he be any good at it now? A leopard doesn't change his spots, after all.

Then again, aside from that night his college buddies brought them, there haven't been any women around. Lexi said he never dates. If he keeps his women away from her, he really must be slowing down because from what I've seen and heard, he's with her all the time.

A loud noise snapped me from my thoughts. I looked at Dan, who was glaring at me.

"What was that?"

"I dropped the weights," he growled. "I'm finished with my routine."

My mouth dropped. "But…" I stammered.

"But what?" He arched his brow. The too-knowing look on his face told me that, once again, my every thought had been obvious.

Not knowing what else to say, I apologized for my lack of professionalism. I'm here to do a job and today, I didn't do it. My apology made Dan's scowl even more pronounced.

"Forget about it."

Those three words couldn't have sounded more formidable if they came from The Godfather himself.

"I really am sorry. This has never happened to me before. I've always been totally focused on my job. I don't know what's wrong with me today."

His intense stare made me feel like a specimen under a microscope. "Your problem is that you're too busy trying to convince yourself that what you're mistakenly thinking is true instead of paying attention to the facts in front of you." Rubbing his hand down his face, he shook his head and stood. "But I'm too tired to rehash this. I'll see you later."

"Let me ice your knee first," I said, attempting to gain some control.

"I'll do it myself," he mumbled, his back to me as he walked toward the steps.

I didn't want to analyze the feeling of loss that came over me, so I decided to exercise. During my teenage years, I would have chosen to eat my way through something like this, but now I deal with things in a more mature fashion… I work-out until I can't move or think.

"Sabrina?"

I don't know how long I was at it when Lexi's voice broke into my routine. Not that it was much of a routine. My body had been on autopilot, performing a series of exercises it knew by heart.

"Hey, Lex." I sat and wiped my face with a towel.

She studied me a minute before asking, "You okay?"

Oh hell, can she see through me too?

"I'm fine." I wiped my neck and chest and dangled the towel between my knees. "Why do you ask?"

She shrugged. "You look kinda sad." After roaming around the room, her eyes met mine again. "So does my dad."

I don't want to hear this, so I tried to change the subject. "What are your plans for the day?"

"Nothing."

"No?" Lexi always had something planned. Whether she was hanging out with one of her many friends, or spending time with Dan or Jeff, she was always on the go.

She shook her head. "I'm just gonna hang out today. What are you doing?"

"Well, right now I think I need a shower. Then I thought I'd head to the mall. Want to come along?"

Lexi's eyes rounded. "Definitely."

"Great. You go ask you dad if it's okay while I shower. I'll meet you in the kitchen in a half hour."

I have no idea what prompted me to invite Lexi to go shopping with me. What made me want to go shopping in the first place is another mystery. Not being much of a shopper, the mall is, generally speaking, not my favorite refuge. Yet today, it seemed like the thing to do in order to escape Dan's presence. And since Lexi loves shopping, I invited her along. At the time, I thought she'd be a distraction from the whole Dan situation, but instead she seems to be adding to it.

"Daddy" came out of her mouth more often than not, and if I have to listen to one more story about him, I just might scream. Lexi finished telling me about the time she and Dan won the relay race at her school on field day and before she could start up with something else, I spoke up.

"Are you hungry?"

"Sure."

"What do you feel like eating?"

She scrunched her nose. "Hmmm, maybe pizza. The place in the food court makes really good pizza."

I spotted a sign that directed us to the food court and kept talking, not giving her a chance to start up about Dan again. Only, after having her list all the food choices available in the mall and remarking on our purchases of the day, I had nothing else to say.

We both ordered two slices of pizza and sweet tea then found a table. After taking two bites of the cheesy concoction, Lexi once again relayed a story of Dan. Every word she spoke was pure agony. I had to keep reminding myself that Dan the father and Dan the man are two separate entities. His love for his daughter is obvious to anyone, but would he act the same way with a woman he loves?

Lexi finished her dissertation on every amusement park Dan had ever taken her to.

"You're lucky to have such a great dad," I replied, hoping to put an end to the whole subject of Dan.

"He's really great." She took a bite of pizza, chewed, swallowed, and added, "Don't you think he's nice?"

"Yes, he's wonderful," I said, hoping an eight-year-old wouldn't pick up on the trace of sarcasm in my tone.

"So why are you two fighting?"

"We're not."

"Then why do you both look sad?"

"Oh honey, I'm just tired."

"Then why didn't you talk to him before we left the house? You didn't even say good-bye to each other," she pointed out.

Now I understand why my friends who have children always talk about how "kids can sense things" and how "they don't miss a trick."

"We're not fighting, exactly." I'd hoped that would be a good enough explanation, but from the determined look on her face, it obviously wasn't going to be. I sighed. "We just had a slight disagreement. It's no big deal. Really. Nothing important."

"You sure?" She picked up her sweet tea and took a long draw on the straw until slurping noises were heard.

"I'm sure." I placed our empty plates on the tray in front of me. "Are you all finished?" She nodded. "Good. I think we have time to hit a couple more stores before we have to head out."

Without answering, Lexi picked up our tray, walked to the garbage can, tipped the contents inside and placed the tray on top. "Sabrina," she said as we walked through the mall once again.

"Yeah?"

"I'm glad that you and Daddy aren't really mad at each other." I didn't know how to comment, so I didn't. "I love Daddy, but I always hoped my mom would come back so we could be a real family. I don't want anything to ruin that."

DAN

I FLIPPED the TV on to break the deafening silence. With Mrs. Evans on vacation, Jeff out, and Lexi shopping with Sabrina, I swear I could hear my breath echo through the house. Since I'm generally surrounded by the team or hanging out with Lexi, I usually relish quiet, but today it's driving me crazy. Probably because with the lack of noise, I can hear all the thoughts and doubts running through my head.

What the fuck am I going to do about Sabrina?

I chuckled out loud at my own question. I'm not going to do anything about Sabrina. She made it pretty clear she doesn't want anything to do with me. The fact that she couldn't even pay attention during my therapy session tells how little she wants to deal with me. Even when she first came to work here, she did her job flawlessly. I don't know what to think about what happened in my gym earlier.

The thought of Sabrina leaving in a few weeks is depressing, but something I'm obviously going to have to get used to. I'll just focus on getting better and deal with whatever comes later. What else can I do?

"DADDY!"

Lexi's voice woke me from a dead sleep. I twisted and pushed myself up on the couch just as she entered the room.

"Hey, how was shopping?"

She jumped onto the couch next to me and I kissed her forehead.

"Good. We got our nails done," she said, wiggling her bright pink fingernails in my face.

From the corner of my eye, I saw Sabrina hovering in the doorway. I looked up and said, "What color are yours?"

She blushed and held her hand up, flashing the same nail color as Lexi.

"I hope you don't mind," she said.

"No, nail polish is fine."

"Daddy paints my nails for me all the time," Lexi said. "Sometimes he lets me paint his, too."

I put an arm around her shoulders and pulled her close, tickling her belly.

"That's supposed to be our secret," I said.

She giggled. "Sorry," she said, sounding anything but.

I saw Sabrina watching us, looking uncertain. I guess

that's better than pissed off and hurt like she'd looked last night.

"Lexi, you forgot your bag," she said, holding out a small, blue bag.

"You made Sabrina go to Connie's?" I asked, referring to the little girl's retail heaven whose logo is on the bag in Sabrina's hand.

"She wanted to," Lexi said.

I looked my daughter in the eye. "Really?"

Lexi nodded, then said. "She never shopped at Connie's and I told her how awesome it is and she said she wanted to go."

I looked at Sabrina and raised my brow.

Lexi hopped off the couch and ran to Sabrina's side to get the bag.

"It was fine," Sabrina said. "We had fun. Thanks for letting her come with me."

Lexi returned to my side and pulled out her bounty. A t-shirt with a glittery smiling cupcake, matching socks, and a purple headband. She held the shirt up and said, "Don't you just love it?"

"I do love it," I said. "Do they have one in my size?"

"Daddy!" she shrieked. "You know they don't have clothes for you at Connie's."

"Well, maybe they'll have one somewhere else," I said, making Lexi laugh. Turning my attention to Sabrina, I said, "How much do I owe you?"

She frowned and shook her head. "Oh no, it's my treat." She smiled at Lexi. "To thank Lexi for keeping me company today."

"Did you thank Sabrina?" I asked my daughter, who nodded.

"She did," Sabrina said. "I'm going to lie down for a little while. She tired me out. See you at six?"

I nodded. "Six."

Sabrina's shoes clicked on the floors, then the stairs, before being muffled in the carpet as she reached the second floor. I turned my attention back to Lexi.

"Are you hungry?"

"No, I'm still full. We had pizza."

"Well, I have a couple hours until therapy. What would you like to do?"

"Can we color?"

"Sure. Go grab your books."

Lexi scrambled around collecting her crayon box and coloring books, and returned, throwing everything on the coffee table. She handed me the superhero book and grabbed the Disney princess one for herself and sat on the floor across from me.

"What did you do when I was gone?" she asked, then picked up a purple crayon.

"Not much. I watched TV then fell asleep."

She paused in her coloring. "Did your leg hurt?"

Lexi has been acting like a mother hen since my accident. It's kind of adorable, but I don't want her to worry.

"No, I was just bored."

"Maybe you can come with us next time."

"Maybe."

She finished coloring the petals of a flower purple and reached into the container for a green crayon.

"Maybe you and Sabrina can go to the mall sometime just together," she said. "Or out to dinner or something."

The red crayon I'd been using to color Spiderman's costume snapped in my hand. Lexi finished coloring the stem and leaf of the purple flower green and glanced at me. The innocent look she didn't quite pull off couldn't hide the hope in her eyes.

It's official…I definitely won't be the only one with a broken heart if Sabrina leaves.

Chapter Twenty

I GOT myself together for Dan's second therapy session of the day. The trip to the mall really helped my mental state. Now I understand why some women find shopping therapeutic. And, while it cleared my head, I also ended up with a few bargains in the process. I'd say that's better than sitting in a shrink's office any day.

Dan finished the last of his leg raises and looked at me expectantly. The therapy session has been unusually quiet. Apparently, he's not speaking to me because, aside from an occasional "okay" Dan hasn't said a word.

"How does it feel?" I asked.

He shrugged. "Okay."

I resisted the urge to scream, and just to give him something else to say, I decided to test his pain level. Grabbing his foot, I asked, "One to ten?"

"Four."

We'd done this exercise enough that he knew what to

expect. I moved his leg in a series of motions and got his feedback on each one.

"Well," I said as I walked to the freezer and retrieved an ice cup. "It's definitely getting better." I knelt down next to him and moved the ice over his knee. "You didn't go above a six, and that was only when I was really pushing you."

Dan didn't comment, though I felt his eyes boring into the top of my head. I wanted to look right back at him and scream, "What?" but I don't think I really want to know. Plus, after the way I acted this morning, I really can't complain about anything. I finished icing his knee in silence.

"Same time tomorrow?" I asked, eager to get away. When he didn't answer, I looked over at him. Big mistake. His eyes were practically glowing, though not with the anger I had expected. I opened my mouth to pose the question again, but the words wouldn't form. Even when Dan stood and walked toward me, I remained silent, my gaze locked on his.

As he stood directly in front of me, Dan's eyes darkened and for a minute I thought he was going to kiss me. He leaned forward slightly then stopped, his brow creasing into a frown. He pinched the bridge of his nose between his thumb and forefinger, then rubbed his hand across his forehead before meeting my gaze again.

"I want to thank you for taking Lexi shopping with you today," he said, his voice husky. He cleared his throat and continued. "She talked about it for an hour and only stopped because I had to meet you for therapy." A smile crossed his face. "I'm sure I'll be hearing more about it when I get back upstairs."

"No need to thank me," I said and looked away before I got hypnotized by his smile. "I had a great time."

"I don't remember you being much of a shopper."

"I'm usually not." I shrugged. "I was just in the mood."

He chuckled. "She told me she wants you to take her school shopping because you don't hassle her."

"She did mention that you give her a hard time with fashion."

He nodded. "She says the clothes I pick out are baby-ish. But some of the things out there are so…" His brow furrowed as he searched for a word. "Small. There's nothing to them. She's eight years old for chrissake."

Dan looked so outraged I actually burst out laughing.

"What?" he asked, around a scowl.

"You're right, she is only eight. What are you going to do when she's eighteen?"

He grasped his chest dramatically, then chuckled. "Don't make me think about that." His expression sobered. "I can't believe how big she's getting." He held his hand up. "When she was born, she fit in the palm of my hand. I don't know where the time went."

"I think every parent feels that way. Hell, my father still calls me his baby girl. I've been begging Kevin to have a baby so that I'm not the baby anymore."

"You'll always be your dad's baby girl."

"I suppose." Wanting to get off the subject of myself, I added, "I'd love to be a fly on the wall the first time a boy knocks on your door."

"I'd better start practicing my scowls and dirty looks."

"I think you're intimidating enough without them."

"Yeah?" He looked inordinately pleased.

I nodded. "You'll have them shaking in their boots."

"Good."

"Lexi's a good kid. I'm sure you won't have to worry about the boys she brings home." He grunted. I took that to mean he didn't believe it. "She really is great. I had a lot of fun today." He didn't say anything, so I decided to voice the thoughts that had been bouncing around my head all afternoon. "I'm sorry about what I said, Dan." His right brow raised, though I'm sure he knew exactly what I was talking about. "I know you wouldn't use Lexi for any reason. She means too much to you and you…" I took a deep breath, "…you're too good for that."

"You really believe that?"

I nodded. "And I don't think you're an asshole."

"No?" he asked on a chuckle.

"Hey, it was your word, not mine."

"Yeah, it was." His smile disappeared. "Thanks Bri, it means a lot."

Again I nodded, afraid I wouldn't be able to speak around the lump that had formed in my throat. When we're not fighting, I'm so drawn to Dan it scares the hell out of me. He must have sensed that because he backed off. Literally. I found myself missing his warmth, his closeness.

"Are you going to be eating with us tonight?" he asked.

"I guess so."

"I threw a pan of lasagna Mrs. Evans made before she left in the oven."

"Sounds good."

"Good, I'll see you then."

I watched him walk toward the stairs, then disappear. The professional in me noticed how much better he was moving around, but the woman in me couldn't help but admire his ass.

It was then I realized how much trouble I was in. For some reason, despite all my reservations, despite everything, I've gone and fallen in love with Dan McMullen.

Again.

If I'd ever actually stopped.

Chapter Twenty-One

"ARE you going home for the Fourth of July?" Dan asked during a therapy session, just two days before the holiday.

We've been getting along remarkably well the past week. I can't help but think it's because I've finally resigned myself to the feelings I have for him. No amount of denial or bitchiness toward Dan is going to change them.

Also, I have—per his request—attempted to judge him on who he is now instead of who he was then. And while I'm still not inclined to get romantically involved with him, I do admire who he's become. His dedication to Lexi aside, he is truly a nice person. His charm notwithstanding, our personalities mesh well and I honestly enjoy being with him.

So, for as long as this assignment lasts, and maybe even afterward, I'll be his friend. I did, after all, make a promise to stay in contact with Lexi and, truth be told, I don't think I could let her out of my life.

Am I looking for trouble here? Probably.

Will I get hurt? Most likely.

Are either of those facts going to stop me? Definitely not.

"Bri?" Dan said, and I realized he was waiting for an answer.

I have no doubt in my mind that he knows I'm in love with him. I've tried to carefully school my features, limit the adoring looks, and hide my feelings, but that's never stopped him from seeing right through me before. But just because I know and he knows, doesn't mean I have to act on anything.

"Sabrina?" Dan said in a singsong voice. I looked at his amused face.

Oh yeah, he knows.

"What?" I'd forgotten the question.

"Are you going home for the Fourth of July or are you staying here?"

"I, uh, I haven't really thought about it." I added five pounds to the weight Dan was lifting. "Why?"

"My family has decided to descend on me for the holiday so we'll be having lots of festivities here." Dan straightened his leg, lifting the weights, not seeming to notice the extra burden. Aside from the fact that he couldn't straighten his knee completely, he didn't seem to have a problem. "I'd like it if you'd stay."

I nearly blurted out, "you would?" in an utterly breathless, totally besotted voice, but managed to stop myself at the last second.

When I didn't answer, he added, "I know my family would love to see you."

"I'm not sure what I'm doing. My mom is probably having something and I should go." I took in a deep breath and let it out on a sigh. "But I don't think I'm up to dealing with everyone right now."

"Everything all right?"

"Everything is fine." I shrugged. "You know how families are. They just got on my nerves last time I was there. Not my mom and dad, but all the aunts and uncles, and of course, the neighbors." I didn't add that the reason they all annoyed me was because they kept asking about him.

"You don't have to explain it to me," he said around a chuckle. "My family invited themselves here for holiday. No 'is it all right' or 'do you have plans,' just 'we're coming, like it or not.'" He sat up on the weight bench and wiped his face with a towel. "I don't really mind though," he admitted. "And Lexi is really excited. We're going for fireworks tomorrow."

"Sounds great."

"Sabrina, I really would like it if you'd stay."

His eyes pleading, his tone sincere.

"I'll let you know," I said, fully intending to be anywhere but here for the holiday.

DAN

"I'M LOADING the cooler with steaks from Marty's," my mother said, referring to the butcher shop she's shopped at as long as I can remember. "And I'll bring the ingredients to make my potato salad."

"Mom, you know Mrs. Evans always has tons of food on hand, and there are grocery stores near my house if we need something. You don't have to lug all that with you."

"It's not the same."

"Suit yourself," I said. "You're bringing chocolate chip bars, right?"

"Four batches." I heard the smile in her voice.

But seriously, my mom makes amazing chocolate chip bars.

"I'll have to grab a batch and hide it in my room," I said. "Or maybe half a batch. I can't get too out of shape."

My mother chuckled, then said, "Speaking of being in shape. How are things going with Sabrina?"

"Good. My leg is feeling great, considering. I'll definitely be one hundred percent for spring training next year."

"That's wonderful, but not exactly what I was asking."

I sighed and rubbed the back of my neck. "I don't know, mom. There's still something there, but I'm not sure if she'll get over what I did back in college."

"Do you want me to talk to her?"

"No," I said quickly…too quickly. "Thanks for the offer, though."

"Okay, but let me know if you change your mind."

"Things are pretty fragile between us. Right now, we're getting along well and she's comfortable with me. I think she still has feelings for me, but I know she doesn't want to and she's fighting it with everything she has." I chuckled. "Which is a lot. She's pretty tough."

"I have faith that it will all work out in the end. You two were so good together."

"Thanks. But don't go too crazy trying to remind her of that when you're here. I don't

want to freak her out too much."

"Okay honey. I promise I won't push."

"Can you pass the word on to my sisters? You know how they can be."

"They just love you and want you to be happy."

"I know, but please ask them to control themselves this time."

"I will," she promised. "If you need us to bring anything else let me know. Otherwise, we'll see you tomorrow."

"Can't wait," I said. "Love you, Mom."

"Love you too, honey."

Chapter Twenty-Two

THE MCMULLEN FAMILY began to descend a few days later, and by nightfall, Dan's house was bustling with activity. First to arrive was his older sister, Patti, her husband, Joe, and their three children.

His younger sister, Megan, and her husband, Paul, were next. They didn't have any children in tow, though Megan was carrying one in front.

Dan's mother, Maureen, soon followed with her "friend" Frank. Everyone seemed to be shocked by the man's presence, but attempted to welcome him just the same. The girls and their husbands did anyway. I saw Dan glaring and snapped him out of it before anyone else noticed.

Various aunts, uncles, and cousins arrived in dribs and drabs throughout the evening with the promise of more to follow the next morning. Dan's father was absent and since there was no talk of him at all, I assumed he wouldn't be coming.

Mrs. Evans had been in her glory all day, cooking enough food to feed an army, which I suppose, wasn't far from the amount of people at the house. The adults helped themselves to her home cooking, while the children ran wild through the house. Dan assured me they'd settle down once the novelty of seeing each other wore off, but I seriously doubt it. Not that they were bothering me. In fact, I enjoyed watching them, and Lexi looked so happy I got choked up.

"So Sabrina," Megan's voice interrupted my thoughts. I looked at her and she patted the empty spot beside her on the sofa. "Come sit and fill me in on what you've been up to for the past ten years."

Megan and I had bonded the first time we met many years ago, but after I broke it off with Dan, it was just too painful to keep the friendship. We kept in touch for a few months afterward, but I found it too difficult and stopped returning her calls and emails. She must have understood —either that or she got really pissed off—because eventually she stopped contacting me altogether.

I complied with her request and settled in next to her. "Not much," I answered. "Working mostly."

"Are you married? Any kids?"

"No and no."

Megan looked poignantly at her mother, who had settled into the chair directly across from us.

"You know," Maureen said, "Dan didn't even tell us you were here. We had to hear the news from Lexi."

"Maybe he doesn't think my presence is newsworthy," I said, hoping to sound cheeky, not bitchy.

"Of course he does, honey." Maureen leaned forward and patted my hand. "Which is why he didn't tell us."

I had no idea what she meant by that, but decided to let the whole subject drop. My gaze dropped to Megan's distended abdomen. "I guess I don't have to ask what you've been up to. When are you due?"

"September twenty-fifth." Megan sighed and patted her round belly. "But hopefully I'll go early. If I get any bigger, I swear I'm gonna bust."

Megan looked like she was going to bust, but I thought it would be rude to say so. While Dan is big, broad, and blond like his father, Megan and Patti are dark-haired and petite like their mother. At five foot seven, I tower over the three of them. I assume Megan's belly looks so large because the rest of her is so small. And she is small. I don't think she's gained an ounce anywhere other than her stomach.

"So are you seeing anyone special?" Dan's mother asked.

"No. No one special." No one at all, but she doesn't have to know that.

Again, Megan and Maureen shared a look, which left no doubt in my mind as to where they wanted this conversation to go. Before I could excuse myself, Megan added, "Neither is Dan."

Okay, it's definitely time to go.

I scooted forward on the couch, but before I could stand, Megan placed her hand on my arm. "I'm sorry, Sabrina. I won't do that again." I must have looked doubtful, because she added, "I promise."

"You have my word, too," Maureen said. "We're just so happy to see you. We've all missed you."

"I tried to keep in touch," Megan said. "But you didn't seem interested." Her sullen expression filled me with guilt.

"I'm sorry about that, Meg. I know I promised we'd remain friends despite everything, but it was just too hard for me. You reminded me of him and I couldn't handle that." I paused for a moment while she digested my words. "Then a few years went by and I thought about looking you up, but felt too embarrassed."

"Oh, I wish you had," Megan said, around her tears. "From now on, we'll be sure to keep in touch. And if you don't return my calls, I'll just show up on your doorstep."

"Jeez Meg, every time I see you, you're crying." Dan's deep timbre rolled over my senses, forcing goosebumps to rise on my skin.

"I know." A fresh gush of tears burst out of Megan's eyes. "I can't help it." She wiped at her cheeks. "It's the hormones."

Dan rested his hip on the arm of the sofa, next to Maureen. "So how is my nephew doing? Still cooking?"

"Yes, and kicking like crazy."

"Yeah?" Dan's eyes lit up. "Right now?" Megan nodded. He jumped off his perch and was hovering over her in a flash. "Where?" he asked, his hands poised over her belly.

"Right up here." Megan took his big hands and placed them on her womb.

Dan stared at his hands expectantly for just a moment before a wide smile split his face. "Holy hell," he said, his tone full of awe.

I couldn't take my eyes off him. Dan turned and met my gaze. I felt poleaxed. The longing in his eyes nearly tore me apart. I had to fight back my own tears.

"Dan…" The tone of Megan's voice told me it wasn't the first time she'd said his name.

"Yeah?"

"I can see you're really enjoying yourself here, but I really have to pee."

"Sorry." Dan moved back and held his hand out to help Megan out of her seat.

"Thanks," she said, then waddled out of the room.

Dan took the seat his sister had vacated, right next to me. I glanced at him just in time to catch the tail end of his grimace of pain.

"Are you okay?"

He nodded and rubbed his leg. "I shouldn't have jumped up like that."

"Probably not," I said, dryly.

He chuckled. "Then why didn't you stop me? You're supposed to be taking care of me, aren't you?"

"I'm off duty," I joked, holding up my bottle of Sam Adams to emphasize the point.

Truth be told, I'd been so wrapped up in Dan's reaction to the baby kicking to think of anything else. He obviously got swept up in the moment and hadn't been thinking either. That fact made me realize how genuine his feelings were.

"How is Dan doing?" Maureen asked, breaking into my thoughts.

"He's uh," I cleared my throat and sat up straight. "He's making remarkable progress."

"Do you think he'll be ready for spring training?"

"Definitely," I answered confidently.

Maureen shifted her eyes between Dan and me several times before she spoke again.

"Well, that's good." She stood. "Now, if you'll excuse me, I'm going to find Frank. Your uncle is probably talking the poor man's ear off." She directed the last comment to Dan, smiled at me, and walked away.

Once she left, I noticed that Dan and I were alone. Sure, there were people milling around, but the person closest to us stood a good six feet away. As I made the observation, Lexi and her cousins ran through the room and out the kitchen door.

"They should sleep well tonight," I said.

Dan nodded. "Lexi loves her cousins. They don't stop the entire time they're together." His eyes crinkled in amusement. "Of course, I remember doing the same thing when I was kid." He took a long pull on his beer. "Now, I get tired just watching them."

"It's tough getting old," I teased.

"As long as I also get wise, I don't mind."

I didn't want to discuss the things he's claimed to have gotten wiser about, so I said, "You really have a wonderful family."

"So do you," he said, as he nodded his agreement.

Our families are very similar, which is probably why we'd always fit in so well at each other's family functions. In high school, I dated a boy who nearly ran out of my house in tears when my Uncle Mark teased him about his spiked hair.

My family is loud and boisterous, and likes to put people through their paces. Dan's is much the same and he hadn't batted an eye when Uncle Mark started on him, nor when the rest of the family joined in.

"It's weird without my dad here." Dan's voice was so low, I barely heard him.

"Did you invite him?"

"If you remember, I didn't invite anyone," he pointed out. "But no, it's too new to have him here with Mom. Maybe someday."

"I'm really sorry. I know how close you and your dad are."

"It's just hard. I mean, on one hand, I want to kill the son of a bitch for what he did to my mom, but on the other..." he gestured vaguely. "My mom told me that everything he did, he did to her, not me or my sisters, but it's still difficult to swallow."

"How do Megan and Patti feel?"

"They don't know the whole story."

"Why not?"

"Mom didn't think she should tell them. She figured it would ruin their relationship with Dad."

"Then why did she tell you?"

"Because she wanted Dad's theory of relationships to stop with me." He cleared his throat. "Once she found out about Dad, she put two and two together and figured out why we broke up. When she confronted me, I couldn't deny it. Then she spilled her guts."

"So, she knows everything."

He nodded, looking embarrassed. At that moment, my armor cracked and I saw Dan's pain. For the first time since I'd arrived, I saw him as a man trying to atone for the sins of his youth. No longer was he the evil creature I'd created in my mind in an attempt to soothe my battered soul. I saw him as a man who made mistakes and is now looking for forgiveness.

The million-dollar question is…can I forgive him?

Chapter Twenty-Three

SABRINA

ONE WEEK LATER, I was still contemplating the answer to the million-dollar question.

Maureen and I had a few words before she left and while she didn't come right out and say it, she gently urged me to give Dan another chance. And I have to admit, the more time I spend with him, the more I'm leaning in that direction.

"Twenty minutes on the bike," I told him in-between my musings.

"Twenty?"

"I want you to add a few minutes each day. We need to increase the motion of that leg."

"You're a slave driver," he teased and started pedaling.

Dan just finished with the bike when Lexi came bouncing into the gym. "Daddy, Tori asked if I could come over," she pleaded. "Can I?"

"I suppose so." Dan looked at the clock. "I can take you in an hour or so."

"Jeff said he'd take me."

"I'm sure he did," Dan said, under his breath. "Okay princess, I'll see you later." He leaned down and kissed her cheek.

"Eewww," Lexi shrieked. "You're all sweaty." She gave him a quick peck. "But I love you anyway."

"I love you, too. Behave."

"I will. Bye, Sabrina," she said as she bestowed a kiss on my cheek.

"Have fun," I said.

Lexi ran out of the gym and up the stairs with more energy than anyone should be allowed to have.

"The girls still don't know about Jeff and Nancy?"

Dan had informed me that Jeff and Tori's mother, Nancy, had started dating about a month ago.

"No." Dan sat on the rowing machine. "How long?"

"Fifteen," I answered and set my timer.

"They want to figure out if things are going anywhere before they tell Tori."

Tori's father had passed away three years earlier, so I could understand Nancy's caution.

"I don't know about Nancy, but Jeff looks like he's walking on air."

"Yeah, love will do that to you," Dan said, through gritted teeth.

"Are you okay?" I watched his motion, looking for signs that he was straining himself. "Don't overdo it."

"My leg is fine."

The tone of his voice stopped me from asking any more questions.

Later that afternoon, Lexi called to see if she could sleep over Tori's. Dan agreed and asked to speak to Jeff.

"You sleeping over too?" I heard him ask Jeff. Obviously, I didn't hear Jeff's reply, but it made Dan laugh. "Does she need clothes?" He paused, listening to whatever Jeff was saying. "Okay bud. I'll see you tomorrow."

"He's sleeping over?"

"No, but he's staying for the moviefest and popcorn, so he won't be home 'til later."

"Oh."

"Do you think it would be wrong for him to stay over?"

"No, I uh, I don't know. I mean, parents do it all the time with the kids at home, so no, I guess I don't." Then, to save myself from sounding like a prude, I added, "They'd just be taking a big chance with the girls there. Considering they want the relationship kept secret."

"Hmmm." I took that as agreement with what I had said and expected him to elaborate, so when he said, "Would you have dinner with me tonight?" I nearly gasped out loud.

"I…" Dan frowned. He was expecting me to make up some lame-ass excuse and turn him down. Not that the thought hadn't crossed my mind, but like I reasoned last time I agreed to accompany him to dinner, I'd rather be alone with him in public than at the house. I shocked Dan by saying, "I'd love to."

"Great," Dan replied in a casual tone, though the look on his face gave away his emotions. He was as excited and nervous as I was. "Italian?"

"Sounds good."

We agreed to go to the hole-in-the-wall Italian restaurant we never made it to a few weeks earlier, thanks to Kent and the rest of Dan's friends. But I decided not to think about that.

"Great," Dan repeated. "I'll meet you in the kitchen around six."

I checked the clock and decided that two hours was plenty of time to talk myself in and out of going a few hundred times. "Six it is."

That settled, Dan made his way to the stairs. His foot on the first step, he spoke again. "Oh, and Sabrina?"

"Yeah?"

"We're gonna get it right this time."

He left me wondering if he was talking about dinner or something more.

DAN

I TOLD Sabrina I'd leave her alone, but I just can't. And like I told her last time I asked her out, we both have to eat…even if I have ulterior motives.

There's just something there between us that I can't ignore, always has been. And, since the 4th of July, she's been more like her old self. She seems more relaxed and things have definitely been less forced between us.

Even though I asked my mother and sisters not to interfere, I doubt they listened. They had Sabrina trapped in conversation a few times, and I'd bet anything my name came up more than once. But if anything they said resulted in Sabrina's new/old demeanor, I can't be angry.

I tried to relax for a bit before getting ready, but was too antsy. This night has to be perfect. I know Sabrina will love Maroni's, and Vince and Rita will fawn all over her. I just have to make sure I don't blow it like I did last time. Hell, I don't care if Babe Ruth himself is reincarnated and shows up at my house, I'm not answering the door.

I took a longer-than-normal shower, letting the warm

water soothe my aching muscles. My workouts have been getting harder lately, so I know my leg is healing well. Which is a good thing. I just hate the fact that my getting better could mean the end of my relationship with Sabrina. Not that we have an official relationship, but it seems we're at least friends at this point. I just need time to convince her we should be more.

After drying off and slinging a towel around my waist, I lathered up and carefully shaved my face to a shiny smoothness. Hopefully all my effort won't be in vain. Then again, as long as I can actually get Sabrina out to the restaurant and through dinner, I'll be happy. Even if she doesn't get to feel the fact that my face is as soft as a baby's ass.

Discarding the clothes I had on last time we were supposed to go out as bad luck, I decided on black dress pants and a pale blue button down shirt. After struggling to get the pants settled over my brace, I shrugged into my shirt, and slipped on black loafers. I'm ready to go, forty-five minutes early.

Oh well, I've waited for Sabrina this long, another forty-five minutes won't kill me. I'll wait for her forever if I have to.

Chapter Twenty-Four

AS PREDICTED, my inner battle raged the entire time I showered and dressed. In the end, I decided to go because (a) I really want to and (b) something tells me that Dan won't let me back down, not after what happened the last time we tried this.

So, at six o'clock on the dot, I closed my bedroom door and made my way to the kitchen. Once again, I had agonized over what to wear, and decided on my all-purpose black dress. For more formal occasions, I dress it up with jewelry or a jacket, but tonight newly-purchased strappy sandals and freshly shaved legs are my only considerations to the fact that this might be a date. I don't want to think about why I slipped on a matching black lace bra and panty set.

Dan's back faced me as he gazed out the window over the sink, so I had a moment to admire his backside. His well-tailored black pants cupped his behind before falling loosely over well-muscled thighs, giving only a hint to their shape. A pale blue linen shirt stretched across his broad shoulders and my fingers itched to explore.

He turned suddenly and I felt a blush creep up my neck and across my face. My embarrassment at being caught in the act didn't make me miss the fact that his front view was as magnificent as the back had been.

"Wow." Admiration shone in Dan's eyes as he walked toward me, using the sleek black cane his mother had given him. He stopped in front of me and let his gaze drift over my body, which definitely responded to his leisurely inspection. My blush intensified. "You look beautiful."

"Thank you," I managed to croak. "You look pretty nice yourself. I like the cane."

Dan's smile practically lit up the room. "It is pretty classy." He pulled his jacket off a stool at the breakfast bar and shrugged into it. "Ready?" I nodded. "Great, I'm starving."

"Me too," I replied, though my stomach was tied in so many knots, I have no idea if I'll be able to keep anything down.

THE RESTAURANT HAD ACTUALLY BEEN someone's home in a past life. Dan led me up the stairs of what appeared to be a large Victorian and through the front door, his right hand resting on my lower back.

A boisterous man with a booming voice greeted us immediately. "Dan, it's good to see you." He slapped Dan on the back as he shook his hand vigorously. "How's the leg?"

"Getting better every day, Vince."

"Glad to hear it. Where is our little Miss Alexis tonight?"

"At a friend's house. I brought my friend Sabrina instead."

Vince looked at me as though he hadn't noticed my presence. "Well, hello Sabrina. I'm Vince Maroni. My wife, Rita, and I own this place." He took my hand in his and raised it to his mouth, lightly brushing his lips across my knuckles. I silently thanked God, because I don't think I could survive one of Vince's handshakes.

"No train room for you tonight. Only the room of romance will do," he declared, rolling his R's dramatically.

Vince instructed us to follow him and we did, to a quiet table for two, set next to a lovely brick fireplace, which in consideration of the season, was not lit. He handed a menu to me, then to Dan and proceeded to list the specials of the evening. With a flick of his lighter, the small votive candle in the center of the table came to light. "Would you like some wine tonight?"

Dan's eyes smiled into mine over the candlelight. "Zinfandel? For old times' sake?" he asked.

I nodded, not trusting myself to speak. Dan had ordered White Zinfandel on our first date. He admitted later that a friend of his had suggested it, that he himself knew nothing about wine. And considering the fact that neither of us was old enough to legally drink at the time, why should we? That aside, I can't believe he still remembers the details of our first date.

"I'll bring that right out for you," Vince said, before turning on his heel and leaving us alone.

I looked around the room and was taken in by its old world charm. Since the restaurant used to be a house, it consisted of a few small rooms instead of one large one. The dimly lit room was very romantic, as Vince had promised.

Light butterscotch paint coated the aged plaster walls. The cozy tables scattered throughout had enough distance between to give space and a sense of privacy. Red checked tablecloths added a finishing touch of traditional charm.

"Dan!" A female voice brought me out of my perusal of the room. I looked up and spotted a petite woman with thick salt and pepper hair and piercing blue eyes rushing toward our table. If it weren't for the ice bucket clutched to her ample bosom, I would have assumed she was a patron. Her casual dress did not mark her as an employee.

"It's been too long," she said, embracing Dan, who was now standing, welcoming her with open arms. "We haven't seen you in so long." Her voice was what I can only describe as smoky, sexy, and exotic.

"I've been kind of tied up," he answered, chuckling.

"How is your leg?" she asked, as she set the ice bucket on the edge of the table.

"Getting better," he said, gesturing toward me. "Thanks to this amazing woman."

The woman's eyes shifted to me, and her pleasant expression put me at ease. "Vince warned me, but I didn't believe him," she teased. I followed her eyes to Dan, who was actually blushing.

"Rita, this is Sabrina Kelly, my physical therapist and date for the night. Sabrina, Rita Maroni, Vince's wife and the main force behind the wonderful food served here."

"Hello Sabrina." Rita extended her hand to shake mine. "It's so nice to meet you." That done, she turned back to Dan. "Sit." He did as she ordered and she pulled a corkscrew out of her pocket and opened the wine. After going through the whole ceremony of allowing Dan to taste it and filling both of our glasses, she set the bottle back in the ice bucket.

"Vince will be out shortly to take your order. I just had to see this for myself," she said, tossing a smile my way.

Then we were alone. Well, as alone as two people can be in a public place. I took a sip of wine, more for something to do than anything else. I felt Dan watching me, and my stomach fluttered. Whether it was from nervousness or anticipation, I'm not sure.

"I take it you come here often," I said.

Dan nodded. "This is one of Lexi's favorite restaurants." He chuckled. "I'm not sure if she likes the food or the fuss they make over her."

"Probably a little of both."

Again, he nodded. He looked like he was going to say something, but Vince returned to take our orders.

Dan and I decided to share an order of stuffed mushrooms for an appetizer. Colossal salads, loaded with a variety of veggies topped with house dressing followed.

I ordered chicken marsala with a side of spaghetti with marinara. It had seemed like a harmless meal until Vince set it down in front of me. A plate the size of a satellite dish held the chicken, which was two full breasts topped with cremini mushrooms smothered with marsala sauce. I thought he'd forgotten my spaghetti until he placed what I would consider a serving bowl down, filled with my "side" of pasta.

The bowl that held Dan's chicken and fettuccine Alfredo was so large I could barely see him over it. Well, maybe that's a slight exaggeration, but I swear there has to be two pounds of pasta in front of him.

"Is everything all right?" Vince asked a while later.

"Delicious," I answered, around a mouthful of the best chicken marsala I'd ever tasted.

"Can I get you anything else?"

Dan and I both told him he couldn't and Vince told us to yell if we needed him.

"I'll never finish all this," I said, looking at the mound of food on my plates.

"They do give healthy portions."

"I don't know if I would use the word healthy to describe this meal, but there sure is a lot."

A loaf of crusty Italian bread sat in a basket between us. Dan picked up the basket and held it out to me. "Bread?"

"Not just yet, thanks."

He set the basket down, took a piece of bread for himself, and proceeded to butter it. I stared, fascinated by his hands, his long, broad-tipped fingers as they held the knife. Images of those hands touching me flashed through my mind, heating my skin. No man's hands had ever felt as good as Dan's. No one else ever made me feel like he could with the slightest touch. I returned my attention to my food.

We ate in silence for some time before he spoke again. "I'm sorry about the fuss."

"Fuss?"

"The fuss Vince and Rita are making."

"That's okay."

"Lexi's the only female I've ever brought here." He thought for a moment then added, "No, scratch that. I brought my mom once."

The way he said the last word made me think the experience hadn't been pleasant.

"Once?"

"She and Rita hit it off instantly and kept trying to fix my life for me."

"What's wrong with your life?" I don't know what possessed me to ask.

He shrugged. "They think I need a good woman."

Okay, time to change the subject.

"So, Lexi really likes it here?" My voice sounded an octave or two higher than normal.

"Yeah, she does," Dan answered. I thought I was home free until he added, "I told my mom that I'd had a good woman and let her go."

I nearly choked on my pasta. He went back to his fettuccini. We ate in silence for a bit, then Dan resumed the conversation on a lighter note, asking questions about my career and family, and other normal date topics.

After a loud good-bye with Vince and Rita, which included hugs and a promise that I'd return, Dan and I shared a quiet ride home. He seemed to be lost in his own thoughts and I didn't feel the need to fill the air with needless chatter.

I used the time to evaluate the evening as a whole. The restaurant was charming, the food amazing, and Dan had been the perfect date. And yes, I readily admit that it was a date. I had truly enjoyed myself and planned to admit as much to Dan.

Resting my head against the window, I allowed my mind to wander to the past. How many nights had we shared like this very one?

More than I can remember.

With or without dinner, our time together had been easy. We never ran out of things to talk about, yet we also weren't afraid of quiet times. Like now, neither of us feels the need to speak and the silence seems neither oppressive nor uncomfortable.

The car stopped and I realized we were back at the house. The garage door closed behind us as Dan unbuckled his seat belt and I did the same. Suddenly, the awareness between us was so overwhelming, I opened my door in order to drag fresh air into my lungs.

"You okay?" Dan ran around to my side of the car. Well, ran as well as any man with a leg injury using a cane can.

"Fine. I just needed some air."

He studied my face for a moment and nodded. His hand reached out and held mine, helping me out of the car. Our hands remained clasped as we walked through the garage and through the door into the kitchen.

The house was quiet.

Dan squeezed my hand before releasing it and asked, "Would you like a drink?"

I really didn't want the evening to end, which immediately made me want to decline. I don't want to want him. But I do. Maybe it's time to face that head on.

"I'd like that," I answered.

"Great." He'd obviously expected me to head straight to bed, even though it was barely ten o'clock. "Have a seat. Would you like more wine?"

While that was tempting, I figured I'd had enough alcohol. "Sweet tea is fine."

I sat on the couch and watched Dan fill two cut crystal glasses from the pitcher of sweet tea Mrs. Evans somehow kept filled at all times. I wondered how he was going to carry both and use his cane, and smiled when he placed both glasses in the palm of his right hand, before picking up the cane and heading toward me.

"Thank you." I took a token sip and placed the glass on the coffee table in front of me. "I had a great time tonight. Thank you for asking me."

From the look on his face, I'd managed to shock him again. "The pleasure was all mine," he said once he composed himself. "Maybe we could do it again sometime?"

I wanted to tell him no, tell him not to get the wrong idea, but instead heard myself say, "I think I'd like that."

Dan finished his tea in one long gulp and placed the glass on the table next to mine. He sat back against the cushion and traced the crease in his pants with his index finger. "Sabrina," he started, then cleared his throat. "I want you to know how sorry I am about everything that happened between us." He turned to fully face me. "You didn't deserve it. You didn't deserve the way I treated you when you confronted me, either."

He took a deep breath and let it out slowly. "I've explained to you why I did it, and you brought up a very valid point. The thought of someone else touching you, kissing you would have driven me insane…still drives me insane."

The anguish in his eyes, on his face, is genuine and I know that he's truly sorry. The things that happened between us obviously affected him as much as they did me.

"I just don't want you to think I'm a jerk anymore. I care about you and your opinion too much to let that be the case."

His eyes searched mine, looking for answers to his questions, for reassurances about my thoughts, my feelings. I knew I had to speak and that I had to be honest. The problem is that while my honesty will thrill him, it scares the hell out of me.

"I don't think you're a jerk," I said, my voice a mere whisper. His disbelieving look made me smile. "I really don't, Dan. That's not to say I didn't when I first arrived. But I don't anymore."

"If I followed correctly, I think I like what I'm hearing." His voice raised slightly on the last word, turning the statement into a question.

"You heard me correctly," I assured him. "For ten years, I allowed what happened to fester inside me. In my mind's eye, you turned into a monster who broke my heart. And you were right." He cocked his brow, but didn't say a word, obviously not wanting to break my train of thought. "When I first arrived, I saw you as I wanted to, not as you actually are. You're obviously a dedicated father and if rumors can be believed, you're not the shallow, womanizing creep I'd imagined you to be."

"Thanks for the compliment." Dan chuckled. "I think."

"It was meant to be a compliment, no matter how backhanded it sounded." I leaned forward and took a drink. "Whenever I thought of you over the years, I'd imagined you with a slew of groupies, living a life of never ending orgies."

He seemed to think about that for a minute then laughed. Not a small chuckle, but a full belly laugh.

"What's so funny?" I asked.

It took a second for him to compose himself enough to answer. "While you were imagining that, I was probably covered in spit up, trying to figure out how to change a diaper." He wiped tears from his eyes and sobered. "Seriously Sabrina, it was never like that. Even back in college, it…" he stopped and rubbed his eyes. "There just weren't as many girls as you seem to think there were." He held up his hand at my indrawn breath. "Now, before you go berserk, I know there shouldn't have been *any*, that even one was too many. I know that now. Hell, I knew that then, if my guilt was an indicator." He ran a frustrated hand through his hair. "I'm really messing up here."

"No, you're not," I reassured him. "Dan, what

happened, happened. Circling around it won't make it go away. That's the mistake I made back then. Instead of talking to you about it, I drew my own conclusions."

"You tried to talk to me. I screwed that up. Remember?"

"Yeah, I remember. But in all honesty, nothing you said that day would have really registered. I was too hurt, too upset."

"Sabrina, I could say I'm sorry a million times and it wouldn't begin to convey how I feel." I nodded, just to let Dan know I'd heard what he said. "Thank you for talking to me about this."

I nodded again, tossing the question around in my mind. Did I dare ask it? Am I strong enough to face his answer? I guess I'll never know if I don't ask.

"Can I ask you something?"

"Anything."

"I was wondering…" I let out a frustrated breath and started over. "The night of the prom, did you…did you go to someone else after you left me?"

Dan looked as unsettled by the question as I'd felt asking it. For a moment, I didn't think he was going to answer, but slowly his features returned to normal, then softened. He inched closer to me and took my hand in his. "Is that what you thought?" Without waiting for an answer, he said, "No wonder you hated me so much." I looked at him with confused eyes and saw the answer even before he said it. "No Sabrina, I never went to anyone after I left you. Not ever, but especially not that night. It was too special, too memorable to tarnish."

"I just always wondered."

Dan stroked my knuckles with his thumb and his smile turned nostalgic. "That night was amazing, Bri. Walking out of that room was the hardest thing I've ever done in my life."

"But you didn't have to," I pointed out. "You could've stayed. In fact, I seem to remember begging you to do just that."

"I know." He leaned closer and cupped my cheek in his big palm. "I know." He kissed my forehead before pulling back and looking into my eyes once again. "That night has haunted my dreams for ten years. Sometimes we finish what we started, but most times I wake up so hard I feel like I'm gonna explode."

His lips gently touched mine. It started as a comforting kiss between two friends, but the old feelings took hold too quickly for either of us to stop them. Dan kissed me once again, this time it was less comforting and more possessive, more complete. I thought I would melt into a puddle right there on the couch.

His hands circled my waist and pulled me closer, our mouths never losing contact. I wrapped my arms around his neck, putting my breasts in contact with his brick wall of a chest. I felt as well as heard his groan before he opened his mouth fully over mine and thrust his tongue inside.

No one kisses like Dan. There must be something addictive in his saliva, because one taste of him and I immediately want more. Dan leaned forward, pushing me against the arm of the couch. I slid my sandals off and put my right leg on the couch behind his back. And the kiss went on.

He settled between my widespread thighs and his erection brushed against my center. Sensation shot through me, then exploded as Dan cupped my breast, and rolled my distended nipple between his thumb and forefinger. I arched my back, telling him in the only way I could that I wanted more. He didn't disappoint.

By slow degrees, he drove me wild. First one breast, then the other received attention. His hips danced a slow, easy rhythm between my thighs and our mouths only parted long enough to allow us to breathe.

I pulled his shirt out of his pants and allowed my hands to roam over the broad expanse of his back. His muscles bunched and flexed beneath my fingers, and I wanted more. I was so into things, it took me a moment to realize that Dan was slowing down, pulling away.

"No," I screamed in my mind and only realized I'd said it out loud when Dan kissed my forehead and whispered reassurances.

"Not like this, Bri," he panted. "Not on the couch like a couple of horny teenagers." His crooked smile looked sexy and seductive, and somewhat evil. "I want to stretch you out on my bed and love every inch of you." His eyes glowed in the darkness and I shivered in anticipation. "Will you let me?"

The word yes was barely out of my mouth before Dan was leading me up the stairs to his bedroom door. A lamp on the nightstand cast a soft glow over the room. The king-sized bed sat in the middle of the room, surrounded by masculine furniture. Family photos hung on the walls, in lieu of the sports awards and memorabilia I'd imagined would be there.

Dan stepped in front of me, putting an end to my perusal. He placed his hands on either side of my face. "Are you sure?"

I didn't have to ask what he was talking about. I also didn't have to think about my answer. "I'm sure," I said. "I've been wanting this forever."

"Me too," he said, before crushing his mouth to mine.

His hands moved down my body, then back up, dragging my dress with them. The kiss ended just long enough to allow him to pull the silky material over my head.

Dan laid me in the center of his bed and looked his fill. Thankfully, I'd worn my sexy underwear.

"You are so beautiful," he said. "Perfect." He stroked his hand across my abdomen. "Soft."

Before he started touching the really good parts, I reached out and unbuttoned his shirt. My fingers itched to touch him, so I did. His skin felt smooth beneath the tawny hair, stretched over well-developed muscles. I leaned forward and placed a kiss just above his right nipple.

He sucked in a breath, then pulled my mouth back to his and proceeded to kiss me senseless. Somewhere in the back of my mind it registered that Dan had unhooked my bra, but it wasn't until I felt his mouth on my naked breast, that I realized it was gone.

As promised, he loved every inch of me. He nuzzled my breasts before moving up to my neck and nibbling on a particularly sensitive spot he remembered. Then back to my breasts where he sucked my nipples into tight, aching points. His hot mouth skimmed down my stomach and nibbled at my belly button.

The man reduced me to a melting puddle of want, unable to do anything but pant, moan, and eagerly await his next touch.

He hooked his fingers beneath the waistband of my panties and pulled them slowly down my legs. He stared for several heartbeats, heating me with his gaze, before he leaned down and kissed my knee. Slowly, deliberately, he inched his way up my leg, alternately kissing and nibbling my skin.

When he settled between my thighs and placed a kiss at their juncture, I nearly jumped off the bed. Dan placed a restraining hand on my belly as his eyes met mine over the expanse of my body. He continued his sensuous torture, laving and nipping and sucking until I didn't think I could take any more.

I closed my eyes as though blocking out the sight of what he was doing would help dull the sensation, giving me a modicum of control. It only intensified the feeling, and when Dan slipped a finger inside me, I shattered. When I came back to reality, he was beside me, naked, condom in hand.

"This time, I'm not leaving," he muttered, before engaging me in a no-holds-barred, tongue-tangling, toe-curling kiss.

"I don't want you to," I panted, ripping the condom from his hand. I pushed him onto his back and proceeded to touch him as I'd wanted to for so long.

I ran my hands over his chest, while nibbling on his neck, behind his ear. Slowly, I moved down, suckling first one, then the other nipple. Moving lower, I nipped his navel, as he'd done to me and was rewarded with a moan. His reaction was probably more due to the fact that my chin had brushed the tip of his penis than belly button sensitivity.

I raised my head and looked down before meeting his gaze. His green eyes glowed, begging. How could I refuse? I leaned down and ran my tongue along the length of him before taking just the tip into my mouth and sucking on it like a lollypop.

"Shit. Bri," Dan moaned. "That feels…" He lost whatever he was going to say when I lowered my mouth, taking in as much of him as I could. I lifted my head, changing my angle, and lowered again, sucking and licking along the way and repeated the process over and over. I moaned deep in my throat, dragging a groan out of

Dan. While I have done this particular act before, I can't say I've ever enjoyed it so much. And Dan's reactions spurred me on even more. I was just getting into it when Dan's fingers tangled through my hair, stopping my movements.

"Stop," he gasped. "Fuck. Please stop."

I looked up. His face was twisted with what looked like anguish. If I didn't know better, I'd think he was in pain.

"Come here," he said as he pulled me up the length of his body. "Do you have any idea what you do to me?" he asked. I assumed it was a rhetorical question, so I remained silent. "It was almost over for a second there," he admitted around a wry smile.

"We certainly don't want that, do we?" I said, as I ripped the condom open. I rolled it down the length of him, caressing along the way. I was ready to play again, but Dan had other ideas. Before I knew what was happening, I was on my back with him leaning over me. His hands pinned mine to the mattress just beside my head.

"I can't have those clever hands on me, or I might embarrass myself." He kissed me and settled between my legs. As his therapist, I should have been concerned about his leg, but I only had one thing on my mind and that was getting Dan inside me. I wrapped my left leg around his right, urging him closer. He complied.

The tip of his cock teased me and I arched my back, wanting him closer still. Again he complied and slipped inside. I gasped at the same time Dan groaned. He moved his hips slightly, barely rubbing himself against me. I reached down and squeezed his ass urging him on. He pulled back slightly, then pushed forward and went nowhere.

"Bend your knees," he panted. I did as he asked then proceeded to wrap my legs around his waist. This time when he flexed his hips, he slipped all the way inside. "Oh man, Bri, you're so tight. So good."

He kissed me and started pumping. I nearly lost it at his first thrust, but figured if he could be strong, so could I.

Dan pulled back and looked into my eyes and I thanked God I wasn't dreaming this time. I'm not going to wake up in a pool of sweat, with the covers tangled around my legs, an unfulfilled longing throbbing between them. There may be heat and tangled covers, but I definitely won't be left unfulfilled.

Dan groaned and picked up the pace. "Sabrina," he said, his voice a mere rasp in my ear.

He pumped in and out in a fast rhythm and I lifted my hips to meet his every thrust. It didn't take much of that before I got sucked into a vortex of sensation. I let out a long, hoarse moan as a fierce orgasm racked through my entire body, shaking me. Some part of my brain registered the fact that Dan had let out his own shout just before he collapsed on top of me.

Dan's weight should have felt oppressive, but I relished in its feel. When he tried to pull off me, I wrapped my arms around his back and wouldn't let him.

"I'm crushing you," he said.

"It feels wonderful. Don't move just yet."

He rested his head on my shoulder for a moment before pulling back slightly and looking me in the eye. "Please tell me this isn't a dream."

I smiled and kissed his chin. "It's not a dream," I reassured him.

"Thank you," he said and settled his head on my shoulder once again.

I can't say how much time passed before I had to allow Dan to move. He shifted onto his side, and after ridding himself of the condom, pulled me into the circle of his arms. I rested my head on his shoulder, trying not to think too much, because if I did, I'd probably regret what just happened. And I don't want to do that…not yet, anyway.

I snuck a quick peek at his face and my heart skipped a beat. His eyes were closed and his mouth curved into a soft, contented smile. My heart swelled. I swear I actually felt it swell in my chest.

It wasn't just good sex—okay, great sex—that put that look on his face, I knew. It was more than simple physical release that made him appear so satisfied. Emotions were also involved. So many emotions. The reason I'm so certain is because I'd bet anything that before the panic took over, I'd had the same exact expression on my face. And before the panic entered my heart, all those emotions had filled me too.

Dan must have felt my gaze, because his eyes shifted my way. He squeezed me closer to him and placed a kiss on my forehead. "Please don't, Bri," he whispered. "It was too special to ever regret."

"I…" I started, but Dan placed his index finger on my mouth, stopping the words from spilling out.

"Sabrina, I saw your face. You looked like a deer caught in a pair of quickly approaching headlights." His sweet smile calmed me a bit. "Do you want to talk about it?"

Now there's a question. Do I want to talk about it? Yes. No. Maybe. Hell, I don't know. I do know that I have to be honest with him if we're going to have any kind of chance.

I stiffened. Where the hell did that thought come from? A chance? A chance at what? Just because we had sex doesn't mean we'll live happily ever after, no matter how bright the afterglow.

"Don't shut me out." Dan said. His fingers exerted

pressure on my chin, bringing my eyes into contact with his. "Please talk to me."

Between his pleading tone and his even more pleading gaze, how could I refuse? I cleared my throat then pulled away from the safe harbor of his embrace. His eyes are distracting enough. I don't need his touch muddling my mind.

"I don't regret this, Dan. I'm just…" I gestured vaguely. "Confused, I guess is as good a word as any."

"What about?"

"You. My reaction to you." I shrugged. "Everything." I'm normally a very articulate person, but now I don't have a clue how I can make him understand the turmoil I feel.

"Dan, for two years I loved you. You were as essential to me as air. I didn't think I could live without you. But I had to, and I did. And then I hated you for ten years." I averted my gaze and focused on the blue sheet covering our bodies. Anything was better than seeing his reaction to my words. But hey, he asked.

"In my mind, I recreated you as someone I could hate, someone horrible, someone I could never love. I blamed you for every bad experience and failed relationship I had, when in fact it was my own insecurities that were at fault." I chuckled. "Though some of the guys were jerks."

"I'm sure they were," Dan agreed, humor lacing his words.

His voice relaxed me, and I wanted to open up to him. I wanted him to understand how I felt all these years, why I reacted to him like I did when I first arrived.

I met his eyes again, knowing he'd be able to read my feelings even as he heard my words. "After I broke up with you, I was shattered. Thank God it was the end of the semester because I was an absolute mess. I went home and holed up in my room for a month. Kevin dragged me out and made me go places, but my heart wasn't in it."

I took a deep breath and let it out slowly. "I pulled myself together in time to go back to school, but when I returned it was awful. Everything reminded me of you. That's when I created mutant Dan in my mind. It helped me get through senior year, but did very little for my personal growth."

"What do you mean?"

"I shut myself off. Not from my family or friends, but from men." He probably didn't want to hear this, but he was going to anyway. "I didn't give them a chance. I mean, on the surface I did, but in the back of my mind, I was always waiting for them to screw up, or at the very least do something I could turn into a major screw up." My laugh sounded humorless. "The poor soul I dated right after you must still think I'm a psycho."

"Why's that?"

"Because I went from hot to cold and back again in the blink of an eye. I tried to convince myself I was going to be casual about relationships, but that's just not me. So one minute I'd be telling him we didn't have to spend every waking minute together and the next I'd be grilling him about his whereabouts. Do you know what happened when I decided to have sex with him?"

Dan flinched at the question, but nodded anyway.

"I practically jumped him, but once it was over, I cried like a baby. He tried to talk to me, find out what was wrong, but I tuned him out. He left and called me the next day and told me he thought it would be best if we took a break." I snorted. "Of course, I twisted it into he got his and now he wants out."

"Why did you cry?"

"What?"

"Why did you cry? Did he hurt you?" The last question was asked through gritted teeth.

"No, nothing like that."

"Then why?"

"Because he wasn't you." My voice was a mere whisper.

Dan remained silent and I looked up to see if he'd heard me. Oh yeah, he had. His eyes glowed with emotion. Before I could sort through them all, he pulled me to him and engulfed me in his embrace.

"I am so sorry, Sabrina." His voice sounded thick. "I never meant to hurt you like that. You have to believe me." He pulled back just enough to look into my eyes. "Please say you believe me."

"I believe you." And I honestly do. He looks too tortured to be lying.

"Thank you," he said against my lips.

The kiss that followed was so sweet I nearly burst into tears. The loving that followed so languorous and tender, I actually did.

Dan kissed each teardrop away and smiled. "You don't have to cry Bri, it's me. And I'll never hurt you again. I promise."

DAN

I LISTEN to Sabrina's slow, easy breathing and pull her closer to my side. She let out a little snore and snuggled in closer.

When I asked her out to dinner, I never dreamed our night would end like this. Making love to Sabrina had been better than I'd ever imagined…and Lord knows I've imagined. In my dreams, I've kissed and touched her entire body, had her in every position humanly possible. But even the basics with Sabrina far surpassed any kinky fantasy I could dream up.

She's amazingly responsive and so goddamn tight, I nearly lost it with the first thrust. Thankfully I was able to hold on so I didn't totally embarrass myself.

Sabrina snuggled closer still, wrapping her arm further across my waist. Her contented sigh tugged at my heart. I pulled her in tighter and kissed her forehead. She started and looked up at me.

"Sorry, I didn't mean to wake you."

"It's okay," she said, rubbing her eyes then looking around. "I should probably get to my room anyway."

"Why?"

She moved away from me, putting about an inch of space between us. In my opinion, that's an inch too much, so I shifted toward her until our bodies touched again. I thought she was going to move away again, and was happy when she settled her head down on her pillow. I willed her to look at me, but she stared at the wall across the room.

"Because."

"That's not really an answer." I ran my index finger down her jawline and squeezed her chin, nudging her gaze up to mine. "Why do you think you should go to your room?"

"I don't know." She blinked. "I don't usually…I didn't think you'd want…" She shrugged and her voice trailed off.

I moved my hand back so it cupped her cheek.

"Let's get a couple things straight right from the start here. First, forget about whatever you *usually* do. This is us, and what's between us is so special you can't compare it to anything else." I took a deep breath and cleared my throat. Brushing my thumb against her cheek, I continued, "And second, I always want you with me. Being here in my bed with you in my arms is like a dream come true and I'd like for it to last as long as possible. So please don't go to your room. Spend the night here with me."

Her shy smile flashed before I heard her say, "Okay."

Cupping her face in my hands, I touched my lips to hers. I'd meant for it to be an undemanding kiss, but good Lord, the woman is delicious. I dipped my tongue inside for a better taste. The kiss went from zero to sixty in two seconds and I was lost…in her, in the moment, just lost. Sabrina twisted her hands into my hair and moved closer, wrapping her leg around my waist.

How can I turn down an invitation like that?

Sliding my hand down her back, I cupped her ass, pulling her against my hardening cock. I nuzzled her neck, and she tipped her head, offering me better access. Finding the sweet spot behind her left ear, I nibbled and licked, and she squirmed against me, rubbing her soft core against my now-raging erection. She's already so wet, it wouldn't take much to slip inside, but I resisted the urge. As much as I'd love to feel Sabrina skin on skin, we haven't had that discussion yet, and I won't take advantage. Instead, I moved my hand between us and slid it back and forth, stopping at her clit just long enough to give it a light pinch.

She arched her back, rubbing her hard nipples against my chest. I licked my way down and sucked a hard nub into my mouth as I thrust my middle finger inside her.

"Dan, please."

"Tell me, Bri," I said, as I continued to lick and stroke her. "Tell me what you want."

"Dan." The word was a mere gasp of air.

I chuckled and bit down on her nipple, then soothed it with my tongue.

"Do you want more of this?" I asked, then slid my finger up to circle her clit. "Or this?" Moving my hand, I slipped my middle finger inside, curling it slightly to hit her sweet spot.

Her answering groan ended on a desperate plea. I'd planned to draw this out, to make her tell me what she wants in explicit detail, but her hot little noises and the way her inner muscles clamped my finger changed my plans. I slowly withdrew and plunged two fingers inside, their tips stroking, stroking, stroking, until Sabrina's hips began to rock along with my movements. I shifted slightly so my thumb rubbed against her clit, and I latched onto her nipple, sucking in time with the thrusting of my hand.

Sabrina panted my name, over and over again, until she screamed as her entire body stiffened and her walls clamped down on my fingers. I slowly withdrew, dragging her orgasm out as she sagged into the pillow, a contented smile on her face.

I shifted onto my back, grabbed a condom off my bedside table, opened it, and rolled it on in record time. Taking me by surprise, Sabrina took advantage of my prone position and straddled my hips. With her hands splayed on my chest, she sat back and looked down at me, her tight nipples peeking through her hair.

Grabbing her hips, I pulled her forward, dragging her wetness against my hard cock. She rose up on her knees just enough to allow me to slip into her tight, wet heat.

"God Bri," I moaned. "You feel amazing."

Just when I was getting used to the feel of her surrounding me, Sabrina rocked her hips back and forth, pulling me further inside. She leaned back, digging her fingertips into my thighs as she rode me. Her position thrust her breasts front and center, and I needed to get closer.

Without breaking her rhythm, I sat up and wrapped my arm around her waist, pulling myself deeper into her, while I latched onto one nipple with my mouth and pinched the other between my thumb and forefinger. She whimpered and moved faster.

"You are a fucking goddess," I said before kissing my way across her chest to taste her other nipple. I sucked her deeper into my mouth. "Mmmm. Delicious."

Sabrina arched and twisted her fingers into my hair. Her movements became more frantic and I tightened my grip on her waist.

"Dan."

My name turned into a throaty moan as she tightened around me.

It was my turn to moan. "Come for me, Bri."

She pulled at my hair, tossed her head back, and let out a sexy-as-hell scream as she milked me to my own orgasm.

Wrapping her arms around my shoulders, Sabrina collapsed against my chest, her heart pounding in time with mine. I scooted down until she was resting on top of me, her legs straddling my hips, my cock semi-soft, but still buried inside her.

I stroked my hand from her shoulder to her ass and back again, catching my breath as our heartbeats slowed together. I kissed her forehead and sated blue eyes met mine. I'll admit that a sense of male pride washed over me at the look of pure satisfaction on her face.

"Hey,"

"Hey yourself."

"You okay?" I asked, caressing her cheek.

"Mmm, never been better."

"Me neither." I kissed her forehead, then rolled to the side, resting Sabrina on her pillow. "I'll be right back."

I walked to the bathroom to dispose of the condom. Sabrina's sleepy gaze watched me walk back to the bed. I climbed back in, pulled her into my arms, and dragged the covers up over her shoulders. She rested her head on my chest, relaxed against me, and let out a sigh. Within minutes, her steady breathing let me know she'd drifted off to sleep.

I kissed the top of her head and swallowed the lump that had formed in my throat. If I hadn't been such an asshole, we could have been sleeping like this for the past ten years. Since I can't change the past, I'll just have to make sure things between us are perfect going forward from here.

Chapter Twenty-Five

I CAN'T STOP SMILING. Two weeks have passed since Dan and I first made love and things have been wonderful, amazing even. So amazingly wonderful in fact, I've decided to call Jodi and have her schedule my vacation so I can stay longer. I'm not ready to move in, as he's suggested many times, but I'm not ready to leave either.

Dan's progress has been incredible and I can't justify staying on as his therapist much longer. He knows the routine well enough to do it on his own and now it's only a matter of him building up his strength again, which the team trainers can supervise.

"This is Jodi. Can I help you?" I heard through the phone, dragging me from my thoughts.

"Hey Jodi, it's Sabrina."

"Well, hello stranger. I thought you'd be calling me every hour on the hour for the past twelve weeks."

"That's not my style," I said. "You know that."

"So, how's it going?"

"Good. Great actually. In fact I'd say my job here is done."

"So he's as good as new?"

"Pretty much. He just needs to build up his muscles again and he can do that with the team trainer."

"You're a miracle worker, Sabrina."

"He did all the work."

"Is that admiration I hear in your voice?" Jodi teased.

"Maybe."

"Well, whatever it is, I'm glad everything worked out. I have to admit I was a little worried after your initial reaction to the assignment." I didn't comment. Jodi continued. "Your papers are drawn. You can have someone look at them when you get back, but I think you'll be happy with the terms."

Again, I didn't comment. In fact, I was thinking about the fact that I'd totally forgotten about the partnership when it had been my main reason for coming here. Or was it? I just don't know anymore.

"Sabrina?" Jodi yelled.

"What?"

"I asked when you'll be back."

"That's, uh, that's actually what I'm calling about."

"Well?" Jodi dragged out the word theatrically.

"I'd like to take my vacation before returning. I figure you already have me off the schedule anyway."

"Why?"

"Why what?"

"Why are you taking your vacation now?"

I didn't think that's any of her business, and told her so.

"Something happened, didn't it?" I chose not to answer. "Between you and Dan?" Again, I didn't answer, but Jodi obviously drew her own conclusions. She let out a screech and said, "Oh Sabrina, I'm so happy for you. Jealous as hell," she added. "But still happy."

"Jodi don't—"

"Don't you worry. My lips are sealed," she declared, which basically means that she'll only tell fifty people instead of the usual hundred.

"Do you want your full four weeks?" she asked.

"Put me down for all four weeks. I'll let you know if I'll be in sooner. I know it's easier to add me to the schedule than pull me off."

"Okay. Will do."

I ended the call and placed my cell on the desk, trying not to think too much about what I'd just done. In fact, I've been trying not to think too much about anything lately, because if I do, surely I'll panic. I spun the leather chair around to face the window. Propping one foot up on the sill, I reclined slightly and settled in to enjoy the view.

"There you are," Dan said, from directly behind me. "I wondered where you'd disappeared to." He propped his hip on the edge of the desk as I turned to face him.

"I snuck in here to call Jodi and print a few things."

Dan's smile slipped slightly at the mention of Jodi, but he quickly recovered. "Lexi and I are heading out for ice cream and we were wondering if you'd like to come."

"You two are trying to make me fat, aren't you?"

He held up his hands as if in surrender. "Hey, we just invited you, you don't have to come."

I made a noise that was a cross between a laugh and a snort. "Like I can turn down a brownie a la mode."

He grasped my wrist and pulled me toward him, sliding his hands around my waist. Squeezing lightly, he cocked his head to the side as if trying to decide something. Then he shook his head and kissed me lightly on the lips. "I'd say you're perfect. If anything, you could stand to gain a few pounds."

"God forbid."

"True statement," he said as he moved his hands to my back and pulled me closer still. I wrapped my arms around his neck. "At any rate, it doesn't matter. I'd love you even if you weighed a ton."

His eyes held mine, not allowing me to look away, not letting me ignore his words. The words he hadn't said since we'd gotten back together. The words I knew were true for me as well, yet couldn't bring myself to say back to him. Not just yet.

"Well, that's good to know." I attempted to sound light-hearted, but my voice was too hoarse with emotion to pull it off.

"I do love you," Dan stated, more firmly this time.

I kissed him, hoping to show him what I couldn't bring myself to say just yet. Dan let me take control, following my lead as I slanted my mouth over his, back and forth, enjoying the difference in texture between his soft lips and his five o'clock shadow before opening to get a better taste. Things were kicking up a notch when I heard a noise in the hallway. I pulled back from Dan and, leaning slightly to the side peered around his arm, but didn't see anything.

"What's wrong?"

"I thought I heard someone."

He slid from my embrace and walked to the door. I tried to ignore how cold I felt without his arms around me, but wasn't very successful. Thankfully, he returned to my side—or my front, as the case may be—immediately.

"I didn't see anyone."

"You don't think it was Lexi, do you?"

Dan and I have been trying our best to keep our budding relationship from his daughter. She's too attached to me as it is. I don't want to get her hopes up about Dan and me, and be disappointed if it doesn't work out.

He shook his head then lowered it to nibble on my neck. "She was playing Xbox. Nothing short of a nuclear blast would tear her away." His breath fanned my skin, heating it, raising goosebumps at the same time.

"But what if it was her?"

I tried to keep my wits as he alternately nipped at and laved my neck.

Dan shrugged. "If it was, we'll deal with it." He lifted his head and placed a gentle kiss on my lips. "I don't plan on keeping this from her much longer anyway."

My initial reaction to his last statement was to panic. After all, Lexi has never met anyone Dan's been involved with, a fact that I have not only heard from Dan and various others, but also from Lexi herself.

So why me? Why now? Is he that sure of this relationship? Or is the fact that his daughter is already so attached to me motivating him to tell her about us?

I quickly dismissed the latter thought, knowing it would be much worse if I were to leave once Lexi knows we're involved. I also know that Dan *is* that sure of this relationship. Even before I let him into my bed, he'd laid it all on the line. He wants me in his life. Permanently.

I'm the one with all the issues. I know I love him—have always loved him—but can I trust him? He hasn't given me any reason to believe his intentions are anything but pure, but then he never did. Basically, it comes down to the fact that my heart wants to believe him, but my head doesn't. Which will win out is anyone's guess.

"Bri?" I could tell from his tone that it wasn't the first time he'd said my name.

"Hmmm?"

"Are you okay?"

I smiled in what I hoped was a reassuring way. "I'm great."

Dan's green eyes scanned over me as if to gauge the truth of my words. He must have been satisfied with what he saw, because he smiled then nodded and said, "Then let's go get us some ice cream."

Chapter Twenty-Six

AS WE DROVE to the ice cream parlor, my eyes kept straying to the man behind the wheel. Ray Bans shaded his eyes and a look of utter contentment covered his face. His right hand rested on his thigh, while the left one loosely gripped the wheel, his thumb tapping in time to the song on the radio.

He must have felt me watching him, because he turned his head my way. Even through the dark shades, his gaze burned me. "What?" he asked.

"Nothing."

"Why are you looking at me?"

"Maybe I just like looking at you," I answered, honestly.

He seemed to think about that for a second before flashing a sweet smile. "Yeah?"

I nodded. "Yeah."

He inclined his head slightly toward me and in a stage whisper said, "I like looking at you too."

His smile nearly melted my heart.

Snickering from the back seat pulled my eyes from Dan. I looked back and found Lexi and Tori grinning from ear to ear.

"What's so funny?" I asked, trying to sound light-hearted.

Lexi removed her headphones from one ear and said, "Huh?"

"I asked what's so funny?"

She and Tori shared a conspiratorial look before they both faced me once again. "Something funny happened in the video," Lexi said.

They giggled again as Lexi replaced her headphones and turned up the volume on the iPad she and Tori were both plugged into.

I SPOONED the last of my ice cream into my mouth, then sat back and placed my hand on my overstuffed stomach.

"Why did you let me eat the whole thing?" I groaned. "I feel like I'm gonna bust."

Dan chuckled. "Like I'm strong enough to stand between you and ice cream."

"It's my only vice…well, ice cream and coffee."

I looked up at Dan and gasped. Actually gasped out loud. His eyes were practically devouring me. The air between us felt so charged, I expected the table to burst into flames.

"Did I tell you how beautiful you look today?" My core clenched at his low, husky tone. The abrupt change of subject, not to mention the let-me-fuck-you-right-now look in his eyes made me shiver. My mouth went instantly dry and other parts of my anatomy became instantly not so dry. I blushed, but it was more out of anticipation than embarrassment.

"Well?" he prompted.

"I, uh, I think you mentioned it when you snuck into my room this morning."

"That was you?" His devilish smile made my core clench.

"Don't you recognize me without my messy hair and morning breath?"

He opened his mouth to reply, but was interrupted by Lexi. "Can I have some more money, Daddy?"

Dan leaned forward and pulled his wallet out of his back pocket. Flipping it open, he perused the contents. "Twenty is the smallest I have. Let me go get change." He stood. "I'll be right back."

Once he was away from the table, Lexi jumped into his seat, a smile plastered across her face.

"Having fun?" I asked.

She nodded.

"Where's Tori?"

"She's over there." She pointed across the room. "Playing pinball."

"Pinball?" She nodded again. "I didn't know kids still played that."

She shrugged. "Sure we do." Then, in the next breath, she said, "I saw you and Daddy kissing before."

I tried to remain calm and think of something intelligent to say, but I felt like I'd been sucker-punched. "You did?" was all I could manage to squeak out.

She bobbed her head up and down. "Uh huh."

I glanced in the direction Dan had disappeared, hoping to find him coming my way. I sighed. No such luck. I looked at Lexi's smiling face again.

Well, at least she's not upset about it.

"Do you guys do that a lot?" she asked.

"What?"

"Kiss."

"Uh, no." It wasn't exactly a lie. After all, we don't kiss half as much as I'd like to.

"Why not?" She actually sounded disappointed.

I prayed for Dan to return. "Uh, I don't know."

"Is it 'cause of me?"

"No, definitely not."

"Because if it is, I want you to know that I don't care. If you kiss, that is."

"You don't?"

She shook her head and I watched her brown curls tumble around her shoulders. "I've been waiting for it to happen."

"You have?"

Her head bobbed up and down again, and the curls tumbled back and forth. "For a long time." She leaned forward, her elbows resting on the table between us. "I knew you'd come back."

Before I could ask what, exactly, she was talking about, Dan reappeared and handed her a cup of tokens.

"Thanks, Daddy." That said, she hopped off his seat and ran toward the game room.

"Why the frown?" Dan asked, as he slid into his seat.

"Lexi *was* outside the office earlier, and she saw us kissing."

Dan's eyebrows raised. "What did she say?"

"Well," I dragged out the word. "She asked if we do that a lot, and when I told her we don't, she told me we should. Then she said she's happy."

Dan let out a breath and sat back in his chair. He appeared to be deep in thought then he smiled. "Good."

He leaned forward and took my hand in his, then waggled his eyebrows. "And I agree with her…we should do it more often."

I smiled at his words then frowned at my thoughts. Dan reached out and smoothed my brow.

"What's wrong?"

I shrugged. "It's probably nothing."

"If it's bothering you, it's not nothing."

"It's just something she said." His brow arched, urging me to continue. I told him the last two sentences his daughter had uttered and asked what he thought she meant.

"I have no idea," he admitted, after thinking about it for a minute. "Maybe she's still talking about when you went home for the weekend."

"Maybe."

"I'll try to feel her out without sounding like I'm badgering her." He took a drink of water. "I'm just glad she's okay with our relationship. After all, she's had me all to herself for eight years."

"I really do admire you for all you went through to keep her in your life." When he didn't comment, I went on. "I imagine being a single parent is difficult enough, but with the life you lead, it must be near to impossible."

Dan's jaw tensed.

"The life I lead?" he asked, looking ready to pounce.

I nodded and took a sip of soda. "The travel, odd hours…"

"The parties, the women?" he asked.

"I didn't say that."

"You implied it."

"I did not," I said, utterly confused by his abrupt mood change. "I was trying to give you a compliment." I felt my own temper rise, and fought like hell to tamp it down.

Dan's glowing green gaze seared me. After what seemed like forever, he spoke in a semi-civil tone. "Do you think you'll ever totally trust me?"

"I—"

"Are you going to try to deny the fact that you still doubt my sincerity?"

What could I say? I can't lie, the man reads me like a book. And it's not that I doubt his sincerity, I'm scared it's not going to last. But that's my issue, not his.

"I'm trying, Dan," I said, not really answering the question, but hoping to placate him.

"Well, try harder," he growled.

Chapter Twenty-Seven

DAN

WHAT THE FUCK is wrong with me? Sabrina made an innocent comment and I jumped down her throat. And I have no doubt her comment was meant to be a compliment. I don't know why I reacted the way I did.

That's not true. I do know why. I'm not sure if she'll ever trust me…really trust me…and it scares the hell out of me. Without a foundation of trust, we'll never survive, especially considering my profession. I don't want her ever wondering if I'm being faithful when she's not with me. She needs to know deep in her heart that I'd never ruin what's between us for anything.

What can I do to make her understand? Make her believe?

Those questions had occupied me all through dinner and even through my evening workout. The only answer I came up with is that there's nothing I can do. I can only love her the best I can and hope she gets it.

With that settled, I made my way to Lexi's room to deal with the next issue that's been on my mind. She had already taken a shower and was waiting for me to tuck her in and read with her.

"Hey Lex," I said, pushing her unlatched door fully open.

"Hi Daddy." She sat cross-legged in the middle of her bed and struggled to run a brush through the full length of her hair.

I walked in, sat on the edge of the bed, and patted the spot next to me.

"Scoot over here and I'll give you a hand."

She crawled over, handed me her pink brush, and sat right in front of me. I slowly ran the brush through her hair, careful to avoid pulling the knots too hard. Instead, I gently worked them free until I could go smoothly from root to tip before moving on to another section to repeat the process.

"Sabrina said that you told her you saw us kissing today," I said. She nodded, pulling the brush from my hand. It snagged on a knot and hung in her hair. I chuckled. "Keep your head still."

I untangled the brush and started the process of working through the knots again.

"Is there anything you want to ask me?" I asked. "Anything you want to talk about?"

She shrugged. "Not really."

"Nothing at all?"

I know my daughter and can't imagine she doesn't have something to say.

"Are you guys gonna get married?" she finally asked.

"I don't know," I said. "It's still pretty new. We're just dating right now. It's a little different because she's living here, but we're still getting to know each other."

As I made a last pass through her now-smooth hair, Lexi turned to face me.

"But you already know each other," she pointed out.

"Yes, but that was a while ago. We need to get to know each other now."

It was obvious she didn't totally understand that, but didn't seem like she was going to question it further.

"Honey, what did you mean when you told her you knew she'd come back?"

Lexi shrugged. "She was gone, but I knew she'd come back."

"You mean when she went home for the weekend?"

She hesitated, then nodded.

"Are you sure?"

She nodded again.

"And you're sure you're not upset about this?"

She smiled, jumped up to her knees, and hugged me. "I'm not upset. I love Sabrina and I hope she stays forever."

That makes two of us.

Feeling good about this conversation, I squeezed her and said, "What book are we reading tonight?"

She pulled away from me, turned around, grabbed a yellow book from the bedside table, and handed it to me. I stood and pulled back the covers.

"Scoot in," I said.

After she was settled, I pulled the covers up to her waist, then climbed onto the bed beside her and opened the book. Lexi read the first couple pages, but then snuggled down into the covers and asked me to take over. I got through the rest of the first chapter before her breathing turned deep and slow.

I closed the book and rolled off the bed. Walking over

to the other side, I placed the book on the bedside table, leaned down, and kissed Lexi on the forehead.

I turned on her nightlight, walked to the door, and turned off the overhead light.

As I closed the door behind me, I prayed the next conversation I need to have goes as smoothly as this one did.

SABRINA

I STARED at the ceiling and tried to figure out exactly where things had gone wrong at the ice cream parlor. We'd been having a great time, then one sentence—which I *had* intended as a compliment—changed everything.

The rest of the day was filled with tense silence. Even Dan's workout suffered. He was obviously pre-occupied with his thoughts and his form was off. I cut the session short and retired to my room, coward that I am.

Dan's right about the fact that I have trust issues where he's concerned, but I don't think I've been obvious about it. Truth be told, I haven't had a reason to be obvious about it. For the most part, we've been secluded from the outside world. The only woman around on a daily basis is Mrs. Evans, and I don't think slightly chunky, white-haired, sixty-something women are Dan's type.

A light tap on the door broke into my thoughts. I got off the bed and turned the knob. Even before the door was fully open, I knew Dan was on the other side. His spicy-citrus scent filled my nostrils as soon as the door cleared the jamb.

"Can I come in?"

I stepped aside and swept my hand in a welcoming gesture. After closing the door behind him, I sat down on the edge of the bed. He followed suit mere inches from me. Taking my hand in his, he studied my fingers for several seconds before speaking.

"I'm sorry about this afternoon, Bri." He brushed his thumb across my knuckles and squeezed my hand before lifting his head and meeting my gaze again. "I acted like a real ass."

I had to laugh at his choice of words. "I did mean it as a compliment," I said.

"I know, and thank you." He dropped his gaze and studied my fingers again. "I just hate the fact that you don't trust me."

I wanted to deny his words, but how could I? I don't trust him, not totally anyway. Certainly not the way I should. I've changed in the past ten years, so it only stands to reason that he would, too. Logically, I know this, but emotionally I can't help myself from reverting back to a twenty-year-old with a broken heart. It's not something I'm proud of, but it's a fact.

Dan's eyes met mine and my chest tightened. The look of anguish and longing on his face nearly broke my heart. It only got worse when he spoke.

"Do you think you'll ever totally trust me?" His voice was soft, almost hoarse.

"I'm working on it," was all I could say.

Dan pulled me into his arms and kissed me softly. The loving that followed was so slow, so languid, so sweet that I was moved to tears. We didn't speak afterward. No words were necessary. All our thoughts and feelings had been conveyed through touch. I rested on my side and Dan curled his body around mine, holding me as though he'd never let go. And, at that moment, I gave up a prayer in hopes that I could let him hold me forever.

DAN'S SMILE greeted me in the kitchen the next morning, and due to the early hour, we were alone. He walked around the island and stopped directly in front of me. His eyes roamed over my face, seeming to devour me before his mouth settled on mine and did just that.

"Good morning," he said when we finally managed to pull apart.

"Mmm hmmm," I muttered, as I slipped my arms around his waist and rested my head against his chest.

"Sorry about my disappearing act last night." He kissed the top of my head. "More than anything I wanted to wake up with you in my arms, then make love to you all morning." His arms tightened, pulling me closer. There was a distinct bulge pressing into my stomach. I rubbed against him and smiled at his groan.

"I understand," I said. "Though what you just described sounds like heaven."

Dan pulled back and looked into my eyes. "You think so?"

"I do."

If his kiss was any indication, I'd say my answer pleased him. His mouth opened over mine, hungry and demanding, and I responded in kind. Tongues tangling, hands roaming, passions rising, I forgot where we were and lost myself in the sensations overtaking my body.

By slow degrees, Dan ended the kiss and pulled away. I watched through heavy lidded eyes as he drew a deep breath in through his nose and let it out slowly through his mouth. He ran a frustrated hand through his hair, then let it drop to his neck and rubbed there.

"We'd better put a stop to that before I drag you to the table and bury myself deep inside you." The way he said it sounded like a warning. Heeding it, I backed slowly away, hoping some space would cool us down.

Dan cleared his throat. "Mrs. Evans is off today, so if we want breakfast, it's up to us." He glanced at the coffee maker, then back at me. "I made coffee and it's not too bad, if I do say so myself."

His adorable smile took my breath away.

"Bri," Dan growled. All his frustration and love was conveyed in that one short word. "Please don't look at me like that."

"Sorry," I tried to sound repentant, but didn't quite pull it off. My coquettish grin didn't help matters either, I'm sure.

"Uh huh." Dan's own grin was devilish. "So, what about breakfast?"

"What do you usually eat when Mrs. Evans is off?"

"Cereal," he answered. "And if you weren't so busy hiding from me all these weeks, you'd know that."

I opened my mouth to protest, but decided against it. As amusing as sparring with Dan might be, my mood is way too mellow to rise to the occasion. Dan must have felt the same, because he let it drop.

"How about an omelet?" he asked, as he opened the refrigerator. "I think I have some ham and cheese."

I couldn't help but admire his backside as he bent over and searched the refrigerator. I was caught ogling when he straightened and glanced my way. I smiled letting him know I'd enjoyed the view.

Dan chuckled and pulled eggs, butter, ham, and a bag of shredded cheddar out of the refrigerator, closed the door with his foot, and placed the items on the counter.

"What can I do?" I asked.

He grabbed various bowls, plates, and utensils from their respective spots. "Sit back and watch Chef Dan create," he said, with a flourish.

"Oh brother." I rolled my eyes and climbed onto a stool.

"Seriously," he said as he cracked eggs—one-handed, I might add—into a bowl and whisked them with some milk, salt, and pepper. "Omelets are one of the few things I can cook well. I'm pretty good at French toast, too…that's Lexi's favorite."

I watched as Dan concentrated on his task. The muscles of his back and arms flexed and bunched with his every move. I remembered how those same muscles felt to touch, to caress, to kiss and my temperature rose a few degrees.

"Bri?"

"Hmmm?" I practically purred.

"Do you want toast?" he asked around a knowing smile.

I nodded and stood. "I'll do it."

His eyes roamed over my face before he smiled again. "Great."

Once I stepped around the island and into the working area of the kitchen, the intimacy felt a bit suffocating. With trembling hands, I took two slices of bread out of the bag and placed them in the toaster. It was after I turned the toaster on that I realized Dan was watching me.

"You okay?" he asked.

I nodded and concentrated on wiping the deer-in-the-headlights look off my face.

Dan placed his hand on my shoulder and his thumb traced slow circles as he kissed my lips. He pulled back and smiled. "It's okay, Bri." Another light kiss was placed on mine before Dan pulled me into his embrace. "We're just cooking breakfast here."

I nodded again and snuggled into his chest. His words told me he understood my fears. And between his words and the warmth of his arms, I relaxed. Dan kissed the top of my head.

"Better?" he asked.

"Much," I answered, before pulling him down for a soul-searing kiss.

We managed to pull apart before our food burned. After plating everything, we made our way to the table.

"So you talked to Jodi yesterday?" Dan asked from his seat across the table from me. He cut his omelet into bite-sized pieces and popped one in his mouth, his eyes prompting me to answer his question.

"Yes, I did." I cut a piece off my own omelet, but only had a chance to spear it with my fork before he spoke again.

"How much longer do I have you for?"

Leave it to Dan to get straight to the heart of the matter. I lifted my napkin from my lap and wiped my mouth. "Four weeks."

Dan blinked. From the look on his face, I knew I'd shocked him. He opened his mouth to speak, closed it, then blinked again.

"Four weeks?"

"Four weeks," I repeated.

He shook his head slowly. "Huh."

"Is that good or bad?" I asked around a nervous laugh.

"Oh honey, it's definitely good," he quickly assured me. "I'm just surprised." The tips of his ears reddened. "I read your last report." He shrugged. "It was on the desk and I couldn't resist."

"And?"

"From what I gathered, your time here is just about up. Did I misunderstand?"

"No," I said. "No, you didn't misunderstand."

"Then I'm confused. Did you send in a different report?"

"No, the one you saw is the one Jodi and the team received." He opened his mouth to speak, but I stopped him with a halting hand. "I told her I didn't think you needed me as your therapist any longer. You know the routine, and you're healed enough to do strength training on your own."

"Then I definitely don't understand. You said you're staying another four weeks."

"I am, but not as your therapist." I pulled my bottom lip into my mouth and dragged it back out through my teeth, feeling uncertain. After all, I made my plans without even consulting him.

"Then as what?"

"I have four weeks' vacation and I told Jodi I wanted to take them now." I paused for a moment to let my words sink in. When understanding dawned in his eyes, I continued. "So I guess I'll be here as, well, uh, as your girlfriend." My tone raised an octave or two on the last word, turning my sentence into a question.

Dan's green eyes filled with such intense emotion, they trapped my gaze and held it captive. "You're staying here because you want to?" I nodded. "Not because you have to?" I shook my head. "You'll be here of your own free will, not out of obligation or because of any partnership?"

"I'm staying because I'd like to. But if you'd rather I didn't, I can change my plans."

Dan jumped out of his chair and was at my side, lifting me out of mine before I knew what was happening. He pulled me into his arms and slanted his mouth against mine. Intense, passionate, and so damn hot, the kiss ended only when we were both about to pass out from lack of oxygen.

I rested my head against Dan's chest and listened to his heart pound in rhythm with mine. He pulled me closer and kissed my forehead, before dragging in a deep breath and letting it out by slow degrees.

"Thank you," he sighed.

Chapter Twenty-Eight

I ROLLED over and punched my pillow. Though physically exhausted, sleep was beyond my reach. I couldn't stop thinking about Dan and Lexi, and my feelings for them both.

In the two weeks since I relinquished my title as therapist and became an official girlfriend, the three of us have spent nearly every waking moment together, and I've loved each and every one of them.

I'd never really pined for marriage and family, but I'm not so sure that's the case anymore. I could very easily see myself slipping into Dan and Lexi's lives as wife and mother.

I fell in love with Lexi shortly after I met her, and despite all my resolve not to, I opened my heart to Dan once again. Although I still haven't said those three little words out loud, there's no doubt in my mind that he knows.

I rubbed my cheek on the pillow attempting to get comfortable. Never, in my wildest dreams, did I think I'd be in this situation again. Not with Dan or anyone. I've been too gun-shy since college to let myself get this emotionally involved with a man.

Though, truth be told, Dan is the only man who ever elicited any kind of real emotion from me. I've never bought into the whole soulmate thing, but if there is one for me, it most definitely is Dan. That last thought was running through my head when the object of my musings let himself into my room and closed the door behind him. Dressed only in a pair of blue plaid boxers, he made his way to the bed and sat on the edge.

"I didn't wake you, did I?" he asked.

I shook my head. "I couldn't sleep."

"No?" His sly grin told me he knew exactly why I couldn't sleep and that he was quite pleased with the fact.

Again, I shook my head.

"Maybe I could help you out," he said.

"And how would you do that?"

"Well," he said, dragging out the word. "I could tell you a bedtime story. That always works for Lexi."

"As nice as that sounds, I don't think it'll work in this case."

"Hmmm." He rubbed his chin. "I could run down to the kitchen and warm some milk. That was one of my mom's favorite remedies for insomnia."

"I don't like warm milk."

"You are a difficult case," he said, an adorable smile punctuating his words. "Let me think." His eyes roamed over my body, causing goosebumps to break out on every inch of my skin. "I suppose I could give you a nice, slow massage to relax you." He leaned closer and whispered in my ear, his warm breath tickling my neck. "And if that doesn't do the trick, I could love you until you pass out."

My answering groan elicited a chuckle from Dan. "We finally found one you like." He leaned down and nipped my earlobe. "Let's get rid of some of these clothes and get started."

The words were barely out of his mouth before he had my top off. It was his turn to groan. "You are so beautiful, Sabrina." He kissed the side of my neck down to my shoulder, then shifted me onto my stomach and brushed his lips against each vertebrae of my back. After paying special attention to the dimples just above my ass, he shifted and removed my shorts and underwear in one clean sweep.

Once he had me naked, I expected Dan to crawl back on top of me, and was surprised when I felt his warm hands grasp my left foot and apply a soothing pressure to its arch. I looked over my shoulder and our eyes met. I couldn't help but wonder if my gaze looked as hungry as his.

"What were you thinking about when I came in?" he asked. While his voice was a mere whisper, it commanded an answer. Even if it didn't, I knew I'd tell him anyway. I have to be truthful if this relationship is going to stand a chance. After all, I want honesty from him, can I offer anything less?

"I was thinking about you and Lexi and me."

His hands stilled for a moment. I'd obviously shocked him, but whether it was because I'd actually answered his question or because of my answer, I couldn't say.

"What about us?" he asked, his hands in motion once again, moving his ministrations to my right foot.

"I was trying to sort out my feelings."

"About you and me and Lexi?"

I nodded and enjoyed the feel of his hands, which had moved up and now kneaded my calf muscles.

"Is there so much sorting to do that you're kept awake at night?"

Dan slid his hands up my calves to the top of my thighs in a long, sweeping motion. His thumbs lightly skimming my folds before moving back down toward my ankles.

"Mmm, that feels so good."

Up and down, he continued, caressing and stimulating, moving closer to where I wanted him—where I needed him—with every pass. There wasn't a doubt in my mind that he could feel the wetness that had settled between my thighs.

"Bri?"

"Hmm?"

His low chuckle brought a fresh rush of arousal. Moving on to my lower back, he asked the question again.

"No…Yes…Not really," I answered.

He snorted. "Well that answers that."

"It's not my feelings I question. It's everything else."

"Such as?" Dan's thumbs rotated on either side of my spine, relaxing every muscle in my back, along with my inhibitions.

"I worry about getting hurt again. About hurting you, and hurting Lexi in the process."

"Why do you think anyone's going to get hurt?"

"It's not that I expect it to happen, but it is a possibility."

"Anything is possible, Bri. Maybe no one will get hurt. Maybe we'll all live happily ever after." At this point, his hands were doing more of a stroke than a massage, but I wasn't about to complain. "But you have to be open to all the possibilities before any of them can happen."

I rolled over onto my back in order to face him.

"I am open to them, Dan."

DAN

IT'S amazing how five small words could make me feel like I was punched in the gut. I swallowed hard, trying to dislodge the lump that had formed in my throat as I searched for something to say. But no words came to mind. So I let actions speak for me instead.

I grazed my lips against her belly, chest, then neck before pushing up and meeting her gaze. The love and hope I felt was reflected in her eyes. I lowered my head and did my best to kiss her lingering fear away. And like every other time our lips met, I had to fight the urge to devour her. Then decided I didn't want to resist.

I slanted my mouth over hers, tasting, biting, loving until we both needed to breathe. Grabbing her hands, I entwined our fingers and pushed them up over her head, then shifted myself between her outspread thighs. Startled blue eyes looked up at me.

"Okay?" I asked.

The tension in her arms loosened and her body moved down and pushed against my erection. She nodded, and her nostrils flared as she glanced down at my mouth. "Yes."

Her husky tone vibrated through my every cell. I tightened my hold on her hands and crushed my mouth to hers and thrust my tongue inside. She met me stroke for stroke, humming deep in her throat, squeezing my fingers.

Sabrina rubbed against me as I continued to devour her mouth, licking and sucking, and she stayed with me, giving as good as she got. I shifted her hands into one of mine and dragged the other one down to pinch her nipple between my thumb and forefinger. She pulled her mouth from mine and let out a hoarse moan. I nipped at her bottom lip before sliding over to suck at a sensitive spot I'd discovered behind her ear.

Letting go of her hands, I stroked down her body, then up again to cup her breasts. She arched, pushing herself into my palms. I slid my mouth across her neck, then down her chest, to run my tongue over one hardened tip, then the other. Back and forth, I teased, sucked, savored.

"Feels so good," she whispered. I looked up at her flush face and parted lips, and don't think I've ever seen anything so beautiful. Apparently I appreciated the site too long, because Sabrina opened her eyes and frowned. "Why are you stopping?"

"Just appreciating the sight."

"Well stop," she said, just before her hands grasped either side of my head and attempted to drag me back to the task at hand.

I chuckled at her indignant tone.

"You're adorable," I said, before placing a kiss on her sternum.

"You missed the spot," she said.

Her fingers squeezed my skull as she directed me to her left breast. Talk about an invitation I can't refuse.

I latched on, taking her into my mouth, tugging and sucking, until her nipple stood tall. Then I gave her other breast the same attention. Propping myself on one arm, I reached down between us and circled my fingers around her clit. Her hands dropped from my head and slammed onto the bed beside her. Out of the corner of my eye, I saw her fingers gripping the sheet.

I shifted to my side and dragged my hand down her hip and grab her ass, pulling her against me.

"Bri,"

"Hmmm?"

"Wrap your leg around my waist." She scooted closer and did as I asked. I reached down and thumbed my erection until the tip settled at her entrance. "Look at me, sweetheart." Glazed blue eyes met mine, then widened as I thrust forward.

"Sabrina…Christ, you feel so good."

I pulled back, then thrust forward again and again. It wasn't enough. I needed to be closer, deeper.

"Hold on," I said, as I wrapped my arms around her waist and rolled onto my back, pulling her on top of me. She settled into place, her wet heat clamped around me. "So good," I said, grabbing her ass and pulling her closer. Just when I thought it couldn't get any better, she sat back, pulling me deeper inside.

"You. Feel. So. Fucking. Good."

"God, Dan." Sabrina said, picking up her pace. She rode me, up and down, fast and slow, until I didn't think I could take any more. I ground my molars together, fighting my release. I knew I couldn't hold off much longer, so I reached between us and pressed my fingers to her clit. Her responding contraction nearly finished me off.

I continued to caress her clit until I felt the tight squeeze of her internal muscles. She cried out, her fingers digging into my chest. I savored the feel of her clenching around me for a moment before letting go. My orgasm seemed to last forever, the intense pleasure something I've only experienced with her.

Sabrina collapsed onto my chest, and I kissed the top of her head and pulled her closer. For a long time, we stayed just like that, wrapped together, still pulsing with aftershocks. I rolled Sabrina to her side and withdrew carefully. Her sound of protest when I left her side made me smile.

"I'll be right back." I kissed her on the forehead and was rewarded with a lazy smile.

After disposing of the condom, I washed my hands and caught a glimpse of the lovesick fool in the mirror before making my way back to Sabrina. Crawling back into bed, I molded my body to her back and pulled the cover up over us both. I wrapped my hand around her waist and slid it up to settle between her breasts.

"I love you," I whispered.

Sabrina wrapped her hand around mine and squeezed. Even though she didn't say the words, I know she feels them.

I closed my eyes and fell into a peaceful sleep.

Chapter Twenty-Nine

SABRINA

"MMM, YOU ARE SO SWEET," Dan murmured as he nipped and licked his way across my back.

"You're much better than an alarm clock."

Dan's big hands moved to my waist and rolled me over to face him. His green eyes glowed in the early morning light. "I aim to please," he said, just before his mouth lowered and devoured mine.

And please me he did, for the next hour. With his hands and mouth and body, Dan took me to paradise and back again.

As I rested, sated and content in his arms, I realized that my heart is fully thawed. If I'm being honest, it had thawed a while ago, but I haven't wanted to admit it, to myself or him. But now I know, without a doubt, that I'm truly, madly in love with him. And more importantly, I trust him enough to share the knowledge.

Tilting my head, I placed a series of light pecks on the underside of Dan's jaw. As I'd hoped, he turned his head so our mouths could meet. My kiss must have conveyed my newly-found—or should I say, newly-admitted—feelings, because when it ended, he looked at me with slightly dazed, questioning eyes.

Placing my hand on his face, I met his gaze and smiled. "I love you, Dan," I said, for the first time in ten years.

Dan closed his eyes and placed his hand over mine. I watched his Adams apple bob up and down twice. He turned his head and placed a kiss in the center of my palm before opening his eyes and facing me once again.

"God, Bri." His voice cracked. "You have no idea how much those words mean to me." He slowly drew a breath in through his nose and let it out through his mouth. "I feel like I've been sucker punched." His crooked smile was shy and disarming and oh so endearing.

"And that's a good thing?" I asked, knowing very well that it was.

Dan rolled over and slid between my legs, aligning our bodies perfectly. "That's a very good thing."

His mouth took mine in a powerful, loving, and eminently sexual kiss. Dan's erection brushed against me and I raised my hips to rub against him. I swallowed his moan.

I dragged my hands over his powerful shoulders to his muscled back, finally reaching his taut ass, where my fingers flexed, pulling him closer.

Dan's own hands moved over my body, stroking and loving. Everywhere he touched burned for more. He tore his lips from mine and moved them along the path his hands had just traveled. His hot mouth reached the juncture of my thighs, and I clenched in anticipation. Dan felt it too, I knew, and he looked up and met my gaze as his tongue reached out and flicked at the hard nub that had emerged, eagerly awaiting his touch.

Grinding my head into the pillow, I fought to restrain the moan that was dying to get out. Dan continued to torture me with little nibbles and flicks, putting me on edge, but not quite giving me what I wanted—what, at that moment, I needed—to have.

"Dan, please," I gasped.

His gaze met mine over the length of my body. With our eyes locked, he opened his mouth and settled it over my very core and sucked. My eyes widened as wave after wave of pleasure rolled through my body and Dan's gaze held me captive, not allowing me to look away.

Never in my life have I experienced anything like that. Not just the orgasm—though God knows, it was amazing —but the connection I felt to him as he watched me achieve it.

Dan looked as awestruck as I felt and as he moved up my body and put his arms around me, I felt like I'd come home. A peace I'd never known settled over me like a comfortable blanket. And, instead of questioning the feeling, or trying to fight it, I let myself embrace it. I opened my mouth to try and convey my feelings, but a light rap on my door stopped me.

My startled eyes looked to Dan, who simply shrugged. "Who is it?" I asked.

"Sabrina, it's me, Lexi."

Those four words set both Dan and me into action, hopping off the bed in order to retrieve our scattered clothing. Hastily slipping into his, Dan pointed to the closet and stepped inside.

"Uh, just a second, Lex." I slid into my robe, quickly tied the sash and opened the door.

"What's wrong honey?"

"I had a bad dream."

Her green eyes were wide and her bottom lip quivered. I wrapped my arms around her and kissed the top of her head. "It's okay. You're okay," I reassured her.

I felt her nod against my waist. "I'm sorry I woke you up, but I just had to make sure you were still here."

"Why wouldn't I be?"

She tipped her head back and looked at me, her eyes swimming with tears. "That's what happened in my dream. I came to find you and you were gone." She sniffed. "And you didn't even say goodbye."

The despair in her expression nearly tore my heart out. "Oh honey, that would never happen."

"Promise you won't leave, Sabrina," she pleaded.

It amazed me that such a small child could make such a big request. I felt her anguish and my heart squeezed with her every sob. But I also knew I couldn't promise her anything, because while Dan and I have certainly made a breakthrough in our relationship, no firm commitments have been made. So I promised her the only thing I knew to be true.

"I'll be here whenever you need me."

That seemed to satisfy her. The tension drained from her body and the arms that had been wrapped around my waist in a vice-like grip loosened.

"Come on, let's get you back to bed."

I walked her across the hall and tucked her in. I sat with her until her eyes drifted shut and her breathing became slow and even.

"We need to talk."

Dan stood in the middle of my room, his hands braced on his hips. During my conversation with Lexi, I'd forgotten he was in the room, so his presence startled me.

I closed the door behind me and moved over to the bed, perching on its edge.

Dan's posture relaxed a bit and I knew he'd been expecting me to give him a hard time. If just the two of us were involved, I may have, but with Lexi in the picture, I knew we had to come to some kind of agreement.

He walked across the room and sat facing me. "I love you, Sabrina." He took my hand in his and laced our fingers together then studied them. "And I think we belong together."

He looked to me then, as though he expected me to comment. What could I say? Dan is everything I've always dreamed of, everything I've ever wanted. Even when I hated him, I loved him.

Dan smiled and inched closer, placing his hand on my cheek. "Marry me," he said softly.

I opened my mouth to speak, but nothing came out. I tried again, but still nothing. Dan chuckled.

"I'll take it as a good sign that you're not screaming no."

I couldn't help but smile. "I'm just not sure what to say."

"I think you do, you're just too afraid to say it."

His words were true, so I didn't even attempt to deny them.

"Okay," he said. "It's not very romantic, but let's look at this logically."

"Logically?"

He nodded. "Do you love me?" he asked.

"Yes, I love you, Dan," I answered without hesitation, which seemed to please him immensely.

"Do you trust me?"

If the look in his eyes was anything to go by, the answer

to that question was more important than that of the previous one.

"Yes," I said. "I trust you."

"Thank you." He leaned forward and placed a light kiss on my lips.

He cleared his throat. "Do you think we have a future together?"

"I do, but…"

He placed his index finger across my lips, preventing my words from coming out. "No buts. We'll get to them in a minute."

"Okay."

"I want you with me all the time. I want us to be a family…you, Lexi, and me, and whoever else comes along." His gentle smile punctuated his words. "The thought of making a baby with you makes me feel…" He broke off and looked away for a moment before meeting my gaze again. The emotion in his eyes tugged at my heart. "I can't even imagine how amazing it would be watching our baby grow inside you. But if you didn't want any children, that'd be okay too. We could raise Lexi then concentrate on each other."

"I do want children," I surprised us both by saying.

"Yeah?" I nodded. "How many?

"I don't know," I said around a laugh. "I just recently realized that I wanted any."

"How about if we just wing it?"

"Sounds good."

"Does that mean that you'll marry me?"

"Y—" Before I could answer, Dan jumped off the bed and held up a halting hand.

"Wait! Don't say anything yet." He grabbed my waist and pulled me to my feet. "Come with me." Pulling the door open, he led me out of my room and down the hall to his. "Have a seat," he said, directing me to the bed.

I watched as he opened the top drawer in his nightstand and rummaged through it. I wanted to ask what was going on, but he seemed so intent on his task, I didn't want to disturb him.

"Yes," I heard him say, half under his breath. He straightened and turned around. My breath hitched when he dropped to his right knee directly in front of me.

"Sabrina Rose Kelly, will you marry me?"

My eyes widened as Dan held up a jeweler's box. Nestled inside was an exquisite emerald cut diamond ring.

"Please."

"Yes, Daniel Patrick McMullen, I will marry you."

Dan let out a breath, as though he'd been holding it. As though he hadn't been one hundred percent sure of my answer. He removed the ring from its confines and slipped it onto my finger.

"It's beautiful," I said as I moved my hand from side to side, watching the play of the light on the diamond. "Just the style I've always wanted."

Dan sat down next to me. "Do you recognize it?" I frowned then my eyes widened. "Remember? We picked it out together."

Just before he graduated, we'd gone shopping and stopped at a jewelry store. He prodded me into trying on engagement rings, and asked me all kinds of questions about my likes and dislikes. I told him my grandmother had an emerald cut diamond in a simple setting and I'd always loved it. The jeweler sent his assistant into the back room and when he emerged, he was holding the ring I had just described with a one and a half carat stone. Obviously more than a soon-to-be college graduate could afford, even with a professional baseball contract in his pocket.

"How? When?" I wasn't sure what, exactly, I wanted to ask.

Dan answered anyway. "The day after you picked out this ring, I went back and put money down and set up a payment plan. I continued making payments until I started earning a real paycheck and could buy it outright."

"Why?"

"Because I loved the look in your eyes when you saw it."

"But we weren't even together then."

He shrugged. "I always had hope."

"And you kept it all these years?"

He nodded.

"What if we never…"

"It wasn't something I was willing to think about."

"You're either extremely hopeful or just plain crazy."

"I guess a little of both."

"Thank God," I said before I tackled him and kissed him senseless.

DAN

SABRINA LEFT my room at the crack of dawn. I hated letting her go, but we agreed that we wanted to tell Lexi about our engagement before she comes bounding in on us in bed together.

After shaving, I took a quick shower and threw on gym shorts and a t-shirt, then headed to the kitchen to start breakfast. It seems like a good day to make Lexi's favorite breakfast, which also happens to be one of my favorites, and one of the few things I cook well.

I grabbed all the supplies from the refrigerator and placed them on the counter, then rummaged around for a cookie sheet, a bowl, and the griddle. After whisking together milk, eggs, and cinnamon, I set a few slices of bread into the batter. While that was soaking, I set the bacon on the cookie sheet and placed it in the oven.

The first batch looked good and soaked, so one by one, I moved it from the bowl onto the griddle, then added more bread to the batter.

My cell rang and I saw "mom" pop up on the screen.

"Hey, Mom."

"I'm sorry I missed your call, honey. I went for a walk and forgot to take my phone."

"Mom." I rubbed my brow. "Please remember to bring your phone when you go out. What if something happened and you couldn't call for help?"

"I was with the girls, so I'm sure someone had a phone on them."

"Are you sure about that?"

"Daniel, I've survived most of my life without having a phone on me every minute of the day."

"I just worry about you."

She sighed. "I know you do, but I'm fine. Really." Before I could reply to that, she said, "But something must be up with you since you called me so early. Is everything okay? Is Lexi okay?"

I flipped the French toast, then checked on the bacon in the oven.

"Lexi is fine," I said. "And everything else is good. Great actually."

"Oh?"

"I uh, I asked Sabrina to marry me last night."

"Oh my God," she screamed. "Oh honey, I'm so happy

for you." I heard her gasp through the phone. "She did say yes, right?"

"She did."

"Oh honey," she said again, then I heard a telltale sniff and knew she had started crying. "I'm so happy for you. Have you made any plans yet?"

I chuckled. "No, I just asked her a few hours ago."

I pulled the bacon out of the oven and set it on the counter next to the plate of French toast I was compiling.

"We need to celebrate," she said. "Can we set something up for this weekend?"

"Would I be able to stop you?"

"If it was just me maybe, but not once your sisters find out," she said. "Speaking of your sisters, are you calling them today?"

I placed a few more slices of French toast on the growing stack.

"Give me a couple hours. I want to tell Lexi first."

"When are you doing that?"

"As soon as she wakes up," I said. "And, of course, today is the day she sleeps later than usual."

The words were still hanging in the air when the topic of conversation entered the kitchen, followed by Sabrina. I couldn't help the goofy smile that made its way across my face when I spotted her. I still can't believe I asked her to marry me or that she actually said yes. It's like a dream.

"And here she is."

"Can I talk to her a minute?"

"Sure." I held the phone out. "Lex, grandma wants to talk to you." She ran over and took the phone from me and ran out of the room. "Did you two plan your entrance?" I asked Sabrina, who had settled at the island.

"We met in the hallway," she said, then looked over at my handiwork. "It smells good in here."

I put the last of the French toast on the rest of the stack, shut off the stove, and made my way over the island opposite Sabrina.

"I figured a celebration breakfast was in order," I said. "Unless last night was a dream."

"No, it just feels like a dream." She ducked her head, but not before I saw the blush spread across her face.

Reaching out, I ran my thumb down her jaw, bringing her gaze back to mine. "It does feel like a dream." I leaned forward and kissed her, but pulled back before things could get of hand.

"Did you tell your mom?" she asked.

I nodded. "She wants to have a party this weekend to celebrate. Do you think your family would be able to come?"

"I'm sure they'll make themselves available," she said. "They're thrilled."

"Really?"

She nodded. "My mother said she'd always hoped we'd find our way back to each other."

Before I could respond, Lexi came back into the kitchen and handed me my phone.

"You made French toast!" she said and hugged me, then looked at Sabrina. "He usually only makes it on my birthday or for holidays."

"If I made it all the time, it wouldn't be special," I said.

"So why are we having it today?" she asked and settled onto the chair beside Sabrina.

"Because we're celebrating," I said.

"Celebrating what?"

I looked at my fiancé and smiled. "I asked Sabrina to marry me."

Lexi's eyes widened and she looked at Sabrina, who held her hand up, exposing her ring. "And I said yes."

"So you're getting married?" She looked back at me and I nodded. Then she screamed…loudly…and launched herself at Sabrina, who reacted just in time to keep her seat. "I'm so happy you're staying," she said.

I figured I better save Sabrina from my daughter's death grip.

"Why don't you grab some dishes, Lex, and we can get this celebration started?"

Chapter Thirty

"TO DAN AND SABRINA." Jeff held up his glass, prompting everyone else to do the same. "May they have a long, happy, and healthy life together."

A chorus of "congratulations" followed just before the crowd, which consisted of Dan's family and mine, took a token sip of champagne. I did the same, feeling as though a tornado had taken me up, spun me around, and plopped me right in the middle of the life I'm currently living. Dorothy Gale from Kansas has nothing on me when it comes to being overwhelmed and confused.

My feelings for Dan are rock solid, and I trust we're going to have a wonderful life together. I still have to tie up some loose ends back home, but other than that, I'm ready to start over again with Dan and Lexi. Everything has just happened so fast, it's going to take me some time to catch up.

"Sabrina, I'm so happy for you," my mother said with a 1000-watt smile plastered on her face.

"Thanks Mom."

"You both look so happy," she said. "It's nice to see."

"I'm very happy."

"And that Lexi is such a sweetheart. It's about time you made me a grandmother."

"She's wonderful and I know you'll have fun spoiling her. She loves shopping, by the way."

My mother's eyes brightened. "A girl after my own heart," she said, placing her hand over her chest. "Unlike my daughter, who would rather be out slopping in the mud."

"I never slopped in the mud, Mother."

"Well, you couldn't tell that by the condition of your clothes when you came inside. They were always a mess. I swear, I don't know how I ever got them clean."

Before I could defend myself, Dan sidled up next to me.

After my mother nearly squeezed the breath out of him, and told him of her utter joy of our impending nuptials for the gazillionth time, he turned to me. "Bri, Megan wants to talk to you. I told her I'd send you to her so she didn't have to haul herself off the couch."

"I still can't believe she's here. She looks like she's going to have that baby any minute."

"Maybe that'll be you next year," my mother chimed in.

"One thing at a time, Mom," I said. "I'll go see what Megan wants."

Dan's sister wanted nothing more than to congratulate me in person…again. We sat in a semi-quiet corner and talked about everything from the impending birth of her first child to my wedding. Dan and I had agreed that we didn't want a huge affair, and I even talked him into holding everything at the house. We were planning on having an outdoor ceremony and reception, but the house would be prepared in case of inclement weather.

I looked around the now-deserted living room. Those who weren't spending the night had driven off a couple hours ago, and everyone else was tucked into their rooms. Dan had gone upstairs a half hour ago to make sure the kids weren't doing too much damage in Lexi's room. I was wondering if they'd decided to hold him hostage when I heard him come up behind me.

"Whatcha thinking about?" Dan asked as he wrapped his arms around my waist.

"I don't know. Nothing. Everything."

"Well that narrows it down." Dan kissed my cheek and rested his chin on my shoulder. His warm breath caressed my face when he spoke. "Still nervous?"

I felt the tension in his body despite his soft tone. "No more than any other bride-to-be." I turned in his arms. "It's all happening so fast. Give me time to catch up, okay?"

"But you do want this?" His apprehensive look tore at my heart.

I leaned forward and brushed his lips with mine. "More than anything."

Chapter Thirty-One

SABRINA

"ARE you sure you have to go?" Dan asked, looking way too appealing lying in my bed clad only in a pair of black boxer briefs.

"I'm just going to pack up my apartment." I kissed his cheek. "Then I'll be back to stay."

"But I'll miss you." Dan's exaggerated pout was so adorable.

I stuffed the shirt I'd just folded into my duffel bag before sitting next to Dan. "I'll miss you too, but I have to go tie up all my loose ends."

"Did you see Lexi yet?"

"Not yet. I wanted to talk to you first."

"About?"

"I was wondering if you'd mind if I took her with me."

"Really?"

"I know you can't come along, but if Lexi doesn't have anything going on, there's no reason she can't."

Due to an addition being added onto Lexi's school, classes were starting two weeks later than usual. Since Dan's leg was on the mend, his agent had set up several local events for him to attend and the Waves have a fundraiser planned at the stadium. Of course, they correspond with my trip home. "Are you sure?"

"Yes, I'm sure," I said around an exasperated chuckle. "It'll give us some time to get to know each other better one on one. I think she'll have a good time."

Dan pulled me into his arms. "Good time? I think she'll have a great time and she'll be thrilled." He kissed me breathless before pulling back. "You're everything I've ever dreamed of, you know that?" I felt my face heat. Dan ran his index finger down my cheek. "And you're adorable when you blush."

That was the last thing either of us said for a long while.

"WHAT ELSE SHOULD I BRING?" Lexi asked.

I looked at the suitcase on her bed then shifted my gaze to the full one resting on her floor.

"Is there anything left in your closet?"

"I just want to make sure I have everything I'll need."

"Lex, we're only going for a few days. I only packed a duffel bag."

"Yeah, but we're going to your apartment. You have stuff there."

How could I argue with that logic?

"All set?" Dan asked from the doorway.

"I think so. But Lexi has other ideas," I said.

Dan surveyed the suitcases and chuckled. "That's my girl." He kissed the top of Lexi's head.

"I'm missing the gene that makes women over pack," I

said. "In fact, I'm missing several female genes. I hate shopping, I don't wear make-up most days, and it only takes me twenty minutes to get ready, and that's from shower to door."

Dan's green eyes surveyed my body from my toes to the top of my head before lowering and meeting my gaze straight on.

"But all the important genes are there."

His voice sounded slightly husky and my body reacted accordingly. If Lexi wasn't in the room, we'd have been all over each other by now.

"Why thank you, sir," I said, using my best southern belle voice, trying to cool the room down a little.

"You're more than welcome, ma'am."

Lexi found our performance amusing and giggled, as only an eight-year-old could. Dan moved over and wrapped her in his arms.

"How long do you girls plan on being gone?" Dan asked.

"Three or four days," I answered. "It shouldn't take longer than that."

"Then you'll be here to stay." Though he said it like a statement, it was definitely a question. The longing I saw in his eyes tugged at my heart.

"Then I'll be here to stay," I said.

He held out his arm, inviting me to join his and Lexi's hug. It was an invitation I couldn't refuse. I took the few steps toward them and allowed Dan to pull me into his arms. Lexi wrapped her arm around my waist as Dan's curled around my shoulder.

"I don't know what I'm going to do without you two," Dan said. "I'll miss you." He kissed Lexi and me in turn.

"You'll be busy signing autographs and having people tell you how wonderful you are." I tried to make light of the situation. I mean, really, we're only going for a few days. It's not like we're moving to another planet. And even as my head knew those facts, my heart still felt like it was being squeezed at the thought of leaving Dan for any amount of time.

"You're the only person I want telling me how wonderful I am," Dan said around a smile.

I couldn't help but laugh.

Chapter Thirty-Two

JODI'S EYES twinkled and her smug smile would have bothered me if I weren't so happy. "I take it things are working out." Her gaze fell to Lexi, then to the ring on my left hand.

"Things are just fine," I said, not wanting to give her any more details than I already had.

"When's the wedding?"

"We haven't set a date yet," I said.

"Why not?"

"Jodi, I don't want to play twenty questions with you."

"Then tell me everything so I don't have to ask." The look on my face must have warned her to stop. "Okay, okay. What do you need to know?"

"What's the deal with this partnership?" I asked. "Is it still going to happen if I'm not working here every day?"

"We had a deal, Sabrina. Here's the paperwork." Jodi

patted a fat folder resting next to her right arm. "Just sign and it'll be official."

"That's it?"

"That's it," she said. "I don't know why you're so surprised. Bill's a partner and he rarely comes in."

"Yeah, but Bill's never been around. He put up his money, and you and Jack brought knowledge and experience. He was never meant to work here."

Jodi waved her hand as though swatting a fly. "Regardless, he's not here every day, and you don't have to be either."

"Thank you."

"And it's not like you're going far away. I'm sure you'll be able to make it here for a meeting or two."

"Definitely."

I couldn't hide my joy or relief. I love Dan, and I want to spend my life with him, but I've worked hard for this partnership.

Jodi stood and held up the folder that I knew contained the partnership agreement.

"I'm sure you'll want a lawyer to look this over." She handed the folder to me and stepped around her desk. "Now what do you say we take this little girl out for lunch? She's been so well behaved, she deserves a treat."

"CAN I CALL DADDY?"

"Sure." I looked at the clock. "He should be home by now."

I scrolled through my contacts and found Dan's name, then handed Lexi the phone. She looked exhausted. We'd spent the day running errands or packing, and I couldn't help but wonder if she was regretting her decision to come along.

I folded a pair of jeans and placed them in a packing box. Lexi's face was puckered in concentration as she held the phone to her ear. "Hi, Daddy. Me and Sabrina are home for the night and I just wanted to call and say hi. Call us back when you can."

She ended the call, handed the phone to me, and shrugged. "He didn't answer."

I tossed a pair of socks into the box and closed the lid. "Maybe he's still at an event and can't answer," I said. "I'm sure he'll call back soon."

But my words were false. Dan never called and as moonlight turned into morning light, my phone still hadn't rung. My stomach knotted and I had to force the niggling doubts that played at the back of my mind from surfacing. He probably got in late and didn't want to wake us.

That's exactly what I told Lexi when she asked if he'd called after she fell asleep. She seemed so worried I offered to take her home.

"I don't want to go home. I just wanted to talk to Daddy."

"Are you sure?"

She nodded. "I'm having a lot of fun."

Though I doubted her statement, I didn't ask again. "Why don't you try him now?"

Lexi did as I suggested, but once again left a message. "You don't think anything happened to him, do you?"

Her worried expression tugged at my heart. "I'm sure he's fine, honey." I put my arm around her shoulder and gave her a quick squeeze. "Come on, let's hit the road." In an attempt to cheer her, I added. "Maybe we can stop at the mall on the way home."

I knew she was really worried when even that failed to lift her spirits.

Lexi and I were sitting in McDonald's when my cell

phone rang. One glance at the caller ID told me Dan was on the other end of the line. "Hi."

"Hey, honey. How's it going?"

"Great."

"I'm sorry I missed your calls. I broke my phone at the signing last night. It fell out of my pocket and totally smashed. Then I ended up visiting the children's hospital this morning and wasn't able to get a replacement until now."

"I thought maybe your events ran late."

"They did, but I still would have answered for my two favorite ladies," he said.

"That's good to know," I said, trying to sound like I wasn't swooning. He really is sweet sometimes.

"You two getting along okay?"

"What do you think?" I asked, a smile in my voice.

"Is she behaving?"

"Of course, and she's really a big help. We got a lot of packing done last night. How was the signing?"

"It went well, but I think I need therapy on my writing hand now."

"That many people?"

"A good amount showed up," Dan said.

"Don't let them run you too ragged. If your leg starts hurting, take a break."

"So far, it's okay. And I have a great physical therapist, you know." I heard the smile in his voice.

I would have loved to continue bantering with Dan, but Lexi was bouncing around in her seat as she waited to speak with her father.

"I hate to cut you short," I said to him, "but Lexi is dying to talk to you."

"I'll call you later," he said. "I love you."

"I love you, too."

That said, I handed the phone to Lexi. While she nodded and laughed and told Dan everything we did during every second of our time together, the knot in my stomach disappeared. The reason it had formed there in the first place is something I'm going to have to work on.

Chapter Thirty-Three

I UNDERESTIMATED HOW much help Lexi would be. We'd finished packing up my belongings, besides accomplishing every other task I had on my list, in record time. Dan said he'd have a professional moving company clear out my furniture and other big items and deliver them to his door. What we're going to do with them after that is beyond me.

"Well, Miss Lexi, I think our work here is just about done."

"What about all the other stuff?"

"Your dad is going to hire someone to come get it."

"So what are we gonna do now?"

"I thought we'd stay here tonight and head back tomorrow morning. We should be home by lunchtime."

"Okay."

"Do you want to go out, or order in?" I prayed that if

she wanted to go out, it would be somewhere other than McDonald's.

"Pizza sounds good."

"Great, we'll order a pizza."

I wanted to talk to her, and I figured having a conversation around pizza would lighten things a bit. A half hour later, we were sitting cross-legged on either side of my coffee table, slices of my favorite New York-style pizza in front of us.

"Lex, can I ask you something?"

She nodded and took a huge bite of her slice. "Is this thing between your dad and me really okay with you?"

"Yeah, it's okay."

"You're sure?" She nodded and took another bite of pizza. "Because if there's anything you want to talk about, I'd be happy to listen."

She thought for a minute before shaking her head. "No, I don't think there's anything I want to talk about."

"You're not worried about me moving into the house, into your life?"

"You've been living at the house and it's been great. I think you're great."

"I think you're great, too," I said, feeling very maternal. I imagine my face must be beaming like a proud parent. "I'll be right back. I have something to show you."

I made my way back to the dining room and retrieved the book I'd found shoved into the back of my closet. Returning to Lexi's side, I settled in next to her and opened it.

"Is that you and my dad?" Her eyes opened wide.

"Yep."

Lexi studied the pictures on the first page before moving over to those on the second. My eyes followed the same path as hers, and I smiled. The couple in front of me was so young, so hopeful, so in love. I haven't looked at this scrapbook of Dan and myself in ten years. I almost threw it away a hundred times, but something always stopped me from taking action. Instead, it's been hidden in a box in the back of my closet.

"You played softball in college?" I nodded. "That's so cool."

"It was a lot of fun." And that was the truth. Besides the thrill of playing and the companionship of the team, the men's and women's teams at the college traveled together, increasing my quality time with Dan.

"Is that how you met my dad?"

"Sort of. I worked in the trainer's room, and we met there."

"And it was love at first sight," Lexi sighed dramatically, batting her eyelashes and giggling.

She flipped through several more pages, silently studying them. "I wish you guys stayed together all those years ago. I wish we were a family all this time."

I knew the feeling, but after seeing these pictures again, I realize how young Dan and I actually had been. Maybe we wouldn't have made it if we stayed together back then. And, most importantly, Lexi wouldn't exist if we hadn't broken up.

"We're together now, and that's all that matters."

She nodded. "I guess you're right." Then her eyes widened and she pointed to a picture. "Daddy used to keep this picture in his nightstand."

I glanced over her shoulder to see what she was talking about. Dan and I smiled, frozen in time forever, his arms wrapped around my waist, his cheek brushing mine. It was the first picture we had taken as a couple, and Dan kept it on the nightstand next to his bed the entire time we dated.

"Are you sure?" I asked.

She nodded. "I found it one day and asked him about it, but he never really answered me. The next time I went looking, it wasn't there."

"When was that?"

"Last year."

I couldn't hide my shock at that revelation. No matter what Dan said, I always had trouble believing he's been pining for me for the past ten years. But if what Lexi said is true—and I have no reason to believe it isn't—he has been.

I couldn't stop the warm, fuzzy feeling that stole through me at the knowledge. Suddenly, I couldn't wait to return home to Dan so I could tell him how much I love and trust him, and how I cannot wait to spend the rest of my life with him.

DAN

I MUST BE GETTING OLD. That or I'm really out of shape. For the past few days, I haven't done more than sign autographs, shake hands, and have my picture taken, and I'm wiped out. I even had trouble getting out of bed this morning. Of course, I was up late, then tossed and turned most of the night.

The house is always too quiet when Lexi isn't around, but with Sabrina missing too, it's unbearable. It's amazing how much she's become part of the household in a few short months.

Some of the guys from the team had invited me out with them, but that's not really my thing anymore. And God knows the paparazzi would probably follow us and somehow blow things out of proportion.

So, other than doing press events, I've pretty much been moping around the house.

"Hey." My friend and teammate, Jack Reagan, met me at the players entrance of First Allegiant Bank Stadium. "You look like shit. Rough night?"

"Not like you mean," I said. "I didn't sleep well and had to be up at the ass crack of dawn to do some radio interviews."

We headed to the locker room to change into our uniforms. It's the first time I'll be wearing mine since the accident. Definitely a bittersweet experience. I can't imagine what it will be like when I retire.

The first time we did this event, the players wore shorts and a Waves polo shirt, but the fans made it known they'd prefer to see us in our uniforms. Which I can understand. It's what we're most recognizable in. Hell, Lexi has grown up at the stadium and there are some guys even she doesn't recognize in street clothes.

After taking some razzing from some of my teammates, I made my way over to my locker. One of my other best friends on the team, Cal Chase, was already seated at his locker with Jack next to him.

"Yo," Cal said. He held out his hand to shake, then resumed putting on his sock.

I sat at my locker between his and Jack's.

"How's it going?" Cal nodded toward my leg then pulled a T-shirt over his head.

"Pretty good. Looks like I'll definitely be back next season."

His eyes widened. "I didn't know that wasn't a given."

"You never know with these things," I said. "But it feels good for the most part and I just have to work on building strength."

"I'm glad Sabrina managed to fix you up right."

Jack snorted. "She sure did."

I leaned forward and gave him a dirty look.

"Obviously I'm missing something here," Cal said.

"It's not common knowledge yet, but Sabrina and I are engaged."

"Get the fuck out!" He slapped me on the arm. "Congratulations. I'm glad things worked out."

"Thanks. Me too." I buttoned my jersey. "I don't know what I would have done if she just left."

"Okay," Jack said, and looked at Cal. "Before things get too sappy, can you tell me what the hell you were thinking swinging at that high fast ball last night?"

"You had to bring that up," Cal said.

"It was ball four."

"I know that now, but standing up there with the ball hurling at me 100 miles per hour, it looked good."

"It happens to the best of us," I said. "Don't you remember the bouncing curveball you swung at in New York last year?" I asked Jack.

That led to shit talk about the myriad of mistakes or errors we've each made since we've known each other. And God knows there are a lot.

I just finished tying my shoes, when Jack said, "It's 9:45. We better head to the conference room."

Tucking my cell into my back pocket, I stood and accompanied my teammates out of the locker room, through the myriad of corridors, heading toward the large conference room. Most of the veteran players were already there, knowing better than to not show up on time. The rookies would inevitably show up late, and they'd have to face the wrath of the head of PR, Hannah Adams. We've warned them, but there are things some men have to learn on their own.

Hannah entered at ten o'clock on the dot, and shut the

door behind her. She scanned the room and I imagine she could make a detailed list of missing players just from that quick glance.

"Thanks for coming everyone," she said. " I know there are probably a million things you could be doing on your day off, so the fact that you're choosing to spend it here lets me know how dedicated you are to the Waves' support of the children's hospital. This event is going to be a little more personal than we've done in the past. Instead of having you sitting behind tables signing pictures and balls, you're going to be mingling with the guests…taking pictures, answering questions, and really engaging with the fans."

Hannah had just finished her sentence when seven rookies burst through the door. The look she tossed their way should have knocked them dead. She continued.

"We're providing photos and balls to sign as part of the admission fee, but I'm sure people will bring personal items as well. Every station has an array of Sharpies, so feel free to grab a handful to keep in your pocket." She glanced at the paper in her hand and continued. "There's a full staff here today, as well as extra security in case anything gets out of hand. We're hoping this structure is successful so we can expand on it in the future. I think this personal touch will really resonate with the fans and keep them coming back year after year. That being said, after this is over, I'd love to hear your feedback on how you think this went. Most of you have done enough events to know when something works and when it doesn't."

She looked toward the group of tardy rookies and said, "Those of you who arrived late, please stay for a moment. The rest of you can go. Gates open in a half hour."

Chapter Thirty-Four

"DADDY'S GONNA BE SO SURPRISED," Lexi said.

We hadn't spoken to him before deciding to return home, so he doesn't know we're on our way. Between his local talk show appearances and the charity event at the stadium, I figured he'd be busy and we'd just surprise him.

"He's probably going to be pretty tired," I said. "He had to be at the studio at five o'clock this morning."

I thought she had fallen asleep when she didn't answer, then remained silent for the next several minutes, but I glanced in the rear view mirror and found her watching me.

"Everything okay?" I asked.

Her cheeks flushed and she dropped her gaze to the hem of her shorts. She played with the edge for a moment before looking up again. "I was just wondering," she said and then stopped. I glanced back to find her nibbling on her lower lip.

"What's wrong?"

"Nothing. I mean, I was just wondering."

I looked at her through the mirror again and arched a brow, silently urging her to continue.

"Should I call you Mom once you and Daddy get married?"

I nearly ran off the road at that question. Why did she have to ask that now? Couldn't she have asked last night when I brought the subject of Dan's and my impending nuptials?

"I, uh, I guess that would depend on you."

"What do you mean?"

"If you'd feel comfortable calling me Mom." I studied her through the mirror again. Her brow furrowed. "Do you think you'd want to?"

The frown deepened. "I think so."

"Then, if it's okay with your dad, it's okay with me."

"Do you think he'll mind?"

"I don't know. But I do think you should talk to him about it first."

WITH THE NUMBER of cars in the main parking garage of First Allegiant Bank Stadium, you'd think the Waves were playing a home game. Which is a good thing. The event being held was raising money for a local children's hospital the team has adopted as its charitable cause. Dan told me that even though it takes place on a rare day off, all the players participate.

After driving up and down the rows of all five levels, I was about to give up and drive to another garage when I managed to snag a spot a car had just vacated at the back of the first level.

"Wow, I've never been here before," Lexi said as we

emerged from the garage. "Daddy parks over there," she said, pointing to the parking garage a couple blocks away adjacent to the players' entrance.

"Of course he does. If he parked way back here, he'd be too tired to play after the long walk to the stadium."

Lexi chuckled, then set her hand in mine as we walked toward the entrance.

A woman approached as we entered the gate.

"Hey Lexi."

Lexi let go of my hand and ran into the woman's open embrace.

"I'm happy you're here. Your dad said you weren't coming today. We miss seeing you."

Lexi pulled away and settled in at my side again. She looked up at me. "We got done early and came back."

The woman turned her attention to me. "You must be the famous Sabrina." She held out her hand to shake. "I've heard a lot about you today. I hear congratulations are in order."

Her smile transformed what had at first glance seemed to be an unremarkable face. Warm brown eyes glowed with sincerity from behind the lenses of blue and yellow striped glasses. Talk about team spirit.

I returned her smile as I shook her hand. "Guilty as charged, and thank you."

"I'm Hannah Adams, public relations manager for the Waves."

"So you're responsible for this great turnout?"

She shook her head. "No, I just plan the events and publicize them. The guys are responsible for all this," she said, raising her arm in an encompassing gesture. "If they weren't willing to volunteer their time, no one would show up."

"Don't sell yourself short," I said, having the feeling

this woman did just that on a regular basis. "They couldn't do this without you."

She opened her mouth to speak just as a young man called her name and waved her toward him.

"Sorry, duty calls," she said. "I look forward to seeing you around. Bye Lex."

"Come on, let's go find your dad." I said to Lexi.

I treated Lexi to a pink cotton candy as we wandered around the stadium. The relaxed atmosphere surprised me. I expected to see the players behind a table, surrounded by crazed fans. Some of the players did sit at tables, but they were chatting with attendees or grabbing a bite to eat.

We found Dan standing with one of his teammates encircled by a group of fans. He seemed to be enjoying himself as he engaged with the awestruck children. For the most part, the adults stayed back and let the kids bask in the attention of their idols. Some of the men looked more spellbound than their sons and daughters. A few of the women watched the players with lascivious intent, but neither Dan nor his teammate seemed to notice.

Dan spotted Lexi and me and a smile lit his face. He said something to his teammate, who I now recognized as Cal Chase, third baseman for the Waves, and pulled away from the group.

"Hey, you're back early." He lifted Lexi and wrapped his other arm around my neck, bestowing a kiss on us both.

"Lexi was such a big help, we got done ahead of schedule," I said.

"We wanted to surprise you, Daddy."

"Well, you did," he said and set Lexi on the ground.

"Are all these people here to see you?" she asked.

"Me and the other guys." He smirked and added in a stage whisper. "But mostly me."

"We better let you get back," I said. "Your doting public awaits."

"I'm almost done here. We're meeting in the big conference room for a drink before leaving. Why don't you come along and meet everyone?"

"Are you sure?"

His smile answered my question.

"Lexi can lead the way." He looked to his daughter for acknowledgement.

She nodded. "I know how to get there."

"I'll be there soon," he said, before kissing Lexi on the top of the head. He straightened and brushed his lips against mine before getting back to work.

DAN

WHEN I GOT BACK to the circle of fans, Jack had joined, and two of the more aggressive women had latched on to him. Probably because they hadn't been getting anywhere with Cal or me. Depending on Jack's mood, he may or may not take what they're offering. Normally he picks one woman and spends time with her for the season, but from what he's told me, this year's flavor was starting to get a little needy for his taste.

"Sorry about that folks," I said. "My fiancé and daughter got back to town early and decided to surprise me."

The women oohed and aahed, then asked questions about Sabrina. I kept my answers vague, not wanting to invade her privacy. I'll have to ask her what she's comfortable sharing with the public.

A short time later, Hannah wrapped up the event in her normal no-nonsense fashion. My teammates and I stood near the entrance, shaking hands, and thanking attendees as they exited the stadium. Once it was cleared out, security closed the gates, and the team headed to the locker room to change before heading to the post-event party.

"Would you wipe that silly grin off your face?" Jack said.

"Someday you're going to fall hard and you'll understand," I said.

He rolled his eyes and looked at Cal. "Listen to this sap. He's not even married yet and he's already trying to get me hitched."

Cal gave a half-assed chuckle, but it was obvious to anyone it was fake. I know he and his wife have been having issues, but since I've been MIA this season, I'm not sure what's going on. But I'm sure he'll fill me in when he has something to tell.

"Sabrina and Lexi are coming to the party, so you'll both get to meet her."

"Lexi likes her?" Jack asked.

"She loves her," I said. "And Sabrina is great with her. They've gotten pretty close over the past couple months."

"I'm happy for you. Really," he said. "And I'm excited to meet her. Hell, I feel like I know her already after listening to you whine for the past eight years."

"You're a douche, you know that?"

"I've been told." He chuckled.

Jack's cell buzzed. "Fuck," he said, half under his breath.

"What's up?" Cal asked.

"Cindy is blowing up my phone today."

Cindy, aka this season's girl, apparently wasn't handling

the fact that the season, and their relationship, was coming to an end.

"I don't understand it. I'm very honest about what I'm looking for in these relationships. I've never had this trouble before."

"Women are complicated," Cal said. "Better men than we have failed at figuring them out."

"Please don't bring this subject up around Sabrina," I said, only half kidding.

"I can't make any promises," Jack said. "Come on, let's hit the party."

Chapter Thirty-Five

LEXI LED me through the stadium to a door with a sign that read, "Staff Only." She turned the knob and pulled it open, leaning back with all her weight. I grabbed the door before it squished her and followed into the hallway beyond, feeling like I was entering a secret sanctum.

Enlarged photos of Waves teams and individual players, both past and present, graced the walls. I didn't have time to study the pictures like I would have wanted since I was trying to keep up with Lexi. She led me toward a noisy room with the door propped open.

As she entered, a slender woman with a blonde bob said, "Hey there, Lexi. I'm so glad you're here. We didn't think you were coming." She pulled Lexi into an embrace.

Lexi pulled back. "Hi, Mrs. K. Is Ava here?"

"Right over there." She pointed to group of children huddled in the corner.

Lexi took off, leaving me standing at the door with a stranger. The last time I'd felt so awkward was the first day of college when I entered the cafeteria and didn't know a soul.

"Hi, I'm Natalie Kasprzyk, John's wife."

I shook the hand she'd offered and said, "I'm Sabrina Kelly, Dan McMullen's…"

Before I could finish my sentence, she squeezed my hand and said, "Oh my gosh, you're Dan's Sabrina. Come on, the girls are all dying to meet you."

She led me toward a group of women, each more beautiful and stylish than the other. I felt like Sandra Bullock's Gracie Lou Freebush character in *Miss Congeniality*, pre-makeover. Lexi and I had just stopped in to see Dan. If I'd known I was going to be meeting his teammates and their wives, I definitely would have made different clothing choices and put on makeup. At least my hair isn't awful…Lexi and I are both sporting French braids, per her request.

Natalie introduced me to each woman in turn. They were all friendly and gushed over my ring. And, they all seemed to know a lot about my relationship with Dan. I'm still trying to figure out when he had time to tell them we were engaged, nevermind anything else.

Natalie said, "I'm thrilled Dan found happiness. We've been trying to set him up for years, but he wouldn't cooperate." She smiled. "Obviously he was waiting for someone special."

I smiled back, not sure how to respond. Thankfully, Dan and his teammates arrived before I had to. The noise level increased with their entrance, but Lexi's voice screeched above the din.

"Uncle Jack!"

She ran across the room toward a Ryan Reynolds look-alike, who reached down and picked her up.

"How's my favorite girl?" he asked and kissed Lexi's cheek.

"I'm hurt." Dan placed his hand over his heart. "My baby runs right by and ignores me."

"Daddy, I'm not a baby," Lexi said, dragging out the first word.

"You'll always be my baby," he said, and kissed her on the head as he walked to my side, threading his fingers through mine.

Lexi rolled her eyes, "That's silly. Someday I'll be grown."

"Even when you're grown, you'll be my baby, remember?"

Apparently, they've had this conversation before and Lexi shrugged, seeming to realize she wouldn't convince him otherwise. She looked from Dan to me and smiled.

"Uncle Jack, did you hear the news?"

"What news is that?" He set her on the floor.

"Daddy and Sabrina are getting married."

"As a matter of fact, I did hear that news."

His eyes drifted to our entwined hands then back up to my face. How a man could fit so much appeal into a single glance and small smile, I'll never know. It didn't work on me, of course, but I could understand how he could get women to drop their panties without much effort.

Lexi pulled me from my thoughts when she announced she was going back to her friends. The men watched her walk across the room, then turned back to the conversation.

"Sabrina, this is Jack Reagan," Dan said, finally making an official introduction. "Jack, Sabrina Kelly."

"It's nice to finally meet the woman who whipped Dan's ass back into shape," he said, eyes twinkling. "And who stole his heart. Congratulations."

"Thank you. It's nice to meet you as well."

Jack was about to say something else when his cell phone buzzed. He looked at the screen and frowned.

"Everything okay?" Dan asked.

"For the most part." Jack shrugged. The two men shared a look and Dan shook his head and laughed. "What?" Jack asked.

"You knew your luck couldn't hold out forever."

"Luck? There are rules and agreements. When they're understood and followed, luck shouldn't have to be involved." His phone buzzed again and he cursed under his breath. "I have to go. Congratulations again. I'm going to say goodbye to my girl. We'll have to go out one night and celebrate," he said before walking toward Lexi.

Dan put his arm around my shoulders and pulled me to his side.

"I'm so happy you're here," he said, kissing my temple. "I didn't think you'd get to meet everyone until the wedding."

I looked around the room and cringed. If all the people in the room are invited, along with our families and other friends, we'll need to hold the wedding at the Taj Mahal.

Dan chuckled, reading my mind as usual. "Don't worry, it'll all work out."

"We were just stopping by to say hi, I wasn't expecting to meet people. I'm really not dressed for the occasion."

He took in my blue shirt and khaki shorts. "You look beautiful, as usual."

I tucked my head into his shoulder. "I'm not dressed like them."

"That's why I love you," he said, kissing my forehead. "I always want the real you, not some Stepford wife." He shifted so we stood face to face. "Please don't think I want you to be anything but the amazing woman you are."

I blinked to hold back the tears his words had produced. He really is sweet sometimes, and I told him so.

Chapter Thirty-Six

DAN LED me around the room twice, and I was introduced to players, their significant others, the owners, staff, and management of the Waves.

I'll never remember all these names.

For the most part, they seem like a tight-knit group, and everyone has been very welcoming. The women thought it was sweet that we found each other again after ten years. Dan used the explanation I gave Lexi when asked why we broke up back then.

A man wearing khaki pants and a white polo shirt sporting the Waves logo embroidered on the sleeve entered the room and approached us. Dan introduced him as Max Rigsbee, one of the team trainers.

"It's nice to meet you," he said. "I've wanted to tell you how impressed I am with both the routines you put together and the progress Dan has made."

"Thank you, but I can't take all the credit. He's the one

who had to do the work. Without his commitment, my routines would be worthless."

He smiled and looked at Dan. "I like her, Dan. Be sure you hold onto her."

While Dan responded to Max, he looked directly into my eyes. "I fully intend to."

"Before you leave, would you be able to stop in my office? The team signed some balls for my son's class, but I haven't seen you to get yours. Would you mind?"

"Not at all," Dan said. "I can sneak away now." I nodded when he looked at me for confirmation to his statement. "It shouldn't take long," he said to be both Max and me.

Natalie Kasprzyk approached me when Dan left.

"Is your head still spinning?"

"You could say that." I chuckled.

"I know it's a lot to take in, but for the most part it's a good group. None of the players are prima donnas and the wives are friendly. The team John played for when we first got serious was horrible. It's not fun dealing with players who think the team revolves around them, or women who are always on the make. It's bad enough we have to deal with groupies, but you shouldn't have to worry about another player's wife hitting on your boyfriend or husband."

"I can't imagine."

"Thankfully John got traded to the Waves and things are different. The players are all down to earth, and the wives and girlfriends who come around are focused on their men, not anyone else's."

"And the groupies?"

She wrinkled her nose. "They're always around, unfortunately. It drove me crazy in the beginning, but now I don't pay attention."

"How do you manage that?"

"Well, for one, I have the children now so I'm not around as much to see it." She chuckled. "Honestly, I finally just realized that I have to trust John to do the right thing, even when I'm not there. And thankfully, the guys on this team who hook up with groupies don't bring them around. Jack usually brings whoever the girl of the season is on road trips, but his women are a bit classier than your average groupie."

"Girl of the season?"

She nodded. "Did you ever see the movie Bull Durham?"

"Kevin Costner and baseball? I've seen it a million times."

"Jack is kind of like Susan Sarandon's character, Annie. He dates one girl for the season. Once the season ends, he moves on. Then he'll find another girl for the off-season."

I didn't know what to say to that, so I didn't respond at all. At that point, a couple of the wives joined our conversation and added their thoughts to the subject, and the three of them ended up laughing over stories of "incidents" that had happened over the years. I managed to offer a laugh, but wasn't amused.

I didn't realize it could be so bad. Obviously, I've heard that professional athletes are bombarded with offers of sex, but I didn't relate it to Dan and me. My thoughts and feelings are all over the place. I trust Dan, I do, but I don't want women bribing their way into his hotel room or trying to sneak into our house.

I asked the location of the nearest ladies room and excused myself, leaving the women to their stories. My stomach twisted as I thought about what Natalie and the other wives had said. I wondered if Dan has hooked up with groupies. I know he wouldn't bring them around Lexi, but she wasn't with him on the road. I know if I asked he'd be honest, but I'm not sure I'd be able to handle it if he said he did.

I washed my hands and checked my appearance in the mirror. Considering how shaken up I feel on the inside, thankfully I look relatively normal on the outside.

As I left the ladies room, I met Dan in the hallway as he returned from Max's office. His lingering kiss did a bit to soothe my nerves.

"Sorry about that," he said. "I didn't think I'd be gone that long."

"Duty calls." I smiled, but it must have fallen short.

"Everything okay?"

"Mmm Hmm." I nodded.

"You sure?"

He studied me for a moment and I thought he was going to push for answers, but he smiled and put his arm around my shoulders.

"Let's get back inside and say our goodbyes."

DAN

SOMETHING IS OFF WITH SABRINA. She's smiling and saying all the right things, but I can tell she's shaken about something. But what could have happened in the time I was gone?

I'll have to talk to her later at home. Otherwise it will drive me crazy.

"Daddy, can Ava and the others come over swimming?"

I'm kind of exhausted, but I know Lexi has missed seeing her friends. I looked at Sabrina.

"Are you okay with that?"

She looked shocked that I'd asked, but then nodded. "Sure."

"Thanks!" Lexi took off to her circle of friends to announce a pool party. Of course, I'd have to talk to all the parents to make it official. I spent the next several minutes doing just that, and had it turn into a full-blown picnic, parents and other adults included.

While I was putting together a party, Hannah had taken the opportunity to grill Sabrina on her background information. They were tucked into the corner of the room, heads together, as Hannah scribbled in her ever-present notebook.

I texted Jack, who said he'd try to stop by. When I mentioned it to Cal, he said, "Thanks, but I actually have plans."

"You and Marsha up to something fun?"

He looked down and rubbed the back of his neck.

"Actually, we're separating," he said. "I'm moving out tonight."

"Oh man, I'm sorry. Where are you going?"

"I'm not sure. I'll probably just get a suite at the Marriott."

"Why don't you stay at my place until you figure things out?"

"No, I couldn't. Not with you and Sabrina just getting settled."

"You can stay in the pool house. You'll have total privacy, and you won't have to worry about us getting in each other's way."

"Are you sure?" he asked.

"I'm positive. At least it will give you time to figure out

where you want to go," I said. "And who knows? Maybe things will still work out."

He shook his head. "I don't think so. I'm just not what she wants. And honestly, I don't think I love her like I should. You and Sabrina made me realize that."

"What do you mean?"

"Like you, I screwed up a relationship back in the day. And the thing is, I can't stop thinking about her, even after all this time." He let out an embarrassed chuckle. "My marriage is falling apart, and I can't stop thinking about the girl I left behind at the start of my career. How fucked up is that?"

"Do you know where this girl is? Are you planning on trying to get back together with her?"

"I'm sure I could find her if I wanted to, but no. I need to figure some things out before I'm worth anything to anyone."

"Sounds smart."

"I'm gonna head out and go grab some stuff," he said. "I'll see you later. And thanks again. I really appreciate it."

"No problem." Cal had just left when Hannah released Sabrina. I made my way to her side. "You ready to get out of here?"

"Sure," she said. "How did the party planning go?"

"A good number can make it."

"Do we need anything?" she asked. "I can stop on the way."

"We should have most of the major stuff on hand. Mrs. Evans keeps things pretty well stocked."

"How about desserts?"

"We could probably use some. I'm sure the kids will appreciate that."

"Any requests?"

"No, just use your judgment."

I signaled for Lexi that we were heading out. She said goodbye to her friends and ran to our side.

"Are you coming home with Sabrina or me?"

"Sabrina."

Why did I even ask?

"That's great," Sabrina said. "Because we have to stop on the way home for dessert. You can help me choose."

"Awesome!"

"Come on," I said. "I'll walk you to your car."

"You don't have to do that," Sabrina said. "We're way out of your way."

"Not negotiable," I said, and walked my girls to the parking garage four blocks away. I'll have to remember to get her a pass to the garage adjacent to the stadium.

Chapter Thirty-Seven

CARS LINED the driveway and I maneuvered my way around them to my usual parking space in front of the garage. I stepped from the car and sounds of the party floated from the back of the house.

Dan said he had enough main course and side items, but Lexi and I had stopped along the way to pick up a few desserts. The first supermarket we stopped at didn't have any good options, so we ended up going to a store a little out of our way. The trip was worth it because they had a huge selection, but we ended up taking forever to decide what to get. In the end, I purchased everything that caught our eye. Otherwise, we may have been there forever.

Lexi ran to the front door and through the house, a container of chocolate chip cookies in hand while I followed at a more sedate pace with everything else. I piled my bounty on the kitchen counter next to the cookies Lexi had thrown there. Dan spotted me through the open patio doors and gestured for me to join him at the grill. I made my way across the patio, avoiding getting hit with a beach ball along the way.

Just before I reached Dan, Cal Chase approached from the other side.

"Sabrina, you remember Cal? He's going to be moving into the pool house for a little while."

I'm not sure what I'd been expecting him to say, but that wasn't it.

"Oh, okay." I looked at Cal and smiled.

"It's just temporary, I promise" Cal said.

"No, please, stay as long as you'd like."

"You soon-to-be newlyweds don't need me hanging around."

"Oh please," I chuckled. "You could be living in the house and we could go weeks without seeing each other. Don't worry about being out here."

"Thank you, I appreciate it," he said. "You're a lucky man, Dan," he said. "I'm going to grab a couple bags from the car and put them inside."

"You okay?" Dan asked.

"Never better," Cal replied. "Thanks again," he said to both of us, then he was off.

I turned toward Dan, who was busy flipping burgers. When he turned my way, I raised my eyebrow.

"He and his wife just separated," Dan said. "He's giving the house to his wife and planned on staying in a hotel." He moved chicken legs to one side of the grill and lowered the heat. "We have room here, so what the heck?"

Before I answered, Lexi yelled from the patio door. I glanced over and saw that she had changed into her swimsuit.

"Can you fix my hair?" she asked. It seems that in her haste to get her shirt off, she'd ruined her braid.

"Duty calls," I said to Dan.

With Lexi's hair emergency dealt with, I took the opportunity to freshen up myself. With all my stray hair in place, I reapplied my lip gloss and returned to the party.

There was a different vibe than just fifteen minutes before and I stood on the fringes looking around trying to figure out why. Dan had finished cooking and everyone seemed to be enjoying the food.

I looked over and saw Dan standing next to Jack Reagan, who had a brunette with legs up to her neck hanging on one side and a bleach-blonde on the other. The brunette transferred herself to Dan and whispered something in his ear. He smiled and shook his head, extracting himself from her embrace. She sauntered away, putting an exaggerated swing in her step. I couldn't help but notice the signatures she bore on various body parts. After grabbing a beer from the cooler, she returned to her perch between Dan and Jack.

The two men continued their conversation and I went back inside. I pulled a platter from the top cabinet and filled it with a variety of the desserts Lexi and I had purchased and attempted to compose myself. With the platter full and my riotous thoughts somewhat subdued, I brought the desserts outside and set them on a table.

Lexi and some of the other children ran to my side and attacked the desserts. Natalie walked over to my side and snagged a peanut butter cookie.

"Some of us girls go out for dinner and drinks once a month or so. It'd be great if you could join us sometime," she said.

"I'd like that," I said.

We exchanged numbers and discussed my schedule and availability, and even though I was engaged in our conversation, my eyes were focused on Dan. Of course, Natalie noticed.

"Don't worry about that," she said. "I'm sure Jack is just lining up his off-season and spring companions."

"So these women just make themselves available and hope he picks them?"

"Some of them. Others put themselves in the running with Jack but also keep their options open."

I followed her gaze across the pool where Dan and Jack spoke while the two women hung on their every word. For the most part, the women hung on Jack, but the brunette kept eyeing Dan and allowed her hand to brush his bicep twice that I saw. He wasn't encouraging her, but he didn't totally move away either.

"Sabrina." I was pulled from watching that woman eye fuck my fiancé when Lexi approached. "Are there any more chocolate chip cookies?"

"Yes." I put my arm around her shoulder. "Excuse us, Natalie. We have to fetch more cookies."

THE PARTY BROKE up a few hours later and Dan and I carried the remains of the food into the kitchen. Despite Dan's protests, I filled and turned on the dishwasher and wiped down all the countertops. Why should Mrs. Evans have to deal with it in the morning?

Lexi had conked out on the couch shortly after everyone left and Dan went to carry her to her room. I took advantage of the time alone to gather my thoughts and figure out what I wanted to say to him.

We've been living in a bubble, so our relationship has

been relatively easy. Now that Dan is better, events like today's will be a regular thing. I have to be honest with him about my feelings or we won't stand a chance.

I poured a glass of sweet tea for myself and grabbed a beer for Dan and settled into the couch Lexi had previously occupied. He returned a few minutes later and sat next to me.

After taking a sip of his beer, he said, "Ok, what's on your mind?"

Despite my serious thoughts, I chuckled. The man knows me too well.

"I'm not comfortable with the groupie thing."

His eyes widened, then he relaxed. "Bri, that's not something you really need to worry about?"

"Why's that?"

"Because I don't…" he waved his hand around as he searched for a word. "…go there. It's not something I do. I never have."

"What about Jack?"

"What about him?"

"Does he bring women like that around often?"

"No," he said, but didn't sound convincing.

"No?"

"Not exactly."

"What *exactly* does that mean?"

"Jack usually has a woman for each season. Sometimes he brings whoever he's with to events and such, and sometimes he doesn't." He shrugged. "I've never paid too much attention."

"He had two women with him here today."

"Yes he did." He took a long gulp of beer, then picked at the label on the bottle before answering. "He was, uh, trying to decide which one he wants to spend the off season with."

Since Natalie had said as much, his words weren't news to me, but I still snorted.

"Why choose? I'm sure both of them would be happy to service him."

"Jack is what he is, but he's not a total man-whore. He's pretty much a serial monogamist. At this point, he sticks to one woman at a time."

"How big of him."

He rubbed his eyes and sighed.

"Bri, what's going on here? What are you upset about?"

"The whole groupie thing freaks me out. Theoretically, I've always known they existed, I've just never seen them up close and personal or heard first-hand experiences of them."

He cursed under his breath. "The wives do like to talk."

"Dan, this isn't about the wives."

"Then what is it about? And what does it have to do with you and me?"

"You're good friends with Jack."

"Yeah, and?"

"If those women are around him, they're around you."

"I just told you that's never been my thing."

"They're still around. And that brunette was making it known you were hers for the taking earlier," I said. "Christ Dan, she was at your home, putting the moves on you in front of your daughter and fiancée."

"Putting the moves on me?" he asked, obviously getting aggravated. "Bri, that was nothing. You have no idea what some of those women do."

"If those words were supposed to make me feel better, they failed."

He shifted. "Bri, I love you. I lost you once because I

was an idiot, I certainly wouldn't make the same mistake twice."

I nodded and swallowed the lump in my throat. "I'm just not comfortable with it."

He kissed my forehead and pulled me in for a hug, but didn't say anything else. After all, what could he say?

Chapter Thirty-Eight

SABRINA

THE HOT WATER pounded on my neck, draining some of the tension that had collected there. I leaned against the tile and enjoyed the sensation.

I turned the water off and squeezed the excess moisture from my hair. After wrapping myself in my tattered blue robe, I grabbed a bottle of raspberry scented lotion from the vanity and headed to the bed. As I moisturized my still-damp skin, I thought about Dan. You always hear about professional athletes and the women who make themselves readily available to them, but until you see it first hand, it's hard to believe. The wives talked about it so matter-of-factly, it's obviously part of their everyday lives.

The problem is, I don't know if I can live like that. That thought was echoing through my head when I heard a soft knock on the door. "It's open."

Dan entered, looking freshly showered himself.

"Are you okay?" he asked.

I shrugged.

"Honey, I swear I've never hooked up with women like that, and I certainly wouldn't now."

"I believe you, it's just…" I gestured vaguely, hoping my hands could say what I didn't want to.

"What?"

"I hate the fact that women like that even exist," I said.

He shrugged. "It's just the way it is." I snorted. "I'm not saying it's right, but it's a fact of life."

"It's not a fact of my life," I mumbled. But Dan heard.

"It is if you're with me."

I looked directly at him. "What if I can't deal with it?" My eyes filled with tears and his image blurred in front of me.

He blinked several times and straightened. "I guess that's something you have to decide." After squeezing my hand, he stood and left the room.

I burst into tears after the door shut. The waterworks lasted for nearly an hour and when I was all cried out, I felt drained, but my mind was clear. If I can't deal with all this, I have to decide now. It wouldn't be fair to either one of us, not to mention Lexi, if I can't.

I stood and got dressed, then packed a bag. After scribbling notes for both Dan and Lexi, I crept down the stairs and left.

DAN

I KNEW she was gone even before I entered her empty room. I felt her absence as if it was a physical thing.

I found a note lying on her pillow.

Dan,

I'm so sorry. I'm just a little freaked out and need time to think. Please tell Lexi I'll be in touch. I don't want her to think I'm abandoning the two of you. I do love you both, so much.

Sabrina

I crumbled the note and threw it against the wall.

I can't believe this. She just left for no reason. No fucking reason at all.

Part of me wants to choke the wives for telling their groupie tales. But I can't blame

them. If Sabrina can't handle those women being in my presence, how will she deal if things ever get intense? I can control my actions, but I can't stop people from saying things about me. And sometimes those women make up stories to get attention. Nothing has ever gotten out of hand for me that way, but some of the other guys have had things written or said about them that weren't true. How would Sabrina react if a nasty story showed up online?

Better this happen now rather than later, I guess.

Now I can just hope there is a later for us.

I left her room and headed toward the kitchen, where Jeff was pouring himself a cup of coffee.

"Want some?" I shook my head and sat at the counter. "What's wrong? You look like you just ate shit."

"Sabrina's gone."

"What do you mean gone?"

"I mean gone, as in, not here."

"Fuck," he said. "What happened?"

"Jack brought some women to the party last night and it freaked her out. The stories the wives had to tell didn't do much to help the situation." I dragged my hands through my hair and held the back of my neck. "She said she has to think."

Before Jeff could reply, Lexi bounded into the kitchen.

She looked around the kitchen and said, "Do you know where Sabrina is? I was gonna ask her to do my hair."

I looked at Jeff, who cringed.

"Honey, come here." I picked Lexi up and perched her on my knee. "Things have happened kind of fast here, and Sabrina needed some time to think." She scrunched her nose. "So she went back to her place for a little while."

"She left?" Tears filled her eyes as her bottom lip quivered. "Again?"

She jumped off my lap and ran out of the kitchen and up the stairs. I heard her bedroom door slam, then silence.

"Well that went well."

As much as I love her, at this moment I hate Sabrina for hurting us like this.

Chapter Thirty-Nine

SABRINA

"TELL ME WHAT HAPPENED," Kevin urged.

After brooding and crying for two days, I finally called my brother and informed him of my whereabouts. He appeared on my doorstep an hour later.

"I don't want to talk about it," I said.

"I bet it'll make you feel better."

"Bet it won't," I said, sounding like a four-year-old.

"Sabrina, if you don't tell me what happened, I'm going to Dan's and pounding the information out of him."

"This time it's not his fault," I said.

"What happened?" he asked again.

I explained, in detail, about the stories the wives had told me and what I'd witnessed at the pool party.

"What did he say?"

"Basically, that if I'm going to be part of his life, it's something I have to put up with."

Kevin stood and shook his head. Hands on his hips, he said, "I can't believe you just left."

"What should I have done?"

"Figure out how to deal with it." He held his arms out, gesturing as if what he was saying should be obvious. "He's right this time and you're totally wrong."

"Kevin, you didn't hear the stories and see those women. The one did everything in her power—except strip—to get Dan's attention. And I'm sure she would've done that if kids weren't there."

"Did he seem interested in her?"

"No."

"So what's the problem?"

"You make it sound so easy."

He took my hands in his and squeezed. "It is easy."

"Considering our history, it's not."

"Considering your history, do you really think Dan's gonna screw things up again?" I shrugged then shook my head. "And you said the wives were sharing stories, but they're still married. They didn't freak out and leave because groupies exist in the world."

Put like that, I feel like an idiot. Why did I make this out to be such a big deal?

"I just don't want you living in limbo for another ten years," Kevin said. "You deserve to be happy, and I don't think you can be without getting this settled between the two of you."

"I know you're right, but I just can't face him yet."

"But you do plan on facing him."

I nodded. "Eventually."

Kevin and I went out to dinner and thankfully, the subject of Dan had at least been dropped, if not totally forgotten. I returned home and fell into bed. Thoughts of

Dan kept running through my head, and I knew I'd have to go face him sooner or later…if not for Dan and me, then definitely for Lexi. I figured I'd just need a few days to get myself together and work up the strength. Unfortunately, I wasn't awarded that luxury.

Chapter Forty

SABRINA

THE INCESSANT BUZZING was a shock to my system, and no matter how hard I pounded on my alarm clock, it wouldn't stop. I sat up and studied the object of my discontent, only to find that it wasn't making a sound. Still, the buzzing continued and was soon followed by a pounding.

I slipped out of bed and shuffled to the front door. Brushing hair out of my face, I flipped the lock and turned the knob. The door flew open and I jumped back to avoid getting hit.

"Is she here?" The voice registered before the words, and I looked up into Dan's eyes. I was too shocked to speak. "Is she here?" he repeated, carefully spacing the words.

"Who?" I managed to ask.

"Lexi. Is she here?"

"No, why would she be?"

"Because she's not home, and I've looked everywhere else."

My addled brain started working at that point, and his words finally sank in. My heart pounded double-time. "Where is she?"

"If I knew that, I wouldn't be here." Dan said the words as though he was mad at me, as if he had the right to be.

"When did she leave?"

"Sometime this morning. She was playing Xbox when I went to work out, but was gone when I was done."

"You don't think someone took her?" The thought was so horrifying I barely pushed the words out.

Dan shook his head and rubbed the back of his neck. "She left a note."

"What did it say?"

He pulled a wadded up paper out of his pocket and handed it to me. "That she's going to find you."

I scanned the note, confirming his words, my eyes stuck on the last sentence.

I love you, Daddy, but I can't lose my mother again.

"You don't think…" I couldn't even finish the sentence.

"She thinks you're her mother. I should've figured that out before. Some of the comments she made alluded to the fact, but I was too stupid to pick up on it."

"I questioned some of the comments she made, but I never imagined this."

"I should have known what she was thinking. She *is* my daughter." What he left unsaid was that she isn't mine and never would be. Losing Lexi was hurting as much as losing Dan.

"Do you have any idea where else she might be?" I ushered him inside and urged him onto the couch.

"No, this was my last resort. I tried to call, but there was no answer."

I turned away from his questioning gaze. "I, uh, shut my phone off."

He didn't ask why, though I could tell he wanted to. He stood. "I have to find her."

"Let me help."

I saw the war raging within him, but he finally accepted my offer.

"Give me a few minutes to change," I said, before disappearing into my bedroom.

My mind raced as I threw on fresh clothes and pulled my hair into a ponytail. After brushing my teeth, I went to face Dan again.

"Any idea where we should look?" he asked.

He seemed angry with me, and I had to remind myself that the man's daughter is missing. After we find her, I could place blame for my behavior where it belongs, but until then, I'll have to keep my emotions in check.

"Here?"

"Jeff and the rest of my family have the bases covered back home. The parents of all her friends have been alerted, so if they see her, they'll let me know."

"I guess we could check out the mall and the park. They were the only places we went."

Dan nodded and headed toward the door.

My panic increased with each passing minute, so I could only imagine how he must feel. I couldn't help but wonder what would happen if we don't find Lexi. Would she go home? Could she find home if she wanted to? Did someone find her and take her? I stopped my train of thought right there. Thoughts like that wouldn't help the situation. We'll find her. We have to.

After searching the mall, Dan left a picture of Lexi at

the security office along with our cell numbers. Next we headed to the park. It was crowded, so it took us quite some time to determine she wasn't there either. Dejected, we headed back to the car.

"Where to?" he asked, clearly nearing the end of his rope.

"Let me think," I said, racking my brain for ideas.

"You do that," he said. "I'm calling Jeff to see if there's been any word."

I nodded and leaned against the sun-warmed car. Closing my eyes, I tried to recall everything Lexi and I had done the previous week. My cell phone chirped, interrupting my thoughts.

"Hello," I said.

"Sabrina, thank God I got hold of you."

"Jodi?"

"Lexi McMullen is here," she said.

"She's there?"

"Uh huh, and she's pretty distraught."

"I'll be right there." I launched myself at Dan. "I know where she is."

His eyes brightened and he informed Jeff of what I'd said and hung up. "Where?"

"At the clinic. Jodi just called."

"Let's go."

We broke several laws getting there, but we made it to the clinic in record time. Dan and I burst through the back door and Jodi directed us to her office. Lexi sat in the leather chair just behind Jodi's desk.

"Oh, thank God," Dan growled as he grabbed Lexi out of the chair and pulled her into a bear hug. She let out a sob and wrapped her arms around his neck. "Don't ever do that to me again," Dan said, his voice thick.

After nearly squeezing the life out of her, Dan sat Lexi

back in the chair. I took the opportunity to pull her into my arms. "You had us so worried, Lex," I said, the tears I'd managed to hold back since Dan's arrival streaming down my cheeks.

"I'm sorry," she sobbed. "But I had to find you."

"How did you get here?" I asked.

"I got a ride." She looked down toward her lap.

Dan looked at Jodi, who shrugged. "I didn't see who dropped her off."

Dan looked like he was going to lose it at that point, but he stood up and raked his fingers through his hair instead.

"Lex, how did you get here?" Dan practically growled.

"McKenzie's sister drove me."

"McKenzie Moran?" Lexi nodded. "Jesus Christ, she just got her license. She was bragging about it at the meet and greet."

"I'm sorry, Daddy, but I couldn't let Sabrina leave again. I need her." Lexi studied her shoes. "I love her."

My eyes clashed with Dan's at her words. I had no doubt he blamed me for this whole situation, and I can't say I disagree. I shouldn't have disappeared like I did. I knew how attached Lexi was, I should have explained things to her.

"Let's go back to my place and talk this over."

After thanking Jodi again, we piled into the car and drove, in silence, to my house.

After hearing the details of Lexi's adventure, and how McKenize ended up driving her over a hundred miles to the rehab clinic, Dan was forced to address the big issue. "Lex, Sabrina isn't your mom," Dan explained.

"But she has to be," Lexi said.

"I wish she was honey, but she isn't," Dan said. "Your mother and I went out for a short time after I got drafted by the Waves. When she had you, she wasn't ready to be a mom, so I decided to raise you myself."

I watched Dan try to explain the situation to his daughter, and my heart went out to him. It's not a position I'd want to be in.

"But I love Sabrina," Lexi said.

"I love you too, honey, but I'm not your birth mother," I said, my heart breaking for the little girl who would never be mine.

"Will you be my mom?" she asked.

What could I say? I don't want to mislead her, but I don't want to break her heart either.

Before I could do either, Dan cut in. "Honey, why don't you go to sleep? Sabrina and I have a few things to discuss," he said. "We'll talk again in the morning."

Reluctantly, Lexi followed Dan to the guest bedroom. I'd offered Dan and Lexi lodging for the night so they didn't have to endure the ride home after such a stressful day.

Lexi wrapped her arms around my neck and kissed my cheek. "I love you, Sabrina."

"I love you too, Lex."

Their images blurred as they left the room. Once they were out of sight, I allowed the tears to fall down my face.

DAN

"IS SABRINA COMING HOME WITH US?" Lexi asked, tearing my heart out again.

"Sabrina and I have some things to talk about. But no matter what happens, we both love you," I said. "And you have to promise me you'll never do anything like this again."

"I promise," she said, looking down at her hands. When her eyes met mine, they were filled with tears. "I was really scared when Sabrina wasn't at work."

"You should have been. Thank God Jodi called. I was going crazy."

"I'm sorry." Two fresh tears rolled down her cheeks and plopped onto her chest.

"You understand that Sabrina isn't your biological mother, right?"

She nodded. "But I really wish she was."

"I know. Me too." I kissed her forehead. "Get some sleep. You've had a long day."

"Will you stay with me until I fall asleep?"

"Of course." I pulled the covers over her shoulder and settled on the bed next to her. Almost immediately, her breathing turned slow and even, letting me know she was asleep. I stayed there a while longer, trying to figure out what to say to Sabrina while I attempted to calm my temper.

Once I worked out a basic script, and had myself under control, I headed to the living room. Unfortunately, all was lost when I spotted Sabrina.

Chapter Forty-One

WHEN DAN RETURNED to the living room, I still wasn't sure what to say. He saved me from worrying. "What the hell is your problem?" His green eyes glowed with anger.

"What's my problem?"

"That's what I asked." He stood directly in front of me, arms folded across his chest looking like he was about to explode.

Any remorse I'd been feeling since my conversation with Kevin evaporated in the face of his attitude. I understand I shouldn't have taken the coward's way out, but his question really pissed me off.

"I can't believe you asked that as though I'm the only one with the problem," I said.

"If the shoe fits," Dan started, but cut himself off. After thrusting his fingers through his hair, his eyes met mine again. "I called you here and on your cell. I even tried the clinic, hoping someone knew where you'd disappeared to. I was worried sick, and Lexi has been inconsolable since you left. I finally got hold of Kevin, who told me you were holed up here."

"I left a note," I said, knowing I sounded overly defensive.

"Yeah, a note that said you didn't know if you could deal and that you had to think."

"Where did you think I'd go?"

"I figured you'd come here, but when you didn't answer the phone, I was ready to put out an A.P.B."

"I'm sorry you were worried."

He nodded and ran his hands through his hair again. Tears glistened in his eyes when they met mine. "So I guess we're back where we started."

The tone of his voice made the hair on the back of my neck stand on end.

"Not necessarily."

"Bri, how can we have any kind of relationship if you don't trust me?"

"I trust you, but…"

"If you really trusted me, this wouldn't even be an issue." The pain I saw in his eyes matched what I was feeling in my heart. "I've got a little girl in there who loves you so much, she left home alone to come and find you. I can't take the chance that you're gonna run every time a pretty woman looks my way. I have to know you love and trust me enough to stick around no matter what." He stepped closer and placed his hand on my cheek. "I love you, Sabrina, and I want to be with you more than anything, but I don't know if you're really ready for it. Maybe I rushed you into this."

"No, you didn't." I felt my whole life being pulled out from under me, and I was powerless to stop it. Dan was speaking nothing but the truth. I'm embarrassed by my actions.

Ten years may have passed since I faced a similar situation with Dan, but obviously my maturity level hasn't grown. I handled things the same way I did back then. It's amazing how hindsight puts things into focus.

"I don't know what to say." My voice was barely a whisper. I'm actually surprised I got the words past the lump in my throat.

"There's not much to say." Dan sounded as choked up as I felt.

That said, he went to join Lexi in the guest room.

Chapter Forty-Two

SABRINA

THE NEXT COUPLE weeks followed in a blur of tears, sleep, and pints of Ben & Jerry's Phish Food. Once again, I was holed up in my house, but this time I had only myself to blame for that fact.

Before Dan and Lexi left for home, the three of us sat down and had a long talk. Mostly Dan and I explained the situation to Lexi, but Dan's words left no doubt in my mind about the state of our relationship. I couldn't ignore the irony that he's the one who wanted into this relationship, and I'm the one who fought it with all my strength…now I'm the one wishing he were here.

I was throwing a one-woman pity party when my ringing cell interrupted the festivities. I had let Kevin's two previous calls go to voice mail. If I did the same for this one, he'd probably call the police.

"Hello," I said.

"What are you doing at your apartment?" Kevin asked.

"Uh, I live here." I loaded my spoon again and shoved it in my mouth.

"I just called Dan looking for you."

"Why'd you call him?"

"Because, when you didn't answer my calls, I'd hoped you two worked things out."

"Well, obviously we didn't." My words were forced out through a mouthful of ice cream.

"Sabrina," Kevin sighed, "put down the Phish Food and call the man."

I looked at the half-empty pint in my hand. My brother knows me way too well.

"That sounds wonderful, Kev, but he's not speaking to me." I punctuated my words with a heaping spoonful of ice cream. Granted, Kevin couldn't see my defiant gesture, but it made me feel better just the same.

"What's that supposed to mean?"

For the next fifteen minutes, I detailed the events that led to the demise of my relationship with Dan. Aside from an occasional "uh huh" or "right," Kevin remained silent. When I finished my sad tale, I waited for him to comment, yet he didn't.

"So?" I prodded.

"So what?" he said.

"What do you think?"

"You really want to know?"

I blew out frustrated breath. "Would I have asked if I didn't?"

"Okay, but remember you asked," Kevin pointed out. "I think the ball is in your court. I think you need to go win him back the same way he did you. You need to convince him that you love and trust him," he said, putting a distinct emphasis on trust.

"I don't know how to do that," I said.

"I'd say begging would be a good start," he said around a chuckle. "Seriously Sabrina, you have to be willing to eat a little crow. Maybe a lot of crow."

"I could eat five courses of crow, but how do I convince him that I trust him?"

"Dan's a pretty smart guy. I'm sure he'll be able to figure it out."

"I don't know."

"Look, if you want to sit there drowning in Ben & Jerry's for the rest of your life, that's your business." My eyes slid to the nearly-empty pint and I flushed. "But I love you and want you to be happy, and I know Dan makes you happy."

"I'm not denying it," I said.

"Then go after him." Kevin paused for, what I'm sure was, dramatic effect. "Call me when you get things straightened out."

That said, he hung up.

Kevin's words flowed through my head all night long. I knew he was right, but still thought he was oversimplifying things. I can't imagine Dan falling at my feet just because I show up pledging my undying love and trust. After all, look at the hard time I gave him when he did it to me. The fact that Lexi is involved just complicates things.

I tossed and turned searching for a solution in my sleep-deprived, sugar-saturated brain. Somewhere around dawn, I made up my mind and finally fell into a sound, untroubled sleep.

Chapter Forty-Three

DAN

I DON'T THINK I've ever been so miserable. I've been doing my best to act normal, hoping it will break Lexi out of her funk, but so far I haven't been too successful. She's way too perceptive, and I'm not that good an actor.

She spent a couple nights at my mother's and now Jeff has her at Tori's. At this point, the less time she spends around me, the better.

I'd hoped Sabrina would call so we could work things out, but that hasn't happened. I've picked up the phone a hundred times to break the silence, but put it down each time. She needs to come back on her own.

My profession can be hard on relationships. I've seen it with my teammates and have heard their stories. If we're going to survive, I can't have Sabrina doubt me or us.

For the third time in the last half hour, I opened the refrigerator and dismissed its contents. I need comfort food. Some calorie-filled, make-you-fill-better, greasy goodness. Maybe I'll take a page from the women's playbook and grab some ice cream on the way home, too.

I grabbed my keys and headed to the door. When I opened it and walked onto the porch, I crashed right into Sabrina, nearly knocking her down the steps.

SABRINA

I STARED at Dan's front door, willing my hand to raise and ring the bell. My inner battle was halted when the door swung open and Dan bounded through it, crashing right into me. His hands gripped my shoulders, holding me steady.

"Sabrina." If his tone was anything to go by, he was both surprised and happy to see me. At least we're off to a good start.

"Hi."

During the drive, I rehearsed what to say, but nothing was coming to mind at the moment. When I realized we were standing there staring at each other, I asked, "I'm sorry, are you going somewhere?"

"I was just gonna grab dinner, but that can wait. Come on in." He stepped aside and gestured toward the open door. "Would you like a drink?" he asked as we entered the kitchen.

"Some water would be great," I said.

Anything to postpone the inevitable.

Dan retrieved two bottles of water from the refriger- ator and asked me to follow him into the family room. I settled onto the love seat. Dan seated himself directly across from me on the sofa. I took a sip of water and looked around.

"It's awfully quiet around here."

"Mrs. Evans is gone for the day, and Lexi and Jeff are over Tori and Nancy's house."

I flashed a knowing smile. "I guess things are still going well."

Dan nodded. "They told Tori and Lexi about their relationship a few days ago, so I guess it's getting pretty serious."

I was about to ask another question about Jeff's love life when Dan asked one about my own. "Why are you here, Bri?"

I placed my bottle on the coffee table and tried to remember my carefully orchestrated speech, but not a single word came to mind. So I decided to keep it short and to the point. "Because I love you." You couldn't get shorter and pointer than that.

Dan's smile was sad. "I know that, but it's not really the issue."

"I know." I stood and joined him on the sofa. I took his hand in mine and felt a surge of satisfaction when he didn't pull away. "I'm sorry I freaked out."

"I can't live the rest of my life worrying it'll happen again."

"It won't." I shook my head emphatically.

"How do I know that?" he asked.

"Because I'm telling you it won't," I said.

"How can I be sure?"

He was determined to make this difficult. Time to pull out the heavy artillery.

"You just have to trust me. The same way you're asking me to trust you." He opened his mouth to speak, but I raised a halting hand, stopping the flow of words. "I know what happened ten years ago and I'm trusting it won't happen again." I stared him down. "Ever." The edges of Dan's mouth kicked up at my not so subtle warning. "I love you more than life, and I want you and Lexi and me to be a family. I want to wake up with you every morning and go to bed with you every night. In between I want to love and laugh and raise our children." I paused, trying to think of something else to say.

"Are you finished?" Dan's words cut into my thoughts. I wasn't, but I nodded anyway, figuring I should give him some floor time. "Good." He put his hands on either side of my face and placed his mouth on mine. I moved in to deepen the kiss, but he pulled away.

"I love you too," he said. "And for the record, you had me convinced with your first sentence."

"I did?"

"Uh huh, but the rest was nice."

"I meant every word."

"And don't think I won't hold you to each and every one of them."

That said, he took my mouth in a fierce, possessive kiss, leaving no doubt in my mind that he'd forgiven me.

"Come on," Dan gasped. "Let's get upstairs before I bury myself inside you right here." He stood and pulled me up the stairs. "And once we've had our fill of each other, we have a wedding to plan."

I settled into the middle of his bed and watched him pull his shirt off. "So you still want to marry me?"

"More than anything," he said, as he stripped off his jeans. "Why would you doubt it?"

"Well, I know your theory of women," I teased. "And with what we're about to do, not to mention what we've been doing for the past few months, I didn't think I'd still fall into the 'girls you marry' category." My eyes danced with amusement as Dan's darted up to meet them. His frown evaporated when he saw my teasing expression.

"You're definitely enough woman to fall into both categories."

Then he proceeded to make love to me until I couldn't help but agree with him.

Are you ready for Jack's story?

Epilogue

Jack

"Congratulations to Dan and Sabrina." I raised my glass then looked at my best friend's fianceé. "And I want to personally thank you for agreeing to marry this guy. Now we won't have to spend another season listening to him whine about you."

The five of us clinked our bottles together to toast then Cal and Monte added their own smack talk to the conversation. We were on a road trip to the West Coast when the happy couple held their engagement party so now that the season is over, we all finally managed to get together to celebrate with them.

What I said wasn't an exaggeration. I've been listening to Dan lament about Sabrina since we met, usually after he had a few drinks. I'll admit that I thought his memory of her was skewed by nostalgia, but she really is great. They're perfect together and the fact that she treats Lexi like a princess makes her okay in my book.

My phone buzzed and I pulled it out of my pocket and

cursed under my breath when I saw Cindy's name on the screen...again.

"Problem?" Dan asked.

I shook my head and set the phone down then finished my beer in one long gulp.

"Nothing I can't deal with."

It buzzed again and I declined the call.

He glanced at my phone then back at me.

"You sure?"

"Positive."

Dan blinked at my harsh tone and I realized our whole table had gone quiet. I grabbed the pitcher and refilled my glass then topped off everyone else's.

"Tonight isn't about me, it's about you and Sabrina," I said with a forced smile.

"If there's something you want to talk about, we can. Either of you," Sabrina said then shifted her eyes toward Cal. "Dan and I don't have to monopolize the whole night."

"No, Jack is right," Cal said. "We're here to celebrate, not discuss divorces or crazy ex-girlfriends."

Thankfully the waitress arrived with our appetizers, pausing the conversation. Unfortunately, the food didn't stop my mind from racing.

If I could go back in time and avoid getting involved with Cindy Parker, I absolutely would. Looking back, I still don't have a clue where things went wrong with her. Despite what people might think, I'm pretty selective about who I get involved with. I'm not looking for a relationship and make sure to find like-minded women.

I've always been very honest about the fact that any relationship with me starts with a set end date. That might make me sound like a dick, but I feel like it's better than leading them on, and something long-term just isn't in the cards for me. I'd rather lay things on the table so no feelings get hurt in the end. That's worked for me for years. I guess I've just been lucky.

"So when is the big day?" Monte asked, pulling me from my thoughts

"The second Saturday in November," Dan said.

Cal's eyes rounded.

"Wow, that's only seven weeks away. That's going to take some quick planning."

Since Cal's the only one of us who's been married, it makes sense that he'd comment on what it takes to plan a wedding.

"We're having it at the house, so that makes it a lot easier," Sabrina said.

"Hannah hooked us up with a great caterer and a place that rents tables, chairs, and tents."

"Now all we really have to worry about is the weather."

"We have the tents if it rains," Dan said. "And the house is big enough for everyone if it gets really bad."

Our waitress approached again and in the time it took her to serve our entrees, Cindy had called twice more. I shoved the phone into my back pocket.

I'm not really sure why she thinks acting like this will make me want to get back together. Then again, nothing about her makes sense to me at this point. Like I said, I was up front with her about what I was looking for in a relationship and she was fine with that. Or so she said. Then about halfway through the season, she started getting clingy and pouty, two things that drive me absolutely crazy. She'd rein it in just enough so I didn't call things off but as the end of the season neared, things got worse. Again, I'm not sure why she'd think acting like that would make me want to keep her around.

I took a deep breath, slowly let it out, and picked up

my fork. I'm not going to let thoughts of Cindy distract me from my friends or the perfectly good steak in front of me.

"Lexi told me all about your dress shopping adventure," I said to Sabrina. "Sounds like it was a great time."

"It was a lot of fun, even though we had a little trouble finding a dress that's appropriate for her. When we agreed to have her be a junior bridesmaid instead of the flower girl, I didn't realize we'd have such a big issue with size and style. I think she tried on every dress in the store before we decided to have one custom made. Which she's even more excited about."

My phone buzzed again, but this time it was accompanied by a beep, letting me know the caller is my agent, Craig Yates. I put down my fork and set my napkin on the table.

"This is Craig. I better take it," I said, then stood and pulled my cell out of my pocket.

I don't need to explain to my friends why I need to take a call from my agent when we're starting to negotiate my next contract with the Waves.

"Hey," I said as I made my way out of the dining room. "I hope you're calling with good news."

"I wish."

I'd just stepped outside, but the chill running down my spine had more to do with his words than the cool air. It never occurred to me that the Waves might not want to renew my contract, but Craig sounds kind of distressed.

"The initial negotiations didn't go well?"

"Initial negotiations went just fine, but I just got word of something that might change that."

"I can't imagine what. My batting average was up this year, I did well—"

He cut me off before I could list my accomplishments on the field.

"Rumor has it Cindy Parker is writing a tell-all book about you."

I took in long, deep breaths and slowly let them out, trying to stave off the punched-in-the-gut feeling his words had brought. The nausea slowly subsided but I felt light-headed and leaned against the side of the building.

"Jack? You still there?"

"I'm here."

"From what I understand, the book is scheduled to be released right before spring training."

"Do you know what's in it?"

"Not yet, but I'm working on getting an advanced copy when one is available," he said. "Is there anything I should know in the meantime?"

"Nothing I can think of." I dragged my fingers through my hair. "I don't do drugs, performance enhancing or otherwise, I stick with one woman at a time, and my partying days are long behind me. I can't think of anything anyone would pay money to read about."

"You're a professional athlete. For some people, that's reason enough."

"This explains why Cindy's been blowing up my phone."

"Well whatever you do, don't answer if she calls again and definitely *don't* call her back. We don't need her to add anything to whatever she's already written."

"What *should* I do?"

"Nothing for now. I'll keep moving forward with your contract negotiations while I wait to get more details about the book. I just wanted you to know what's going on and make sure there's not anything she'd include in the book I should be prepared to deal with."

I looked up at the dark sky and shook my head.

"Honestly, I can't think of anything."

"That's good. Now we just have to hope she doesn't get creative with the facts."

"Shit, I didn't even think about that. As crazy as she's been acting the past couple months, it's not out of the realm of possibility that she'd make shit up."

"Once I find out more, we'll come up with a game plan. Just stay cool."

"Staying cool is easier said than done."

"You know I've got you covered. I'll work on finding out what's in the book. Until then, just go about your business like I never called," he added with a chuckle.

"Again, easier said than done."

"I'll be in touch."

That said, he hung up.

Lowering the phone from my ear, I stared at the screen until it went black then shoved it back into my pocket. My mind raced trying to figure out why this is happening, but I honestly don't have a clue. What I do know is that Cindy Parker is going to upset my controlled, well-ordered life more than she already has.

"*Fuck.*"

Bonus Epilogue

Dan

I tugged at my tie and looked out the bedroom window, watching the guests arrive. Sabrina and I wanted our wedding to be intimate and semi-casual, and found a wedding planner who transformed our backyard and pool area into the perfect venue. The weather is even cooperating, so we won't need to use the tents we have on standby.

Now if I could only breathe, things would be perfect. I reached for my tie again.

"Will you stop messing with your tie?" My best man and best friend, Jack Reagan, chastised me from across the room.

Shoving my hands into my pockets, I paced along the wall of windows, glancing down with every pass. Jack sat sprawled in the chair over in the corner, enjoying every second of my discomfort. I'd punch his smug face if I thought it would make me feel better, but I know it won't. Besides, Sabrina wouldn't be happy if our best man showed up for the ceremony with a bloody nose or black eye...or both.

I started to drag my fingers through my hair but stopped myself at the last minute. I don't want to look like a total lunatic when Sabrina sees me for the first time today. Speaking of that...what idiot came up with the rule that the groom can't see the bride on the wedding day?

We've been living together for months and on one of the most important days of our lives, we can't see each other? That's shit.

I was banished to Jack's house last night and he brought me home a couple hours ago to get dressed. I'd hoped to see Sabrina for a minute or two but both her mother and mine are taking the whole no seeing each other thing pretty seriously. So I'm basically being banned from my own bedroom where Sabrina is getting ready with Lexi and all the bridesmaids. Right now I just want to see her, talk to her, touch her.

"Maybe if you go knock on the door and say you need to speak to Sabrina, she'll come out into the hallway and I can see her."

Jack stared at me with one eyebrow raised and slowly shook his head.

"There's no way in hell I'm risking my life going down there," he said.

I stuck my fingers under my collar then yanked at my tie again.

"This collar is cutting off my oxygen supply and the tie is strangling me."

Jack stood and walked over to me. He checked my collar and adjusted the tie.

"The collar is fine and so is your tie. What's going on?"

I looked down at the floor and shook my head. Taking

in a long breath, I let it out slowly and looked up at him again.

"I don't deserve her. She's way too good for me." I swallowed then put my worst fear into words. "What if this time apart makes her realize that and she calls off the wedding?"

Jack blinked then looked at me like I'd grown another head.

"You think that after being with you for six months that —" He dramatically looked at his watch. "—sixteen hours apart is going to make her call off the wedding?" I nodded, happy he understood. "Well, you're right about one thing. Sabrina *is* too good for you. But for some reason, she loves you and no time apart is going to change that. And not only that but she agreed to marry your sorry ass." He patted me on the back. "So why don't we head downstairs so you can stand there with a sappy smile on your face while you watch your bride walk down the aisle toward you?"

"You're an asshole, you know that?"

"I'm aware, but for some reason, you keep me around anyway."

"Lexi likes you."

"You keep telling yourself that."

I leaned over and gave him a hug. A real hug. Jack is the brother I never had and I honestly don't know what I'd do without him most of the time. Hell, he's the one who convinced me to try to get Sabrina back after he'd listened to me talk about her for years.

"Thank you for that."

"Anytime."

"I promise to return the favor when our roles are reversed."

"Don't hold your breath for that, buddy. I'm never getting married."

"And I never thought I'd get Sabrina back, yet here we are."

Jack rolled his eyes, opened the bedroom door, and stepped aside for me to pass.

"Let's just go get you married."

I walked past him and he followed me into the hallway.

"Do you have the rings?"

He dramatically patted his pockets and I stopped in my tracks. Looking back over his shoulder at me, he held up the box.

"You really are an ass, you know?" I shook my head.

****

I stood off to the side with Jack and Monte and watched Cal seat my mother in the front row next to her boyfriend Frank. My dad sat a few seats away with his latest fling. I'm not thrilled he brought her, but won't let it ruin my day. He is my father and while I realized a long time ago that I don't want to be anything like him, I won't banish him from my life.

When Sabrina's brother Kevin walked their mother up the aisle and sat her on the other side, my heart pounded, not from fear but from excitement. With her seated, the bridal party would be next and then I'd finally see my soon-to-be wife.

Jack clasped his hand on my shoulder and smiled. "Ready?"

I nodded and we walked over to stand next to the minister. Cal and Kevin fell in line as the attendees took their seats. The band began to play *Pachelbel's Canon* and I saw the bridesmaids lined up behind the curtain that's dividing the ceremony and reception areas. Kevin's wife Maggie was first in line and she slowly walked down the aisle, followed by my sisters Megan and Patti, Sabrina's friend Jodi, and finally Lexi, whose smile lit up her face. She's beyond thrilled that Sabrina and I are getting married. She's also happy that instead of dressing her as a flower girl, we agreed to let her be more of a junior brides-maid so she's wearing a modified version of the women's dresses.

I smiled and winked at Lexi when she took her place and glanced over at me. She looks stunning and way too grown-up for my peace of mind. The first eight years have flown by and I know I'll blink and she'll be old enough to date. I'm at least comforted by the fact that I'll have a whole baseball team of guys to help me intimidate any walking hormone that comes knocking on our door.

The band paused for just a beat and the attendees stood as the *Bridal Chorus* began to play. I turned my head and froze in place as my gaze locked onto Sabrina's at the end of the aisle. She held her father's arm and as they slowly walked toward me, I felt like I'd been sucker-punched and had to remind myself to breathe.

My heart pounded, drowning out the sound of the music as Sabrina's image blurred. I fought the urge to blink, not wanting to miss one millisecond of this moment. She's a vision in white. Her gown is both elegant and sensual made of a top layer of delicate lace over a silk gown that skims her body to mid-thigh before slightly flaring out into a long train.

I stared mesmerized, taking in all the details. The simple fitted shape shows off her curves perfectly and sits off her shoulders, giving a modest glimpse of her wonderful creamy skin. With her hair pinned up in a mass of curls, her neck looks impossibly long.

I'm so happy she decided not to wear the veil over her face, because I would have hated to miss the shine in her beautiful blue eyes or the megawatt smile on her glowing face as she made her way down the never-ending aisle. I shifted in place, fighting the urge to run and meet her halfway. But that's not how we rehearsed it last night so I focused on my beautiful bride as she took what seemed like forever to finally reach me.

I took two steps toward her and as she turned to face her father, I noticed that her dress has tiny buttons going all the way up the back. I seriously hope they're either an illusion and there's a zipper under there or they're not difficult to open, otherwise we'll have buttons scattered all over the floor later. There's no way I'll have the patience to loop a thousand tiny buttons through their holes.

Her father tenderly kissed her cheek and I smiled and nodded in his direction as he passed her left hand over to me. The symbolic gesture choked me up last night and it's even worse now. I blinked to clear the tears from my eyes and discreetly cleared my throat so I don't sound like a pubescent boy when I have to speak.

Sabrina squeezed my hand. "You okay?" she whispered.

Her image blurred in-between blinks and I smiled. "Never been better."

And that's the truth. From the very first moment I saw her back in college, I knew Sabrina was the one for me. If I'd realized back then how fucked up my father's thinking was, I wouldn't have idolized him like I did and messed things up with her. We could have been married for years now, with a family of our own. But then I wouldn't have Lexi.

What-could-have-beens are a slippery slope to go down, so instead of lamenting over them, I focused on the here and now, on the amazing woman standing next to me, and our future together.

We turned toward the minister as he signaled for everyone to be seated.

"Ladies and gentlemen, we are gathered together here on this glorious day to witness the union of Daniel Patrick McMullen and Sabrina Rose Kelly."

While he went through his spiel, I mentally recited my vows. We'd decided to forego the traditional route and had written our own. It had taken me forever, but I'm happy with the end result. I included some personal thoughts as well as more established words.

The minister stopped speaking and I realized it's my turn. I squeezed Sabrina's hands and looked deep into her eyes.

"Sabrina, I knew from the very moment I laid eyes on you that I wanted to spend the rest of my life with you. Through our years apart, I never lost hope that someway, somehow I'd get you back into my life and make you mine. And here we are today and you're making all my wishes come true. I promise to spend the rest of my life loving you and proving that I deserve this second chance you've given me."

I looked down at our joined hands and cleared my throat. Blinking away the tears I've been fighting all day, I met her gaze again and continued.

"I promise to be your faithful partner in sickness and in health. I will protect you, trust you, and respect you. I'll stand by your side in good times and in bad, to share your joy and sorrow. I promise to love you unconditionally and support your goals and dreams. I'll laugh and cry with you, share my life with you, and keep you safe at my side. All that is mine is now yours. I give you my hand, my heart, and my love from this moment on for as long as we both shall live."

Sabrina squeezed my hands and blinked away tears.

"Dan, you're the only person I know who's as stubborn as me. And as we stand here today, I thank every deity known to man for that because, even after years apart, you never gave up on me, on us. Because of you I laugh, smile, and feel alive in a way I didn't when you weren't in my life. I know I'm not perfect, but I love that you treat me like I am."

She removed her hand from mine and reached up to wipe away a tear that had escaped before entwining our fingers together again. After taking in a breath and letting it out, she continued.

"I promise to trust and respect you, laugh and cry with you, dream with you, celebrate with you, and walk beside you regardless of any challenges that come our way. My heart is entirely yours and I will cherish you always and love you faithfully for the rest of our lives."

While Sabrina and I had written our own personal vows, we decided to say the same words while exchanging rings and had written them together. The minister looked to Jack, who handed him the rings. He pulled them from the box with his thumb and index finger and held them up as he spoke.

"As the years go by you will change, but your rings, which represent your vows, will be constant. The promises to love, cherish, and respect one another no matter what life brings or what paths you take will always be worn around your finger. Your love will be constant as you walk together into the unknown."

He held out Sabrina's ring and I let go of her right

hand to take it from him. Holding up her left hand, I set the ring at the end of her fourth finger.

"Sabrina, I give you this ring as a token of my love and devotion to you. Let it be a reminder that I am always by your side and that I will always be your faithful partner. On this day, I gladly marry you and join my life to yours."

I slid the ring down her finger, then lifted her hand and placed a kiss on top of it. She offered a wobbly smile before turning toward the minister so he could hand her my ring.

Taking my left hand in hers, she slipped the platinum band onto my ring finger.

"Dan, I give you this ring as a token of my love and devotion to you. Let it be a reminder that I am always by your side and that I will always be your faithful partner. On this day, I gladly marry you and join my life to yours."

I've never worn a ring in my life so it should have felt foreign when Sabrina slid it down my finger, but it didn't. It felt natural, like it belonged there.

I held onto Sabrina's hands, waiting for the minister to pronounce us man and wife and finally tell me I could kiss my bride. Instead, she glanced over my shoulder at Jack then released my hands and took a small step back.

My smile slipped as I stared at her, trying to figure out what's going on.

"Before I pronounce our happy couple man and wife and let our very anxious groom kiss his bride, she wanted to say something," the minister said.

He held out a small box and handed it to Sabrina. She turned and gestured for Lexi to join us. My heart skidded to a stop, then pounded so hard I'm sure it's visible through my jacket. Tears had threatened since last night's rehearsal, but I'd managed to keep them at bay...for the most part anyway. But this...I'm not gonna survive this.

Sabrina knelt down in front of Lexi, who didn't seem as shocked as me about this change in the program.

"Lexi, you are so amazing. You've been generous enough to share your dad with me after having him to yourself your whole life. And I can't tell you how happy I am that marrying your father makes the three of us a family. I made some promises to your dad today and I want to make some to you, too. I promise to remind you every single day how truly loved you are. I promise to teach, guide, and respect you. And I vow to never treat you as anything less than my own child, for you truly are my daughter from this day forward."

Once Sabrina was done speaking, Lexi threw her arms around her neck and hugged her. I held back my tears until that happened, then they fell down my cheeks faster than I could wipe them away. I'm pretty sure I even heard Jack sniffling behind me.

Lexi stepped back and wiped her face with the back of her hand. Sabrina dabbed at her cheeks, then opened the box she was holding and held it up.

"Your dad and I exchanged rings today, and this is for you."

She pulled out a necklace and held it up for my daughter, who looked down at it and seemed to be reading.

"What's it say?" my mom yelled from the front row.

Lexi looked up at Sabrina, who nodded. Then my brilliant eight-year-old daughter described what she was looking at loud enough so everyone could hear.

"It's a heart locket. When you open it, there's a removable heart inside that has today's date and says, 'Today I tell your father I do, but I promise to love you forever, too.'"

Sabrina stood and told Lexi to turn around while she secured it around her neck. When that was done, Lexi wrapped her arms around Sabrina's waist and I heard her say, "I love you, Sabrina."

"I love you too, Lex." Then she leaned down and whispered something in Lexi's ear that made her laugh and nod.

Looking down at her new necklace, Lexi stepped back into place next to Sabrina, who turned back to face me. Her eyes widened, most likely because I looked like a blubbering fool. But how could I not after that?

"Ready?" the minister asked, so just the two of us could hear.

We nodded and smiled at each other.

"By the power vested in me by the State of South Carolina, I now pronounce you husband and wife." He looked at me. "You may now kiss your bride."

He didn't have to tell me twice. I wrapped my arm around Sabrina's waist, pulled her to me, and placed my lips on hers. I'd debated on how to handle this kiss and figured I'd keep it rated G, but once I felt her mouth against mine and heard the hoots and hollers from my teammates, it crept into PG-13 territory.

I leaned into her, bending her back over my arm and opened my mouth over hers. Thankfully she responded in kind. I slipped my tongue inside for a quick taste before pulling her upright and dragging my mouth from hers. There'll be time for that later.

"I present to you Daniel and Sabrina McMullen," the minister said.

Our guests stood and clapped as we made our way back down the aisle. One nice thing about having the ceremony and reception at the house is that I can drag my new bride away for a private moment without having to search for a spot.

Holding onto Sabrina's hand, I dragged her across the

yard, through the open patio doors, across the living room, and up the stairs into our bedroom.

"Dan, what are you doing?"

I slammed the door behind me and stalked toward her. Placing my hands on either side of her face, I tilted her head back and pulled her in for a kiss. A real kiss. One with open mouths and tongues and roaming hands. I cupped her ass through way too many layers and squeezed, then slowly inched my fingers down her thighs, dragging the dress up so I could get a better hold. My fingertips grazed silk stockings then I felt the bare skin of her thighs.

Dragging my mouth from hers, I pulled back and looked into her eyes.

"Sabrina, what are you wearing under this dress?"

She gave me a coy smile. "You'll have to wait to see."

I narrowed my eyes. There's nothing I love more than a challenge.

Dropping to my knees, I lifted the front of her dress up to her waist, revealing pale pink thigh high stockings with garters and a matching thong.

I looked up at her, shifting my gaze from her chest to her eyes.

"What's on top?"

"It might be a matching corset." She shrugged. "I got dressed so long ago, way back when I was single, so I'm not sure. It's hard to remember."

"It's hard all right."

"Daniel!"

Right now, there's nothing I want to do more than stick my head under her dress and slide my tongue against her until she comes, but that will have to wait until our guests leave. I don't want to embarrass Sabrina by getting her all sex-rumpled for our wedding reception.

I stood and smoothed her dress back into place.

"You look so beautiful Sabrina and you've made me the happiest man in the world today." I took her hands in mine and realized she was still wearing her engagement ring on her right hand. Slowly sliding it down her finger, I reversed the process on her left hand until it rested flush against her wedding band. Blinking away more tears, I met her gaze again. "And what you said to Lexi—Jesus Bri, why didn't you give me some warning?"

"I wanted it to be a surprise."

"She didn't seem as surprised as me and obviously Jack knew."

"Jack only knew I had something to give her and I told Lexi I was saying something to her during the ceremony, but didn't give her details."

"What did you whisper to her when she hugged your waist?"

"I promised to French braid her hair whenever she wants."

This woman. Could she be any more amazing?

I wrapped my arms around her and pulled her in for a hug so she couldn't see that she'd made me cry again. We just stood there holding each other while I got myself under control. When I finally did, I kissed her on the cheek and pulled back just enough to see her face.

"You're perfect, you know that?"

"Like I said in my vows, I'm really not but I love that you treat me like I am."

"Well, you're perfect for me and you're perfect for Lexi."

"I'm glad you think so because I love you both very much."

"I love you, too." I leaned down and gave her a soft kiss. "I'll show you just how much in a couple hours, but right now we have a reception to attend." I pulled back and reached for her hand. "Are you ready to go greet our guests, Mrs. McMullen?"

"Absolutely, Mr. McMullen."

I opened the door and led my wife back down the stairs to celebrate this happy occasion with our friends and family.

Chapter 1

Jack

I walked through the office doors and nodded at the receptionist before continuing toward the stairs to Mr. Hanover's office. Normally I'd stop and talk with the staff, but I'm not in the mood today. I've punched up my workouts getting ready for spring training and I'm sore as hell, plus I haven't been sleeping so I'm tired. The former is something that gets worse as the years go on and the latter is because of that damn book.

In my fourteen years with the Waves, I've done my best to avoid being singled out by the team owner. Aside from a warning about partying too much my rookie year, I've been successful. And now this. It's bullshit.

I worked to keep my temper in check as I made my way through the hallway toward Mr. Hanover's office. I'm sure whatever happens at this meeting is only gonna piss me off so I can't start it with a hot head.

Stepping in front of the double doors, I took a deep breath and knocked three times. The door opened immediately. Ken Hanover Jr., heir apparent to the Waves stood in the doorway, blocking my view of the office.

"Kenny," I said.

"Come on in, Jack."

He moved aside and I stepped into the office. Mr. Hanover sat in an oversized chair behind his gigantic mahogany desk.

"Come have a seat," he said.

The thick, blue carpet cushioned my steps as I crossed the room. I settled into one of the visitor's chairs directly across from him and Kenny sat in the chair on my right.

"How've you been doin'?" Mr. Hanover asked. "You're lookin' good. Must be workin' hard." His good ol' boy accent and small talk weren't fooling me. The man didn't call me in to tell me how good I look or ask about my workout routine. But I'll play the game.

"I'm good," I said. "Just ramped up my workouts getting ready for the season."

"Well it shows."

"Thank you, sir."

My words still hung in the air when Hannah Adams, from the public relations department, stepped into the office.

"Sorry I'm late," she said.

She gave me a small smile and sat in the chair to the left of me. Dressed in her usual bland attire, bright red glasses added the only color to her face.

"Jack, we asked you to come in today so we can discuss this book of yours," Mr. Hanover said.

I wanted to point out the fact that it's not my book, but figured he wouldn't appreciate that. Instead I focused on keeping a neutral face.

"Now I'm a live and let live kind of guy. Who you spend your time with off the field is your business. But once it affects this team, we have a problem." He leaned back in his chair and steepled his fingers in front of his chest. "When the book first came out, we decided to ignore it. But that's not working anymore. Now it's a best seller and that woman's been all over the local circuit. Word on the street is she'll be on *Good Morning America* next week. And if she's heading to New York, that's probably not the only show she'll be hitting."

Shit.

When Cindy released that book, I thought it was a joke. Turns out, the joke is on me.

"Sir, I—" He held up his hand, halting my words.

"The problem is that this book is taking focus off baseball," he said. "We're gearing up for spring training and it's all the reporters are asking about. The phones are ringing off the hook with requests for interviews and comments.

Not to mention the fact that the staff is tittering about it instead of working."

Mr. Hanover's face reddened with each word. He sat forward and took a deep breath, dragging his fingers through his hair. Resting his elbows on the desk, he looked at me again.

"Son, I understand you didn't ask for this, but you got it anyway," he said. "There's nothing we can do about the book. It's out and doesn't look like it's going away anytime soon. So, we'll just have to give them something else to focus on."

"Like what?"

"That's where Hannah comes in," he said. "She has some ideas for a, whaddyacallit?" Looking over at her, he raised his brow.

"A PR blitz," she said, shifting slightly in my direction. Clearing her throat, she continued. "We want to get you out there having a positive impact. If we show all the great things you're doing in the community, the media will look petty if they keep focusing solely on the book."

"There are tons of pictures of me visiting the children's hospital, and once the season starts, I'll be engaging with the fans like usual. What else did you have in mind?"

"You've been great with the children's hospital and we'll be able to use that. And you're always a fan favorite so that's something we can definitely highlight. But I know there are other causes you support that you've never wanted us to capitalize on. Now's the time to do that."

How the hell does she know what I support?

"I've kept them off the radar for a reason," I said. "They're not things I want to discuss."

"You wouldn't have to discuss them necessarily, just let it be known you're doing them."

"I don't want to do that, either."

She opened her mouth to speak, but it was Mr. Hanover's voice that filled the room.

"You don't have much of a choice here," he said. The fact that he didn't raise his voice didn't lessen the impact of his words. "We're trying to focus on baseball and the reporters are asking about what kind of underwear you wear instead of how the team is shaping up for God's sake."

I doubted that was true, but thought it best not to state it out loud.

Instead I said, "I apologize for that sir, but don't you think this will die down with time?"

"From what we've heard, she's making the most of the fifteen minutes of fame she's getting with this book. And once the season starts, the press will link every little thing you do to that book, stoking the fire. I'm not willing to have my **PR** department stomping out brush fires all year. Hannah here thinks we should hit this head on."

"She does, huh?" I asked, not quite keeping the sarcasm out of my tone. It's not Hannah whose ass will be on the spot answering probing questions. And no matter what she says, I know the questions will be asked.

"If you have some time before you leave, I can explain the ideas I've come up with so far and maybe we can think of a few more," she said.

I opened my mouth to answer, but once again, Mr. Hanover pulled his ventriloquist act.

"Son, I can see you're not quite on board with this, but understand, it's not an option. You know Hannah is good at her job, so let her do it. You've been a valuable asset to this team for a lot of years. I'd hate for this unfortunate incident to put a bad color on our future negotiations."

Did he just threaten my contract renewal?

His steely eyes told me he did just that.

Well damn.

Mr. Hanover prides himself on keeping the team's reputation flawless and in his opinion, this book is threatening that. I've played my whole major league career with the Waves, and plan on retiring from the team. Until now, that was never in question. I guess I'll have to play nice.

"I understand," I said to Mr. Hanover, then turned to Hannah. "I don't have any plans, so I'm yours for the rest of the day."

Hannah

"Great," I said. "We can head to my office now if that works for you."

"I'm all yours," he said with a slight bow.

After wrapping things up with the Hanovers, Jack and I exited the owner's office and stepped onto the elevator. As we stood side-by-side in silence, his sweet, spicy scent found its way to my nostrils making me want to bury my face in his neck and deeply inhale.

And maybe lick.

Oh, who am I kidding? Definitely lick.

How am I going to survive this?

Despite the fact that Jack Reagan is everything I don't want in a man, my heart goes pitty-pat every time he's near. And it pisses me off because at this point in my life, you think I'd be immune to men like him.

I mean, I've been working for the Waves for nearly ten years. I shouldn't be susceptible to the charms of any of them. Not to mention where and how I spent some of my teen years. Beautiful people shouldn't even cause a blip on my radar because I know the reality behind all the glitz and glamour.

We exited the elevator on the third floor and walked down the hall to my office, fourth door on the right. I stepped behind my desk, hoping it would provide a barrier to Jack's magnetism. No such luck.

Maybe it's because he's a professional athlete and a dead ringer for Ryan Reynolds that tips my scales. It's like a double-punch to my sound judgement.

Jack slouched into the visitor's chair across from me and crossed his ankle over his knee. I assume he's trying to look relaxed, but the man is practically vibrating.

"I have a few ideas to start with and we can add on as the season progresses," I said. He didn't answer or react, so I forged on. "I know you've been a silent supporter of a variety of anti-drunk driving organizations as well as the anxiety and depression associations here and in your home state."

He sat forward. "How?"

"Excuse me?"

"How do you know that?" he asked. "No one knows that."

"It's my job to know," I said, leaving it at that.

He doesn't need to know that I stumbled on both of those facts while obsessively creeping on him a few years back. Most people don't look past the first few pages of an internet search, but the last few are where you can find some of the best stuff.

Sure, Jack is obsessive about keeping his private life private now, but back in the beginning of his career, he didn't cover his tracks as well. Which led me to the little tidbits I just shared. A few follow-ups and voila, I've got something to work with. Thankfully he didn't question me further and slouched back in the chair.

"Can't you just find me something else for me to do?"

"I can and I will, but if that's all we have, it looks like we're doing it just to up your image."

"But that's exactly what we're doing."

I chuckled, both at his words and the incredulous look on his face.

"Yeah, but we don't want the public to know that."

He sat forward, resting his elbows on my desk.

"Hannah, the reason I support those groups is personal and I really don't want to discuss it," he said, then added. "With anyone."

His New Hampshire accent appeared when he stated my name, a definite tell of how upset he is about this. But I have to say, *Hanner* never sounded so sexy.

Mentally shaking myself, I accepted his point and told him so. "I'm sure there will be some questions about why you're supporting those specific groups, but you don't have to tell the whole story. They're both very worthy causes. Why wouldn't you support them?"

"I guess."

"Considering the time of year, I think we should focus on the drunk driving groups first. With proms coming up in the next few months, their campaigns will be in full swing. I've contacted a few schools and groups around St. Pete to work with during spring training. There's also a local event prior to that you can attend."

"What kind of event?"

"A dinner at Lucca. It had sold out but I managed to convince them to squeeze another table in for us to purchase. I was thinking maybe you and some of the other players could attend. Do you think Cal and Dan would go? They're really good with the public."

"What about you?"

"What about me?"

"You're not just going to set me up for all these things and not come along to babysit, are you?"

The twinkle in his eye mingled with that wicked grin nearly gave me an orgasm. I cleared my throat and struggled to sound professional.

"You're great with the fans. I have no doubt you'll be able to handle it without a babysitter."

"Oh no, if I'm stuck doing all this stuff, you're going to be there every step of the way."

In all my years with the Waves, I've managed to minimize my alone time with Jack Reagan. His mere presence is enough to scramble my thoughts, and his scent...well, I think I've already mentioned that. Being in close proximity to him on a regular basis will not be good for my peace of mind.

"I figured I'd set up everything, give you the details, and you could take it from there. I'm just a phone call away if you need me."

"Oh I'll need you," he said. "In fact, I'm going to tell Mr. Hanover that you'll have to be available for every little thing I do."

God help me.